EV4.00

MRS. JEFFRIES
and the
SILENT KNIGHT

MRS. JEFFRIES
and the
SILENT KNIGHT

EMILY BRIGHTWELL

BERKLEY PRIME CRIME, NEW YORK

THE BERKLEY PUBLISHING GROUP
Published by the Penguin Group
Penguin Group (USA) Inc.
375 Hudson Street, New York, New York 10014, USA
Penguin Group (Canada), 90 Eglinton Avenue East, Suite 700, Toronto, Ontario M4P 2Y3, Canada
(a division of Pearson Penguin Canada Inc.)
Penguin Books Ltd., 80 Strand, London WC2R 0RL, England
Penguin Group Ireland, 25 St. Stephen's Green, Dublin 2, Ireland (a division of Penguin Books Ltd.)
Penguin Group (Australia), 250 Camberwell Road, Camberwell, Victoria 3124, Australia
(a division of Pearson Australia Group Pty. Ltd.)
Penguin Books India Pvt. Ltd., 11 Community Centre, Panchsheel Park, New Delhi—110 017, India
Penguin Group (NZ), Cnr. Airborne and Rosedale Roads, Albany, Auckland 1310, New Zealand
(a division of Pearson New Zealand Ltd.)
Penguin Books (South Africa) (Pty.) Ltd., 24 Sturdee Avenue, Rosebank, Johannesburg 2196,
South Africa

Penguin Books Ltd., Registered Offices: 80 Strand, London WC2R 0RL, England

This book is an original publication of The Berkley Publishing Group.

First edition: October 2005

Library of Congress Cataloging-in-Publication Data

Brightwell, Emily.
    Mrs. Jeffries and the silent Knight / Emily Brightwell.
        p. cm.
    ISBN: 0-425-20558-4
    1. Witherspoon, Gerald (Fictitious character)—Fiction. 2. Jeffries, Mrs. (Fictitious character)—
Fiction. 3. Police—Great Britain—Fiction. 4. Women domestics—Fiction. I. Title.

PR6052.R4446M64 2005
823'.914—dc22

                                                                        2005047514

PRINTED IN THE UNITED STATES OF AMERICA

10   9   8   7   6   5   4   3   2   1

In loving memory of Robert Eugene Lanham

CHAPTER 1

"It's not my fault the cat has gone missing," Nina Braxton said to her sisters. "I don't know why father always assumes that everything that goes amiss in this house is my responsibility. I've nothing to do with the wretched animal." She put the copy of the *Financial Times* she'd been reading down on the table and stood up. Nina was a woman of medium height and frame. Her eyes were blue, her complexion pale, her features ordinary, and there were a few strands of gray in her light brown hair. She glanced around the small drawing room, staring at her two sisters as they finished their morning coffee.

Lucinda Braxton, the oldest of Sir George Braxton's three daughters, shrugged her shoulders. "None of us have anything to do with the beast," she said. "And personally, I don't care if the stupid creature ever turns up. But I suspect it's in all our interests to make sure he does." She glanced at the third woman in the room. Charlotte Braxton, the middle sister, was reading a novel and appeared to be taking no notice of the conversation. "Father will want to know if you've seen Samson," Lucinda said, raising her voice to get Charlotte's attention.

Charlotte sighed and put down her book. She had more than a few strands of gray in her dark auburn hair, and there were fine lines around her brown eyes. She was a bit shorter and heavier than her younger sister, but not as short or heavy as Lucinda. "This is becoming tiresome. I've already told you, I haven't seen hide nor hair of the stupid cat. Have you asked Mrs. Merryhill or either of our houseguests?"

"Of course I've asked Mrs. Merryhill," Lucinda snapped. "She hasn't seen him, and neither have any of the other servants. Father had them out searching this morning at the crack of dawn. I don't care if you find this tiresome or not, I'll not have Raleigh disturbed over this matter because you don't want to get your nose out of a book long enough to discuss it properly."

"Have you spoken to cousin Fiona?" Nina interjected. "Perhaps she's seen Samson."

Lucinda glared at her sister. The question sounded quite reasonable, but she knew Nina was being malicious in bringing Fiona into the conversation. "You know very well I haven't spoken to Fiona. I've no idea why she's even here. I certainly didn't invite her to spend Christmas with us."

"Father did," Charlotte snickered, "and you really ought to be nicer to her. You've barely spoken to her since she got here."

"If I'd had my way, she'd not be here at all," Lucinda cried. "I don't know why Father insisted on inviting her this year. It's not as if he's overly fond of her."

"Father isn't overly fond of anyone," Charlotte said softly.

"Not even us." She picked her novel up and commenced reading again.

"Put down that book," Lucinda ordered. "We've got to think of how to find Samson."

Charlotte ignored her and kept on reading.

"You're being quite silly about this matter," Nina said calmly.

"If we don't find that wretched cat, everyone's Christmas will be ruined," Lucinda snapped. "So whether you think I'm being silly or not, I would suggest you get up and help me locate Samson. As Charlotte is too busy reading to care about the matter, it's going to be up to the two of us to keep Father from ruining our holidays over that stupid cat."

"I wasn't referring to the cat," Nina continued. She smiled slyly. "I was referring to our houseguests."

Lucinda felt a flush creep up her cheeks. She took a deep breath, trying to calm herself and keep her face from turning that mottled crimson color that was so unbecoming to a woman of her age. She cringed as she thought of her age. Forty-three wasn't really old, but then again, Fiona was only thirty-five.

"Don't be absurd. I'm simply being a good hostess. Of course I don't want Raleigh's Christmas ruined over a stupid cat and you know what Father's like. If Samson isn't found, we'll probably have to go without Christmas dinner."

"I'm glad to hear that your concern extends to Fiona as well," Nina said. She was only thirty-eight, but unlike her sister, she had no prospects for marriage on the horizon. Nor did she want one, either. Being under her father's authority was bad enough. Why on earth any woman would deliberately put herself under a husband's authority was beyond her.

"I don't care if Fiona falls into a well," Lucinda shouted. "I do care if I'm humiliated in front of my fiancé."

"Oh, you're engaged?" Nina asked archly. "When did that happen? I certainly saw no evidence of it at breakfast this morning. Odd that Raleigh didn't mention it when Fiona asked him to accompany her to the Waifs and Strays Society subscription dinner."

Lucinda's face turned beet-red, and she glared at her sister. "You're impossible," she cried as she stomped her foot. She charged for the door. "I don't know why I even bother speaking to either of you." She slammed the door hard as she left.

"That was rather mean," Charlotte said. "But very funny."

"Yes, wasn't it?" Nina grinned. "And even better, it'll keep her away from both of us for the rest of the day. I don't know about you, but I'm busy. I've a number of things to see to today."

"As do I," Charlotte murmured.

"I do wish people would stop slamming doors." Sir George Braxton stepped into the room and gave both his daughters a disapproving frown. "What's wrong with Lucinda? Has she lost what little good sense she ever had and gone completely mad?" He was a short, stocky man with a heavy mustache, ruddy complexion, and watery blue eyes. He was also going bald. "Charlotte, I thought I told you to clear out all that junk in the attic. It can be sorted and sold. There's no use letting perfectly good items sit up there doing nothing."

Charlotte looked up from her book. "That's Mrs. Merryhill's job," she said. "And most of the things in the attic are broken or useless."

"Mrs. Merryhill has enough to do around here," he snapped. "And I'll thank you not to talk back to me. Not if you want your quarterly allowance."

Charlotte who'd opened her mouth to reply to him, thought better of it and clamped her lips shut. Finally, she said, "I'll see to it this afternoon."

"See that you do." Sir George turned his attention to his youngest daughter. "I want you to come into my study this afternoon at four. The builder's coming to give me an estimate on the cost of tearing down the conservatory. You're best at dealing with tradespeople. So make sure you're not late."

"Yes, Father," Nina replied. "I take it you've told Clarence you're selling it. He'll need to make arrangements for all his plants."

"His plants!" Sir George snorted. "Seems to me they're my plants. I bought and paid for every single one of them. Don't you worry about what I've told Clarence. You just be there at four and don't make any plans for tomorrow morning, either. My broker is coming in at half past ten, and I'll need you there to decipher what the fellow's talking about. You can never get a straight answer out of those chaps." He stomped toward the door, then turned. "Have either of you seen Samson? I can't think where he's got to."

"I haven't seen him, Father," Charlotte said.

"Nor have I," said Nina. "Why is your broker coming? Is something wrong?"

"I've no idea what the fellow wants. He said he needed to see me, that's all."

"He probably has a good investment idea for you," Nina said cheerfully. "Oftentimes one has to act quickly to take full advantage of a good situation."

"Humph, we'll see." Sir George's broad face creased in a worried frown. "It's odd Samson going off like this, it's been miserable outside, and you know how he hates bad weather. He's been gone for two days now, and that's simply not like him. Can you two have a look about the place for him? I've had the servants and Clarence out looking, but they're useless."

"Of course, Father," Charlotte said softly. "I'm sure he'll turn up."

"He'd better," Sir George muttered. "The paper predicts snow for tonight."

"It's going to snow tonight," Mrs. Goodge, the cook for Inspector Gerald Witherspoon said to the housekeeper, Mrs. Jeffries. "I can always tell."

"Can you really?" Mrs. Jeffries said. She looked up from the list of provisions she'd been writing. "How?"

"My bones start to ache," the cook replied. "Not the kind of twingy ache you get when it rains, but a different sort, deeper and kind of dull-like, if you know what I mean." Mrs. Goodge was a stout, elderly woman who'd cooked in some of the finest houses of all England. But this, her last and final position, was by far the best she'd ever had. "And it's not like when my rheumatism acts up," she continued. "It's a different sort of feeling altogether."

Mrs. Jeffries nodded. "Perhaps it's just as well we've nothing to investigate, then. Slogging about in the snow wouldn't be very amusing."

"I'd not mind," the cook grinned. "I do all my investigatin' from right here, where it's always cozy and warm. It's been far too long since our last case. It's boring."

"True," Mrs. Jeffries replied. "But it's Christmas. It's dreadful to think there's murder about at what should be the season of forgiveness." The moment she said the words she realized she was being ridiculously sentimental. She was the widow of a Yorkshire policeman and the leader of the inspector's household. She knew that the season of forgiveness had no meaning for some individuals. She'd been involved with enough homicides to know that murder knew no season. It happened all the time. As a matter of fact, she'd noticed that murder tended to happen more often when family and friends spent substantial amounts of time with one another.

Betsy, the slender blue-eyed, blonde-haired maid brought her cup of tea to the table and sat down in her usual place. "I'd not mind slogging about in the wet if it meant we were on the hunt, so to speak. It does keep life interesting, doesn't it? Besides, a bit of snow never hurt anyone."

The maid was engaged to the coachman Smythe, and their wedding was set for June. Because of Smythe's economic circumstances, she knew that once they were married, her days investigating homicides might be numbered. She wanted to get in as many cases as she could before it all came to an end.

"That's true, but it's not very pleasant to be out in the wet," Mrs. Jeffries replied. She was a plump woman of late middle age with auburn hair and brown eyes. She'd been housekeeper to Inspector Gerald Witherspoon for several years now, and she, along with the rest of the household, was very involved in helping to solve their inspector's murder cases. Of course, he'd no idea he was getting their assistance, and they were determined to keep it that way. But Mrs. Jeffries secretly took a great deal of pride in knowing that their small band of dedicated sleuths had sent him from the Records Room to being the most famous homicide investigator in all the country. "I wonder where Wiggins and Smythe have got to? They promised they'd be back for tea this afternoon."

"Smythe's gone to Howards' to make sure his darlings are warm and snug in their stalls," Betsy grinned. Her beloved was quite fond of the inspector's two carriage horses, Bow and Arrow.

"And I sent Wiggins over to Luty's with some of my chicken broth," the cook added. She frowned slightly. "Luty isn't getting over her cold, she's had it now for two weeks."

Luty Belle Crookshank and her butler Hatchet were two special friends of the household. They'd gotten involved in one of the inspector's earlier cases, and they'd insisted on being included ever since then. Both of them had taken to homicide investigations like ducks to water.

"Sometimes it takes the elderly a bit more time to recover," Mrs. Jeffries replied. "She's under a doctor's care."

"Yes, but is she actually doing what the doctor tells her to do?" Betsy mused. "You know how stubborn she can be."

"She's stayin' abed most of the time and takin' her medicine, not that I think all them potions and pills doctors use nowadays do all that much good," Mrs. Goodge put in. "That's why I sent my broth along, it'll fix her right up. Mind you, I expect it'll put that nasty cook's nose out of joint. But I don't care. Luty must get well, and those fancy French chefs haven't got any idea about what a body really needs when it's feelin' poorly."

They heard the back door open and the sound of heavy footsteps coming along the back hall. "Cor blimey." Smythe pulled off his hat and brushed the snow off of it as he headed toward the coat tree. He was a tall, muscular man with harsh features, dark brown hair, and kind brown eyes. "It's startin' to come down fast out there."

"How are the horses?" Betsy asked as she reached for the teapot and poured him a cup. "Nice and snug in their stalls?"

"They are now." Smythe slipped into the chair next to Betsy. "The stable lads aren't used to this kind of weather, and the owner is out of town for the day. No one 'ad thought to make sure there was a bit of 'eatin' in the stable. But I soon set them right." He glanced around the table, his brown eyes narrowing in concern as he saw Wiggins' empty seat. "Isn't the lad back yet?"

"Don't worry, Smythe," Mrs. Jeffries said. "I'm sure Wiggins has enough sense to stay at Luty's if the snow comes down hard."

Smythe didn't look convinced, but he held his peace. "What 'ave you ladies been talkin' about?" he asked as he took a sip of tea.

"We're complainin' we've not got a murder," Mrs. Goodge said quickly. "It's right borin'."

The cook had once been something of a snob in the way that only an English servant could be. Before she'd come to this household, she'd have been scandalized by the very idea of being associated with something as vulgar as a murder. But she'd changed a great deal since being here, and she wouldn't trade this position for anything, not even if the queen herself offered her a post.

Mrs. Goodge had a vast network of former associates, tinkers, deliverymen, match sellers, flower girls, and mush fakers that trooped through her kitchen on a regular basis. She fed them tea and pastry, and they fed her clues about the suspects in whatever case the household happened to be investigating. Nothing she'd ever done in her life made her feel as proud as helping with the inspector's cases.

"Murder or not, I don't know that I'd like to be out in this." Smythe jerked his thumb toward the windows over the sink. "I've never seen this much snow in London."

"I do hope the inspector gets home soon," Mrs. Jeffries murmured. "The roads will be a bit of a mess. But I expect he'll take a hansom if it gets too bad."

" 'E'd probably do better walkin'," Smythe retorted. "The roads are already a mess. Where'd he go today?"

"He's at the Yard," she replied. "There was some sort of meeting with Chief Inspector Barrows."

The back door opened again, and they heard footsteps, just as their mongrel dog, Fred, who'd been sleeping peacefully on the rug, shot to his feet and ran toward the back hall.

" 'Ello old feller," they heard Wiggins say. "You been waitin' for me, 'ave ya. Brrrr . . . it's gettin' right cold outside." He came into the kitchen with Fred trotting at his heels.

"It's about time you got home," Mrs. Goodge chided. "We were starting to worry."

"I'm sorry, I got back as quick as I could." He hung up his hat, coat, scarf, and gloves, and then hurried over to the table and slipped into his seat. "I've never seen it comin' down like this. You ought to see the traffic on Holland Park Road, it's a right old soup, it is. A hansom's lost a wheel, and a cooper's van went up over the pavement trying to get 'round it."

"I hope no one was hurt," Mrs. Jeffries said.

"Nah, there's just a lot of shouting and yellin'," he replied.

"How is Luty feeling?" Betsy asked.

Wiggins took a quick sip of tea. "She's a bit better than she was yesterday," he said. "She was up when I got there, sittin' in front of the fire. Hatchet was 'avin' a right old time tryin' to get 'er to go back to bed." He glanced at the cook. "She was pleased to get your broth. I told 'er it would make 'er right as rain. She's scared we're goin' to get us a murder while she's still ill. When Hatchet went out of the room, she made me promise not to leave 'er out in case somethin' 'appens."

"You didn't agree to any such thing, did you?" Mrs. Goodge demanded.

Wiggins looked down at his teacup. "Well, she looked like she were goin' to cry. I 'ad to promise 'er she'd be included, but I don't think it's likely. It's too miserable outside even for a murder."

Mrs. Goodge looked disapproving but said nothing.

"Not to worry, lad," Smythe said quickly. "I'd 'ave done the same. A woman's tears aren't something a man can ignore."

Betsy squeezed his hand under the table. Smythe always knew just the right thing to say.

Wiggins smiled in relief. "Is our inspector 'ome yet?"

"Not yet." Mrs. Jeffries cast another worried glance toward the window. "If he doesn't get here soon, he may get stranded."

It snowed on and off for the rest of the afternoon, but despite the inclement weather, Inspector Witherspoon made it home in time for supper.

"It's dreadful out," he said to Mrs. Jeffries as he handed her his bowler and brushed snow off his heavy black coat. He was a middle-aged man of medium height and a thin build. His eyes were blue, and his dark hair was thinning quite noticeably. He'd inherited his home and his fortune from his late Aunt Euphemia Witherspoon, and as he'd been raised in quite modest circumstances, he'd no idea how to manage a huge house. He'd hired Mrs. Jeffries as his housekeeper, and she kept things running smoothly. "But at least the crime rate appears to have dropped a bit in the last week. I say, is that roast beef I smell?"

"It is, sir." Mrs. Jeffries helped him off with his coat. "Mrs. Goodge thought you could use something substantial this evening. Is the crime rate really down, sir?"

He sighed happily. "It most certainly is, Mrs. Jeffries. The consensus at the Yard is that it's the weather that's causing it. The number of complaints we've had about pickpockets, assaults, robberies, and burglaries have all diminished greatly."

"That's very good, sir," she replied. "If you'll go straight into the dining room, I'll bring your supper up."

"Even the murder rate has decreased," he said as he went down the hall. "Let's hope it stays that way, Mrs. Jeffries. Then we shall all enjoy our Christmas."

"Meow . . . meow . . ."

Sir George Braxton sat bolt upright. "Samson," he muttered as he climbed down from the high bed. "Don't worry, old precious, I'm coming." He fumbled for his spectacles, shoved them onto his nose, and then peered toward the double French doors that led out onto the terrace. He could see quite easily. The snow had settled like a white blanket over everything, and it was quite bright outside. But he saw no sign of Samson. Braxton picked up his wool dressing gown and shoved his arm through the sleeve.

"Meow . . ." the cry came again, and Braxton quickly pulled the gown around him and poked his other arm through the sleeve. "Hold on, old precious, Papa's coming." The gown secured, he dropped to his knees and fumbled under the bed for his slippers. Finding them, he shoved them on and charged for the doors. He threw the bolt, pulled open the door, and stepped outside. "Samson," he called. "Samson, where are you?"

But there was nothing, just silence.

Snow filled Braxton's flimsy slippers as he moved farther out onto the terrace. At least it's stopped snowing, he thought. "Samson," he called again. "Where are you? Samson."

"*Meow.*"

He whirled around to his left, peering in the direction of the conservatory. "Samson? Where are you? Come to Papa, old precious. Come to Papa," he called as he hurried toward the conservatory. He stepped off the terrace onto the grass, and his feet immediately sank even deeper into the snow. It came up past his ankles, but he didn't care, he had to find Samson. No doubt the poor thing was trapped in that wretched greenhouse. Well, by golly, no matter how much Clarence complained, trapping Samson like this was reason enough to sell the wretched thing.

"*Meow, meow . . . meow,*" the cat's cries increased in volume as it heard his master calling. "*Meow . . .*"

"Don't worry, old precious, Papa's co—" Braxton's voice died suddenly, and he heard a loud thud. A roar filled his ears, and his vision blurred. He slumped to his knees, a look of surprise on his face as he flopped to the ground.

A gloved hand reached down, grabbed the dressing gown at the back of Braxton's neck, and pulled him toward the frozen ornamental pond directly off of the terrace. It started to snow again, but the assailant didn't care. The more snow, the better. Within moments, Sir George Braxton was lying face down in a chipped-out hole in the frozen pond.

"*Meow,*" Samson cried piteously as the gloved hand reached down and opened a large wicker basket placed next to the body. With pinned-back ears and an angry hiss, the orange-colored tabby leapt out of the basket. Almost immediately, the animal realized its paws were enveloped in wet, cold snow. Samson leapt upon his master's back and crouched into a sit.

"Thanks for your help," a voice whispered as the gloved hand reached over and stroked the cat's back. "I couldn't have done it without you."

Samson twisted, clawing at the stroking hand as he hissed his displeasure.

At dawn the next morning, there was a heavy knocking at the front door. Mrs. Jeffries, who was already up and dressed, wasn't surprised to find Constable Barnes on the door stoop, blowing air on his hands in a vain attempt to keep them warm. "Sorry to disturb you so early," he said. "But I've got to see the inspector."

Mrs. Jeffries kept her expression neutral, but inside she was overjoyed. There was only one reason Constable Barnes would be here at this time of the day—there was a murder to be solved.

"Go straight down to the kitchen, Constable," she ordered. "You look half-frozen, and I've just made a pot of tea. Help yourself. I'll pop upstairs and let the inspector know you're here."

She'd also awaken Smythe. It might be necessary for him to get out and about to see what was what.

"Ta," Barnes grinned and started down the hall toward the back staircase. "I'm sure you've already sussed out that we've got a murder on our hands," he said softly. "The victim's a baronet so that means there's going to be all sorts of political pressure."

Mrs. Jeffries paused and nodded. Constable Barnes' message was quite clear. He'd have to watch the inspector's back. When it came to bureaucratic politics, Witherspoon was an innocent. Barnes wasn't. The tall, gray-haired constable had been on the force long enough to know how to protect himself and his inspector.

Barnes continued on to the kitchen as Mrs. Jeffries dashed up the staircase. She knocked lightly on the inspector's door, stuck her head inside, and said, "Excuse me, sir, but you'd best get up. Constable Barnes is here to see you."

"What? What? Yes, yes, of course, I'll be right down," he replied groggily.

She closed his door quickly and hurried up to the top floor. Knocking once, she opened the door slightly and said, "May I come in?"

"I'm decent," Smythe said in a loud whisper.

She stepped inside and saw that the coachman was dressed in his trousers and shirt. "Sorry to wake you so early," she said softly. "But Constable Barnes is here, and I may need you to be out and about in a hurry."

"I thought I 'eard voices from downstairs." He pulled on a gray wool sock. "Do we 'ave us a murder?"

She nodded. "Yes, and from what little I know, it's going to be a sticky one. It's a baronet. Do you know if Wiggins is up yet?"

The two menservants used to share a room, but the previous month, Inspector Witherspoon had converted the small attic into another bedroom and insisted that each man have his own quarters.

"The lad's probably dead to the world," Smythe grinned. "He stays up late at night reading. Why? Do you think we'll need him?"

She thought for a moment. "Wake him. We might need everyone. Come downstairs when you're ready. I'll go see what I can get out of Constable Barnes before the inspector gets downstairs."

But Mrs. Jeffries wasn't able to get anything out of Constable Barnes. The inspector, who'd managed to dress very quickly, was right on her heels as she went down the back stairs to the kitchen.

Constable Barnes was sitting at the kitchen table. Mrs. Goodge was coming out the back hall holding a brown bowl covered with a clean white tea towel in her arms. "Morning, sir, Mrs. Jeffries," the cook said. "I thought I'd get the constable one of my Cornish pasties for his breakfast. We've a few left over from yesterday's lunch."

"That's most kind of you, Mrs. Goodge," the inspector replied. "I'll have one as well. I've a feeling we won't have time for one of your delightful cooked breakfasts." He hurried over the table. "Morning, Constable. You're here early. I presume something awful has happened."

"There's been a murder, sir," Barnes replied. "Sir George Braxton was found dead early this morning."

"Where was he found?" Witherspoon asked. He sat down and then nodded his thanks as Mrs. Jeffries handed him a mug of hot tea.

"At his home in Richmond, sir," Barnes replied. "Thank you, Mrs. Goodge," he said as the cook put his pastie in front of him.

"Richmond?" Witherspoon shook his head. "That's out of our jurisdiction."

"It is, sir. But the Home Secretary happened to be visiting at the house next to the Braxton place and when he saw the constables, he went over to see what had happened. As soon as he saw the body, he took control and sent along to the Yard for you to be called into the case."

Witherspoon frowned slightly and took another gulp of his tea. "I expect that didn't go down well with the local lads, did it?"

"They'll do as they're told," Barnes replied. He stuffed a huge bite of pastie into his mouth. It would probably be hours before he got another chance to eat, and he'd been rousted out of his bed in the middle of the night.

"I don't like to be the cause of any resentment," the inspector murmured.

"Not to worry, sir," Barnes said. "Most of the local lads don't want to have to deal with a murder like Sir George's."

"Why's that?" Mrs. Goodge asked. "Oh, sorry, sir. I didn't mean to be so bold . . ." The cook was of the generation of servants that had been trained not to speak unless spoken to when in the presence of their betters. Not that the inspector ran his household in such a fashion, but old habits die hard.

"Nonsense, Mrs. Goodge." The inspector smiled at the cook. "You've every right to be curious." He was a bit curious himself. He couldn't think why the local police wouldn't resent him greatly for taking over their case, especially at the request of the Home Secretary.

Barnes finished off the last of his food. "If they fail, Mrs. Goodge, they'll ruin their chances for promotion. Most detectives aren't like our inspector," he nodded at Witherspoon. "Detectives come from the ranks and it's a good way for working-class men to better themselves. There's lots of lads with plenty of ambition on these local forces. They'll not want a failure like this on their records if they don't catch the killer."

"Surely you're not saying they'd be dismissed if they didn't find the killer?" the cook asked.

"Of course not, they'd keep their positions, but they'd not move up." He glanced at Mrs. Jeffries, and she gave him an almost imperceptible nod indicating that she'd got his message. This case was important. She knew their inspector wasn't overly keen to move up in the department, but his status as a homicide detective would be badly hurt by a failure of this magnitude.

"Well, we'd best be off then," Witherspoon said. He

drained his mug of tea and rose to his feet. "Let's hope we can get a hansom this early."

The minute the two policemen had gone up the stairs, Smythe slipped out of his hiding place in the back hall.

"How'd you get in there?" the cook asked. "I didn't hear you come down the stairs."

"Good, then the inspector didn't, either." He was fully dressed, including his heavy coat. He shoved his hat on and pulled on his gloves. "I'll 'ead for Richmond, then."

"Try and find out as much as you can," Mrs. Jeffries replied. "It'll be this evening before the inspector gets home, and we want to be on the hunt before then."

"I'll try to get back with something by lunch," he said. "If not, I'll be here by tea time. Tell Betsy not to worry, I'm dressed warmly. Under this coat, I've got on a heavy wool vest, two shirts, and my scarf."

The Braxton home was more than a house but not quite an estate. The huge brick monstrosity occupied two acres and was set back behind a set of wrought-iron gates at the end of a long road. The house was a hodgepodge of styles. The main part of the house was Georgian with gracious columns and perfectly proportioned windows and doors, but the effect was ruined by the turrets and gothic wings that had been slapped onto both sides of the house without any thought of depth or proportion. On the far side, a conservatory had also been added. The drive, made up of pockmarked bricks and stone, curved around the front of the house and snaked across the property to end in front of a dilapidated carriage house with a sagging roof.

A young man wearing a bowler hat, a striped scarf, and a brown overcoat stood in front of the open wrought-iron gates at the end of the drive. He was rubbing his hands together and moving in short, jerky motions, probably to keep his feet from freezing.

"Are you Inspector Witherspoon?" he asked as the two policemen got down from the hansom.

"Yes," the inspector replied, "and this is Constable Barnes."

The young man nodded respectfully. "I'm Darwin Venable, from the Home Secretary's office. I'm to offer you any assistance in this matter. Quietly, of course. We don't want it out and about that the Home Secretary thinks the murder of a baronet is more important than the murder of anyone else."

But the Home Secretary obviously does, Barnes thought, as he'd never offered assistance in any of their other cases. But he wisely kept this thought to himself.

"Thank you, that's very much appreciated." Witherspoon murmured. He didn't know what to make of this. Of course he'd do his best to find Sir George's killer, but then, he did his best in all of his cases. "May we see the body, please."

Darwin nodded eagerly and started toward the house. "It's in the back, we'll go straight around. We're familiar with your methods, Inspector. The Home Secretary himself told the local constables not to touch the body until you got here."

"Er, uh, that was very good of him," Witherspoon replied as he followed the young man. "So I take it the police surgeon isn't here yet?"

"We told him there was no rush," Darwin said as he led them up the drive. "We knew you'd want to have a good look at the body."

They cut across the lawn and around the side of the house, going past the conservatory to the back garden. The snow was beginning to melt, and the ground was soaked. A constable was at the end of the terrace, presumably making sure no one from the house came out to disturb the body. Another two constables were standing in the snow next to a small, frozen pond with a statue at its center. One stood on each side of the late Sir George Braxton.

Barnes cast an anxious glance at Witherspoon. The inspector was quite squeamish about corpses, and this looked to be a nasty one. Even from this distance, the constable could see that the back of the victim's head was crushed.

Witherspoon slowed his pace. No matter how awful it might be, he knew he must do his duty. He took a deep breath and steeled himself. He was suddenly glad he'd not had too much to eat this morning. He hoped the pastie would stay put in his stomach. He nodded politely to the two policemen as they reached the dead man's body.

"Good day, sir. I'm Constable Goring, and this is Constable Becker. We've kept things undisturbed, sir." Though the tone was polite, their expressions weren't. Goring was an older copper, with deep-set hazel eyes and a thin, disapproving slash of a mouth. Becker was a fresh-faced lad in his mid-twenties, with blue eyes and dark hair beneath his policeman's helmet.

"Thank you," Witherspoon said. He waited for them to move out of his way. Becker moved immediately, but Goring stood his ground.

Barnes wasn't having that. "If you'll move, Constable Goring, then the inspector can have a proper look," he said. His words were polite, but his tone was hard. He was going to nip this insubordination in the bud before it could take root. He knew the rank and file respected Witherspoon greatly, but he also knew the inspector had a bit of a reputation for being very lenient with the lads. Well, these lads had a lesson to learn if they thought they could get away with out and out disrespect.

Goring hesitated a split second and then stepped to one side. "Yes, sir."

Witherspoon took a deep breath and knelt down by the body. He fought back a wave of nausea and forced himself to make a thorough examination.

The body was face down in the pond. The water was shallow enough that it only came up to his ears, so the inspector could see that the back of the head was horribly crushed. The victim wore a dressing gown over his nightshirt and had slippers on his feet. "It must have been the blow to his head that killed him."

Goring snorted.

"Do you have something to add, Constable," Barnes snapped.

"No, sir," Goring replied.

"Then move off out of our way," he ordered. He knelt down on the other side of the corpse. "I think you're right, sir. I doubt anyone could survive a blow like this. But what do you make of this?" He pointed to the man's head. "His face is under water."

Witherspoon nodded. "And the pond is completely frozen over."

"That means whoever did this had to chip the ice to shove Sir George's head into it." He shook his head in disbelief. "Why on earth would the killer go to the trouble to do that when he must have known Sir George was already dead? This pond is frozen hard, chipping a hole in it wouldn't have been that easy."

Witherspoon shrugged. "Perhaps he didn't know his

blow had been successful. Perhaps he wanted to make sure his victim was dead."

"Then why not whack him again, sir?" Barnes asked. "Seems to me, drowning the man in a frozen pond is doing it the hard way."

CHAPTER 2

"Thanks, mate." Smythe paid the hansom driver and started toward end of the road.

"You've given me too much," the cabbie called after him. Smythe waved him off and quickened his pace. "You earned it, mate. The roads are still a mess, and you got me 'ere lickety-split." He'd gotten to the cab stand on the Holland Park Road and managed to grab one just as he saw the one the inspector and Barnes had gotten into turn the corner. He'd told the driver to stay back but to follow the inspector's cab. The man had done a good job, and Smythe had rewarded him for his efforts. Even better, the cabbie hadn't asked any nosy questions. Besides, Smythe thought as he slowed his pace and examined his surroundings, he had plenty of money.

Smythe noted that there were two constables standing at the drive of the house at the far end of the road. That must be the place. The constables were standing there, not doing much of anything except staring down the road, but Smythe didn't think they'd spotted him.

He stopped and studied his surroundings. Blast, he couldn't go any farther. It was too dangerous. This wasn't a busy street in London where he could blend into a crowd and pick up bits and pieces of information from the locals. This was a road of big houses with lots of empty space between them and not near enough places for a bloke to hide. There weren't even that many trees, and because it was winter, there was very little foliage about to cover him.

He ducked behind the trunk of an elm tree, standing sideways because the trunk wasn't big enough to cloak him completely. He had to think what to do. How to get close enough to suss out what was what. He peeked out and saw one of the constables heading his way. Blast a Spaniard, one of them must have seen him!

Inspector Witherspoon forced himself to look closely at the victim's head again. Bile rose in his throat, but he fought it back. He knew everyone expected him to examine everything where the murder had occurred and then come up with the killer based on "his methods." The truth was he wasn't sure what he was supposed to be seeing and even worse, he wasn't sure what his "methods" were. They seemed to vary from case to case. Except for this, leaving the body where it was, undisturbed. But what a horrid mess of blood, matted hair, and what was probably bit and pieces of the poor man's brain were supposed to tell him, he couldn't fathom. He got to his feet.

Barnes rose as well and turned slowly in a circle, his gaze locked onto the ground. It took a moment before Witherspoon realized what he was doing.

"He wasn't killed here." Barnes pointed to the area by the victim's feet. The inspector looked down at the ground as well and saw the faint outlines of a trail that extended from the tip of the slipper toe outward for a good two feet before disappearing underneath a sea of footprints.

"And we'll likely not know exactly where the poor fellow was murdered." The constable shook his head in disgust. "Not with all these footprints. They're everywhere, sir. The ground by the pond is so covered with them we'd never get any useful evidence; they're all over the terrace. Good gracious, they're even over near the ruddy greenhouse." He glared at the two constables who were standing on the other side of the pond, but were close enough to hear them. "What did you do," he asked angrily, "invite the whole household out to have a good look? Why wasn't this area roped off?"

Becker bit his lip, but Constable Goring didn't flinch. "It wasn't our fault, sir. By the time we got here, the damage had been done. We kept people away as soon as we realized it was murder."

"Realized it was murder," Barnes exclaimed. "Ye Gods, man, the poor fellow's had his head bashed in and stuck in a pond. Did you think it was suicide?"

Goring glared right back. "When the call came in, it just said there was a body here. By the time we got here, the whole household was outside and tramping around the place."

"But no one had pulled Sir George's head out of the pond?" Witherspoon asked. He kept his voice neutral, not wanting to add more tension to the situation. He didn't wish to undermine his constable, he quite understood what Barnes was doing, but on the other hand, he didn't want the local lads to feel bad. He was sure they'd done their best.

"That's odd, isn't it? Generally, family members would have pulled him out, if for no other reason than to make sure he's actually dead."

Goring turned his attention to the inspector. "They had, sir. The Home Secretary instructed us to put the victim back. Your methods have become quite well known, sir. But we'd have done the same without being told."

"So you placed the head back into the pond," Barnes asked, but his tone was a bit less harsh.

"Yes, sir. We took care to put it back exactly as it had been," Goring replied. Some of the animosity had left his voice. "I had the gardener, he's the one who found the body, tell me exactly how the victim looked when he found him. As I said, Inspector Witherspoon's methods have become quite well known, and even without the H.S. intervening, we'd have done it."

"That's quite right," Darwin Venable interjected. "Look, now that you're here, do you mind if I go? I really must get to the Home Office. The secretary's got a very full schedule, and I've so many things to do."

Witherspoon started in surprise. He'd quite forgotten the fellow was still with them. "Yes, of course, do go on your way. We'll not keep you."

"Excellent." Venable beamed his thanks and took off at a fast trot back the way they'd come.

Barnes looked at Goring. "You did well, Constable. That was exactly the right thing to do. But I still wish there weren't so many footprints."

Goring looked as though he couldn't decide whether to be pleased or to continue taking umbrage. But he finally said, "Thank you, sir. We did our best."

"I'm sure you did," Witherspoon said quickly, glad that some of the tension seemed to be fading. "Could you please take care of getting the body to the morgue and notifying the police surgeon that it's been released for the postmortem."

"Yes, sir." Goring hurried off toward the front of the house.

Witherspoon looked at Constable Becker. "Get the lads from the terrace and search the property."

"Do you want me to get the ones you sent out to the front gate?" Becker asked, looking at Barnes.

"No, leave them there for the time being," the constable replied. "We need someone to make sure the press doesn't get in and trample the place down before we've found any evidence that might be useful."

"Yes, sir," Becker replied. "Er, uh, what are we looking for, sir?"

"The murder weapon," Barnes said dryly. "The man didn't cosh himself on the back of the head. But keep a sharp eye out for anything else you find lying about on the ground. Come get us if you find anything, anything at all." He turned to Inspector Witherspoon. "Shall I send someone to the station to get the lads here for a house-to-house?"

Witherspoon looked around the area, noting the distance between the houses. He wasn't certain about what to do. In London, the houses were so close together that people frequently heard or saw something useful. "Do you think anyone would have heard or saw something? I mean, the houses aren't close, and I'm not certain that anyone was awake in the middle of the night. That's probably when the murder happened."

"It couldn't hurt, sir," Barnes said easily. "Sometimes people have strange habits; there might have been someone with a bout of sleeplessness or a case of indigestion up and about. Besides, it'll be good to have the locals doing their fair share."

"Yes, of course, Constable, you're absolutely right. I don't know what I was thinking." He was a bit embarrassed by his behavior. He mustn't keep second-guessing himself, of course there must be a house-to-house, that was standard procedure.

Barnes nodded. "I'll send one of the lads from around the front. One good copper ought to be able to keep the press at bay for fifteen minutes."

Smythe knew he'd have to make a run for it. The copper would be here any second, and the one thing they would be looking for was strangers hanging about a murder scene. They'd knick him for sure, and if the inspector saw him, he'd be done for. There was no reason on God's green earth that he could give for following him to a murder scene.

"What are you doing?" The voice rang out loud and clear from the direction of the house.

"I thought I saw something," another voice replied. "I thought I saw something out of the corner of my eye."

"You didn't see anything," The first voice yelled. "And we can't be caught mucking about again. That old constable that came with the inspector is heading this way, so get back to your post."

"All right, I'm coming. It was probably just a squirrel or the wind or something."

As he heard the footsteps retreating, Smythe slumped against the tree trunk in relief. He knew he had to move. He knelt down and peeked around the tree trunk. Both the constables had their backs turned, their attention on the house. Smythe ran out from behind the tree and ducked into the front garden of the nearest house. He didn't stop, but kept on moving, hoping that no one was looking out a window. Smythe made it to the end of the property and dodged behind a small shed. He leaned against the wood, his heart racing like mad. Luckily, he'd put on his boots this morning, so at least the snow wasn't getting in his shoes, but his trousers were soaked to the knees, and his nose was running. Pulling a handkerchief out of his pocket, he blew his nose and tried to decide how to get closer to the victim's house. Unfortunately, he was several houses away from the Braxton home, and with police activity in the neighborhood, there were sure to be eyes peeking out of windows today. But Smythe wasn't going to let that stop him. He'd figure out a way. He always did.

He pushed away from the shed, looked around to make sure no one was about and then dashed toward the next property. There was a grouping of evergreen trees at the end of that garden, and if he could make it to them without being seen, they'd provide a bit of cover. If he was fast and lucky, he could make his way to the murder house from back here. There were a few fat tree trunks and garden sheds about; he'd just have to make sure he didn't get caught.

Witherspoon sighed and then looked toward the house. Behind him, the body was being loaded onto a stretcher and covered for transport to the morgue. "I suppose we'd best go into the house," he said.

"We've done everything we can out here, sir," Barnes replied. "We've got men searching the grounds and the outbuildings, the house-to-house has been organized, so we'd best get on to interviewing the family and the servants."

"I hate this part of it," the inspector said as he started walking over the now-rapidly melting snow. "It's dreadful watching people grieve over the loss of a loved one, especially when the death is the result of murder."

They'd reached the side door of the house. Barnes pulled

it open, and the two men stepped inside. They went down a dimly lighted hallway toward the front. On the hardwood floor, there was an old threadbare rug, and there were spots on the wall where the damp had seeped in. "You'd think a baronet would keep his property better than this," Barnes murmured.

"He might have been one of those aristocrats that have a title and little else," Witherspoon said quietly. They went past the wet and dry larders, the butler's pantry, and the staff dining room until they came out into the kitchen.

A scullery maid was washing dishes at the sink, and a small, slender woman wearing a cook's cap and a dirty white apron was rolling out dough at a large table in the middle of the room. She looked up at the two policemen. "I expect it's Mrs. Merryhill you'll want to speak with," she said. "Nelly," she called to the girl at the sink, "run and get Mrs. Merryhill."

"There's no need for that." A tall woman dressed in a black bombazine dress strode into the room. She had gray hair and wore spectacles. "I'm already here. I've been waiting for them." She stared at the policemen. "I'm Mrs. Merryhill, and I know who you are. The family is ready for you. They've assembled in the drawing room, but you'd better hurry. The solicitors are coming this afternoon, and the misses will want to speak with them." She jerked her head toward the door, whirled around, and hurried out the way she'd come. "Come along," she called. "It's this way."

"Er . . . Yes." Witherspoon took off after the woman. Barnes followed after him.

Mrs. Merryhill led them down another long hallway, this one in slightly better condition than the one that had led to the kitchen, and around a staircase into a large, rather dark drawing room. The windows were covered with heavy red curtains, and the walls were painted a dull, faded crimson. A gray-and-red patterned carpet was on the floor. The room was furnished with furniture from a variety of eras. Delicate Queen Anne chairs sat next to heavy mahogany tables, an Empire-style French love seat covered in pale cream damask was next to an overstuffed horsehair sofa. At the far end of the room a small fire burned in a dark marble fireplace over which hung a huge portrait of a fat man in elaborate Elizabethan dress.

Three women were in the room. The one sitting on the horsehair sofa glared at them and said, "It's about time. We've been sitting here waiting for ages." She got up and stalked toward the two policemen. "I'm Lucinda Braxton, the eldest of Sir George's daughters."

Barnes resisted the urge to pull his inspector back from the woman, as it looked like she was charging over to give him a good smack for being late. But she wasn't. She was simply going to the sideboard that held a tea service on it and refilling her cup. She was wearing a navy blue dress festooned with lace and overskirts, none of which complimented her short, rather chubby frame. She had dark blonde hair, blue eyes, and a very sour expression. Barnes doubted that she was going to offer them any tea.

"I'm Inspector Witherspoon," he said softly. "And I'd like to convey my condolences for your loss."

"Thank you." She finished filling her cup and stalked back to the sofa. "These are my sisters, Charlotte Braxton"— an auburn-haired woman sitting on the love seat nodded at the two policemen—"and Nina Braxton." The one sitting on a chair next to the sofa also nodded at the two men.

"Is this going to take long?" Charlotte Braxton asked. Her voice wasn't as harsh as her sister's. "We've an appointment with father's solicitors this afternoon."

Witherspoon gaped at them. He wasn't quite sure how to respond. "Miss Braxton, perhaps you don't understand. Your father has been the victim of murder. We must investigate. I've no idea how long I'll need to speak with you, but I assure you, I'll not detain you unnecessarily."

"We know perfectly well that father has been murdered," Lucinda Braxton interjected. "But surely you've some idea how long these sorts of things take. Presumably you've done it before. I believe I heard the Home Secretary mention you were quite good at taking care of these kinds of inconveniences."

Witherspoon gazed at the woman in stunned surprise. He was, quite literally, speechless. He'd never, ever heard a murder referred to as an "inconvenience" before.

"It'll take less time if we get started," Barnes said quickly. He glanced at Witherspoon, who gave him a barely perceptible nod. "Miss Braxton." He directed his question at Lucinda. "Could you give us an accounting of what happened?"

"What happened when?" She put her tea cup on the table and flopped back down on the sofa. "You mean when we found out Father had been murdered?"

"That's correct." Barnes whipped out his little brown notebook. "Do you mind if we sit down, it's easier to write that way."

Lucinda hesitated. "Yes, all right, sit where you please." She waited a moment for the two men to settle themselves. "All right, you'd like to know what happened. I'll tell you what I know. I was awakened about half past four by Charlotte pounding on my door and screaming that something had happened to father."

"That's not true," Charlotte interrupted. "I wasn't screaming. I was quite calm, and I believe my exact words were that I thought there'd been an accident."

"You didn't say that at all," Lucinda retorted. "You said something awful has happened to Father."

"And you were screaming," Nina added. "That's what woke me up."

"I most certainly was not," Charlotte yelped.

"If you could continue, ma'am," Witherspoon said quickly, his attention directed at Lucinda. "What happened next?"

"I put on my dressing gown and opened the door and told Charlotte to lower her voice." Lucinda sniffed disapprovingly. "We have houseguests, and I didn't want them disturbed."

"Weren't you concerned about what had happened to your Father?" Barnes queried.

Nina snorted faintly.

Lucinda shot her a quick glare before answering. "Father's health hasn't been good lately, so I thought perhaps he'd fallen. I didn't think it was anything serious."

"Even though your sister was screaming," Witherspoon pressed.

"Charlotte often screams," Lucinda said. "It's her nature. She's prone to hysterics."

"I am not." Charlotte leapt to her feet. "I'm not in the least prone to hysterics." Her voice rose as she spoke. "And I'll not sit here and be insulted." She charged for the door, swept out, and slammed it shut behind her.

"You were saying, Inspector," Nina Braxton said coolly. "You were asking Lucinda to explain herself."

"I most certainly don't need to explain myself," Lucinda snarled at her sister. "I've done nothing wrong."

Nina smiled faintly. "Then why weren't you alarmed when you heard Charlotte screaming about Father."

"I didn't see you come flying out of your room," Lucinda

shot back. "And I told you, I thought Father had had a fall or something. I didn't think it was serious."

"Miss Braxton!" Barnes yelled. He wanted to get back to their questions. At the rate these sisters were sniping at one another, they'd be here until Boxing Day. "Could you please continue with your account?"

"If my sister would please refrain from interrupting, I'll get to the rest of it." She glared at Nina, who totally ignored her. "As I said, Charlotte was screaming that something had happened to Father. When I came out into the hall, half the household was standing there, Mrs. Merryhill and Cousin Clarence and of course, the gardener."

"They were all standing in the hall?" Witherspoon asked. He couldn't believe it. "Surely one of them must have stayed with the body?"

"No, it was very cold out, you see," she replied.

"The body had been discovered by then?" Barnes clarified.

Lucinda nodded. "Oh, yes, the gardener had already sent the footman off to fetch a policeman. Mrs. Merryhill told me that I'd best come quick, that Father was outside in the ornamental pond. So we all trooped out into the snow and had a look. He was there all right, lying face down in the pond with the back of his skull crushed."

"You saw this?" Barnes prodded. "In the dark?"

"Mrs. Merryhill had brought a lamp. So did Cousin Clarence. But even if they hadn't, you could see quite clearly. It wasn't a particularly dark night."

"What did you do then?" Witherspoon asked.

"I told the gardener to pull Father out of the pond. Well, it looked rather awful, what with him lying there like that, and they did. They pulled him out and flopped him over onto his back."

"By that time, the entire household was up," Nina Braxton added. "They were making an awful racket."

"I'll thank you not to interrupt," Lucinda snapped at her sister. "And if you'd any decent feeling in you, you'd have come right out to see what was wrong. But no, you stayed warm in your bed while . . ."

"Please, Miss Braxton," the inspector pleaded, "do go on with your account."

"As I was saying, they pulled Father out of the pond and rolled him onto his back. It was obvious he was dead."

"What happened then?" Witherspoon was almost afraid to ask.

"What happened? Well, nothing. We stood about waiting for the police to arrive. We're not fools, Inspector, it was apparent Father hadn't died by natural causes."

"Did anyone search the grounds?" Barnes asked.

Lucinda stared at him blankly. "Search the grounds? What on earth for?"

"The murderer," the constable replied. "He might have still been here."

"Oh." She shook her head. "We never thought of that, and, in any case, none of us are properly equipped to deal with a murderer. I should think that was something you chaps ought to do."

"Who actually discovered the body?" Witherspoon asked. He remembered Constable Goring saying that it had been the gardener, but it never hurt to double-check these things.

"I've told you already," she said irritably. "The gardener. Why else would he be in the house at that time of the morning?"

"How did the gardener happen to be outside in the middle of the night?" Witherspoon asked.

"He said he heard something outside and went to have a look. When he saw Father in the ornamental pond, he roused the household."

"I see," Witherspoon replied.

"And they went and got Miss Charlotte?" Barnes had a feeling the sequence of events for the evening might turn out to be important.

"She was already up," Nina interjected again. "She came out onto the landing when she heard all the footsteps. She was already fully dressed."

Witherspoon turned his attention to the youngest sister. "What time was this?"

"I believe Lucinda already said it was about half past four," Nina replied.

"Was it customary for Miss Charlotte Braxton to be up and attired at such an early hour?" he pressed. The inspector was beginning to get a headache. He didn't think there was much fondness between these sisters.

Nina shrugged. "I've no idea. You'll have to ask her."

Both the policemen looked at Lucinda. She, too, shrugged her shoulders. "It's no good either of you looking at me, Charlotte's nocturnal habits are her own business. Is that all you needed to ask?"

"We'll probably have more questions for you and your sisters," the inspector said quickly. "But we'll ask them later. I'm sure you've a number of important matters that require your attention now."

"Yes, I must make sure my fiancé hasn't been unduly upset at all the commotion. Raleigh's got a very delicate constitution."

"Is the gentleman staying here at the house?" Barnes looked up from his notebook.

"He's here for Christmas." She hurried out the door.

Barnes glanced at the inspector and then at the last remaining sister. "May I have the names of everyone who was in the house last night?"

"Certainly," Nina smiled coolly. "There were the servants, of course. Mrs. Merryhill can give you their names. Then there were the three of us, Cousin Clarence, Raleigh Brent, Fiona Burleigh, and Father."

"When was the last time you saw your father alive?" Witherspoon asked. He normally wouldn't be quite so blunt in his questions, but he was of the opinion that none of the victim's daughters were overly upset by the poor fellow's sudden death. They were acting as if it were just an inconvenience rather than a tragedy.

"At dinner," she replied. "Father retired right after the meal was finished. He wasn't in the best of moods, but then again, Father was rarely in a good mood."

"Was there anything specifically bothering your father?" the inspector shifted in his seat. The cushion was quite hard.

"His stupid cat had gone missing."

"And that had your father upset?" Witherspoon pressed. "Was there anything else bothering him?"

"Something was always bothering the man," Nina said impatiently. "He was constantly complaining about how much the household cost to run or how much he had to spend on our wardrobes. But that was just his character. He was genuinely upset about Samson. The silly cat had been gone for two or three days. We told him not to worry, that the animal would come home when he got hungry enough, and sure enough he did."

The door opened, and Mrs. Merryhill stuck her head inside. "The solicitors are here, ma'am," she said to Nina Braxton. "Shall I put them in—"

"Put them in Father's study," Nina interrupted, "and tell them I'll be in directly."

"Yes, ma'am." Mrs. Merryhill started to withdraw. "Shall I get Miss Lucinda and Miss Charlotte?"

Nina sighed heavily. "I suppose you'd better, otherwise I'll never hear the end of it." She turned to the two policemen. "You'll have to continue this another time, I must speak with the solicitors."

"Of course, Miss Braxton," Witherspoon replied. He wondered why the solicitors were here so quickly. He made a mental note to make sure he had a word with them as well. Though with lawyers, one never knew how much information one could actually get out of them. "If you don't mind, could you please direct us to your father's room before you go?"

She looked puzzled. "Why do you want to go there? By the looks of it, he was murdered outside."

"It's standard procedure, miss," Barnes said politely. "Your father was wearing his nightclothes when he was killed, so we're assuming something or someone roused him from his bed."

Smythe knew he couldn't hang about any longer. He ducked behind a tree trunk and took one last, hard look at the Braxton property. So far, the only thing he'd found out was that the constables were searching the grounds and that their search was bringing them closer and closer to his hiding place. They were searching systematically, fanning out in a wide pattern, poking through the rapidly melting snow and peeking behind every tree, bush, and shed.

It had taken ages to work his way down here without being seen and much as he wanted to find out what was what, he didn't dare. He stuck his head out from behind the trunk and made sure none of the constables were coming in his direction. But they were all still in the area just off the terrace and behind the conservatory. He knew that wasn't going to last much longer, so he eased out from behind the tree. He wasn't sure he ought to go back the way he'd come. There had been a close call with a spaniel at one of the houses, and he wasn't sure he'd be so lucky this time.

Suddenly, a constable broke ranks and headed directly toward the copse of trees where he stood. He turned, and moving as quietly as he could, he ducked and broke into a run. He made it to the edge of the property without hearing an alarm raised, so he slowed and risked a glance behind him. The constable was now at the copse of trees. Smythe ducked lower, almost flattening himself behind a bush. He peeked out and saw the constable turning his head slowly, his gaze traveling from bush to bush and tree trunk to tree trunk. Smythe sucked in air as he flattened himself completely on the ground, and within seconds the snow penetrated through the layers of clothing he wore. What on earth was he to do? He couldn't make a run for it; the copper would see him for sure. He began to inch his way backward, toward a low wooden fence that framed this end of the property.

"Evans, what the blazes are you doing there?" asked an irritable voice belonging to one of the constables still fanning out behind the house. "Get back here."

"But I thought I saw someone," Evans replied.

"Yes, and you thought you saw someone earlier," the voice chided. "But it was just the wind blowing a leaf. Now get back here and help us search these grounds. It's bloody cold, and I want to get this done quickly."

Evans, with one last look, trudged back to the others. Smythe was up and over the fence in an instant.

He made it back to Upper Edmonton Gardens by lunchtime. Everyone was already at the table when he walked inside.

"I'm so glad you're back," Betsy exclaimed. "We were so afraid it would be tea time before we saw you." She got up and rushed toward him. "You look half-frozen. Take off your coat and get out of those wet boots."

"I'm fine, lass," he replied, but he was delighted at her fussing. He shrugged out of his heavy jacket and sat down to unlace his boots.

"You've either found out an enormous amount of information in very little time, or you've found out nothing," Mrs. Jeffries said.

"I found out nothin'," he admitted. "I couldn't get close enough and the inspector 'ad the constable searchin' the grounds, so I couldn't even get close enough to have much of a look at anything." He frowned. "Where's Luty and Hatchet?"

"We decided to wait a bit before we told 'em," Wiggins answered. He brushed a lock of his brown hair back off of his forehead. "Luty's still pretty ill, and we didn't want 'er climbin' out of 'er sick bed." He'd reluctantly gone along with the others when they'd suggested the idea of keeping quiet; after all, he'd promised Luty he'd tell her if they had a murder. But the others had convinced him it might do her a great deal of harm.

"Cor blimey, I forgot about that. Luty'll not like havin' to stay abed while the rest of us is off on the 'unt."

"That's why we're going to avoid telling her for a day or two," Mrs. Goodge added. "I think we ought to keep it from Hatchet as well. She'll notice if he's gone."

Mrs. Jeffries looked uneasy. "I don't feel right about this, but I suppose we've no other course of action."

"I don't feel right about it, either, but Mrs. Goodge is right," Wiggins said. "Hatchet's nerves is already strained a bit and he'd be out of that 'ouse like a shot if 'e knew we 'ad us a murder. Besides, it don't feel so much like I'm breakin' my promise to Luty as long as Hatchet doesn't know about the case, either."

"Luty been runnin' 'im ragged," Smythe chuckled. "That's not surprisin'."

"At first Hatchet was so worried about 'er, 'e wouldn't leave 'er side," Wiggins explained. "But now that Luty's out of danger and just needs bed rest, she's bored and miserable. She's not bein' mean or nasty, she just wants a bit of attention."

"Then it's settled," Mrs. Jeffries said firmly. "We'll wait until tomorrow to contact Hatchet about the murder. But contact him we must, we don't wish to offend him."

"And we're likely goin' to need both he and Luty's information about the deceased on this case," the cook said stoutly. She looked at the housekeeper. "You did say the victim was a baronet, right?"

"That's right," she glanced at Smythe. He pulled one of the chairs out from the table and pushed it toward the oven, then he set his wet boots on it. "Can you tell us the basics, at least."

"I've got enough for us to get started." He sat down next to Betsy. "The house is on Derby Hill Road, which is just off the Upper Richmond Road. It's at the end of the street and sits on about an acre and a half to two acres of land. The other houses along the road are big ones, but they've not got as much property. It's goin' to be bloomin' 'ard to do much investigatin' along that street, it's not like London, a stranger will be noticed right away."

"Cor blimey," Wiggins exclaimed. "What am I goin' to

do? You know it's usually the servants that gives me my bits and pieces."

"Not to worry, lad," the coachman said kindly. "I said it was goin' to be difficult, not impossible. We'll find ways to find out what we need to know. Sheen Common is about a quarter of a mile away, and I expect that's were a lot of the servants go on their day out. Actually, for a place the size of the Braxton house, I didn't see all that many servants."

"I thought you said the constables were searching the grounds," Mrs. Jeffries said. "Perhaps the servants were all inside."

"They were, but generally you'd see 'em comin' to the windows to sneak a peek. But I only saw a maid peekin' out of one of the attic windows."

"Perhaps they're short on staff," the cook suggested. "A lot of these old noble families are stingy and work their servants to death."

"What makes you say it's an 'old' noble family?" Mrs. Jeffries asked curiously. The cook's network of connections was intricate and vast.

Mrs. Goodge shrugged. "I'm not sure; it just popped into my head. Why?"

"Because sometimes we know things without being aware we know them." She shook her head impatiently. "I'm not explaining this very well, but given your extensive knowledge of important families in this country, you may have made the remark because you've heard something about the family without even realizing it."

"The name of the dead man did sound familiar," she admitted, "but I honestly can't remember anything I might have heard about him or his family."

"The house looked old as the 'ills," Smythe remarked. "It was a big brick monster of a place that looked like bits had been added onto it without much thought. There was a terrace running along part of the back of the 'ouse and right next to it, a huge greenhouse or conservatory. It was filled with plants. There was a statue in a pond behind the terrace, and that's where the victim was. I did manage to get a glimpse before the lads hauled the body off to the police van."

"Were there any other outbuildings?" Mrs. Jeffries asked.

"There was a heap of bricks on the far side of the front of the house that looked like they 'ad once been a carriage 'ouse. But the roof sagged, the windows were broken, and one of the big doors was gone. There weren't no carriages inside, nor any others that I could see about the property."

"You'd think a baronet would have a decent carriage," Betsy muttered. "Was the rest of the house shabby?"

"It was a bit 'ard to tell." Smythe shook his head. "There was still a lot of snow about. It was meltin' fast, but it was still on the roofs and window sills. But my impression was the main 'ouse was in good enough condition. The grounds looked really nice, like they'd been well taken care of before winter set in, and the glass in the greenhouse was so clean, you could almost count the flowers."

"You did a fine job of getting the 'lay of the land', so to speak." Mrs. Jeffries drummed her fingers on the tabletop, "That ought to give us enough information to get started."

"Too bad it's in Richmond." Betsy made a face. "That's not very convenient."

"It's not as bad as you think, lass," Smythe said kindly. "There's good train service between Shepherds Bush Station and Richmond."

"Shepherds Bush," she frowned. "Uxbridge is closer, but I suppose it'll have to do."

"You'll take the local shops, of course." Mrs. Jeffries nodded. Betsy had a real genius for getting information out of local shopkeepers.

"There's some along the main road right by the railway station," Smythe said. "I'll show you. We'll go along this afternoon. I spotted a pub off the Sheen Common that I want to 'ave a go at."

"What can I do?" Wiggins asked glumly. "The servants aren't likely to be on the common today, with a death in the 'ouse, they'll not be getting any time out today."

"No, but it's someone's day out. Staff from other houses might be out taking the air on the common or going to and from the train station. Have a go at it, Wiggins. Servants talk to one another, and you never know what you might find out until you look," Mrs. Jeffries said encouragingly.

He didn't look convinced. "Well, I don't know, Mrs. Jeffries. It's a bit of a gamble." He suddenly brightened. "But then again, it's better than sittin' 'ere with Fred waiting for everyone else to come back."

CHAPTER 3

Barnes and Witherspoon waited until Miss Nina Braxton had left them before they opened the door to Sir George's room and stepped inside.

The room overlooked the terrace. Against the wall in the center of the room was a large bed with a canopy and dark maroon side curtains tied back against the side rail. It had been made properly, with the maroon bedspread pulled up over a mountain of pillows against the ornately carved wooden headboard. Next to the bed was a side table with curved legs, on top of which stood a brass lamp and a copy of the *Times*. On the far side of the room was a fireplace with the same dark marble as in the drawing room. Over it was a portrait of an elderly gray-haired woman wearing a blue Empire-style ball gown. Two overstuffed chairs were in front of the fireplace. A set of cut-glass whiskey carafes stood on the top of cabinet next to one of the chairs. The walls were done in an ugly gray-and-blue striped wallpaper.

"Blast," Barnes muttered. "The room has been tidied up. You'd think these people would have enough sense to let things alone when there's been a murder in the house."

"It does muck about a bit with the evidence," Witherspoon agreed. "But perhaps we'd best make sure. I mean, just because the bed has been made doesn't mean that the room's been put right. Perhaps Sir George never got in the bed, in which case, we'd best rethink some of our assumptions."

"I'll go and check, sir."

While he waited for the constable to return, Witherspoon continued to study the room. The bed faced a set of double French doors that opened directly onto the terrace. He wandered over to the doors and examined the area around the lock. The paint was a dull gray color, done to match to walls, but there were no scratches around the lock nor any sign of splintered wood.

Barnes slipped back into the room. "Mrs. Merryhill says the maid cleaned in here this morning. No one thought to tell the girl to leave the room alone."

Witherspoon turned the brass handle. It was good and sturdy. "This appears to be in good working order. I don't think the lock has been forced. Did the housekeeper say whether or not the door was open or closed this morning?"

"It was closed, sir. I asked that question straightaway. So it looks like he went outside on his own and had the foresight to close the door behind him." Barnes frowned. "Now why would an elderly man go out in the middle of the night like that? The weather was miserable, and it was snowing."

"I don't know, Constable," Witherspoon said softly. "But this seems a very strange household. His daughters seem to barely notice the poor man is dead, and getting a reasonable answer out of anyone is almost impossible." He had the feeling this might turn into a really unsettling case. "And I suspect the local lads resent us. I'm not sure that I blame them all that much, either."

"Don't let it worry you, sir," Barnes turned in a slow circle, examining the room for clues. "They'll come around. At least we've not got Inspector Nivens dogging our footsteps, sir. This would be just his sort of case, he likes the ones that get the most press coverage." The moment the words were out of his mouth, he wished he could take them back. Barnes wasn't an unduly superstitious person, but he had a sudden feeling that he shouldn't have even breathed Nivens' name. But he shook the silly superstition off, Chief Inspector Barrows wouldn't let someone as incompetent as Nivens near a murder case like this one.

Witherspoon walked over to the bed and scanned the top of the bedside table. The newspaper was dated December eighteenth, so it was yesterday's, but that told him nothing except that Sir George had read the paper. He yanked open the drawer and rummaged inside, but he found only a tobacco pouch, a coin purse with a broken clasp, and an 1890 copy of *Wisden's Cricketer's Almanack.*

"He must have been keen on cricket," Witherspoon murmured. He picked up the heavy book and fanned the pages. But nothing fell out.

Barnes had gone to the tall wardrobe and pulled open the double doors. The constable reached inside and pulled out the first garment. It was an old-fashioned frock coat. He laid it across the bed and began to methodically check the pockets. The inspector went to the bookcase, pulled out the first volume on the top shelf, and fanned the pages.

They spent the next hour searching the room but found nothing that could constitute a clue. Witherspoon sighed as they stepped out into the hall. "Let's go talk to the servants, Constable. Perhaps someone saw or heard something that might be useful. We'll start with the gardener and see what he has to say. Then we'll speak to the houseguests and Cousin Clarence."

Ten minutes later, they were in the butler's pantry. A slender, brown-haired man wearing a navy coat, workboots, and carrying a workman's cap in his chapped hands stepped inside the room. "Mr. Clark said you wanted to see me."

"Are you the gardener, the one who found the body?"

He nodded.

Witherspoon gestured at the empty chair on the other side of the scratched table. "Please sit down. Could you please tell us your full name and how long you've been employed here?"

"Name's Randall Grantham, and I've been here about three months," he replied as he took a seat. He looked down at the tabletop and began running his index finger over the deep scratch marks in the wood. "I started on September twenty-fifth."

"And you're the gardener?" Barnes clarified. He looked up from his notebook. There was something about the man that sent his copper's whiskers bristling. Had he seen him before?

Grantham snorted and jerked his attention away from the tabletop. "If you can call it that," he said sullenly. "That's what I'm supposed to be doin', but Mr. Clark, he fancies himself one of them naturalists or botanists or some such thing. He generally has me fetchin' and carryin' and doin' for him out in that conservatory of his. Then I catch it from the old man or Mrs. Merryhill because the hedges ain't been trimmed nor the leaves raked."

"Is Mr. Clark your superior?" Witherspoon asked.

"He's some sort of cousin to Sir George." Grantham sniffed loudly and yanked a dirty handkerchief out of his pocket. He blew his nose. "And he fancies that he runs everything outside the house, I can tell ya that."

"I see." Witherspoon didn't see at all. But he decided he'd try and sort out the intricacies of the chain of command in the gardening world at a later time. "Can you tell us about finding the body?"

"It was disgustin', it was." Grantham said firmly. "A person doesn't like to see that sort of thing, especially not in the middle of the night."

"Yes, I'm sure it was quite unsettling," Witherspoon said sympathetically. "Could you please give us a few more details of how you came to find Sir George?"

"It was really more early this morning than the middle of the night," he said. "I was lyin' there tryin' to keep warm." He snorted derisively. "It was bleedin' cold last night, but do you think the old blighter'd give me a bit more coal for the fire, he bleedin' well wouldn't, and Mr. Clark wouldn't give me any, either, and he had plenty, 'cause there'd just been a delivery to the greenhouse so he could keep his stupid plants warm, but do you think he'd part with a lump or two . . ."

"Isn't the house kept reasonably warm?" Witherspoon interrupted.

"How would I know?" Grantham blew his nose again. "I sleep out in the shed and believe you me, by the wee hours of the mornin' it was cold enough to break the balls off a bull—"

"We understand it was cold, can you get on with it," Barnes pressed.

"But bein' cold is the important bit," Grantham cried. "That's the reason I was awake. Despite how miserable I

was, I'd managed to fall asleep, but something woke me up,
I think it was one of them ruddy icicles falling off the side of
the shed. They do that when they get too heavy. Anyway,
something woke me up, and it were so cold I couldn't get
back to sleep. I laid there for awhile, then I 'eard something
outside."

"What exactly, did you hear?" Witherspoon asked.

"The cat," Grantham's eyes narrowed. "It was that
bleedin' beast that belonged to Sir George. The dumb thing
'ad finally found it's way home and was caterwaulin' like a
banshee to be let inside."

"You don't like animals?" Barnes asked curiously.

"I like a nice hound or a good horse as well as the next
man," Grantham said. "But I hated that ruddy cat. Samson's
the meanest thing on four legs. He'd just as soon scratch
you as look at you. You'd try and pet him, and he'd almost
take your arm off." He shook his head. "Everyone but Sir
George hated the ruddy thing, and everyone was glad when
it looked like he'd run off. But the gov' loved him, so we all
put up with the beast's nasty manners. Well, we'd no choice
in the matter, had we?"

"Did you go to let the animal inside?" Witherspoon
probed. He did wish the fellow would get on with it. At the
rate these interviews were going, they'd be here until the
spring thaw.

"Nah, I thought I heard a door slam, so I figured someone else had let it in." He shrugged. "I rolled over and tried
to go back to sleep. But a few minutes later, I heard the
bleedin' cat again. I got up, put my clothes on, and went
outside."

"So it was the cat crying that made you go outside?"
Barnes asked.

"That's right, Samson wasn't one to give up when he

wanted to be let in. It's not like the little blighter has anything else to do, is it? Samson was there all right, he was sittin' smack on top of Sir George's body and screamin' like a fishwife."

"The cat was on top of Sir George's body?" Witherspoon was horrified. It seemed so very undignified.

"Huddled right in the center of Sir George's back. Samson was so miserable, he even let me pick him up and take him inside."

Witherspoon couldn't believe it. "You took the cat inside before you tended to Sir George? Good gracious man, why would you do such a thing?"

"I had to," Grantham exclaimed. "I tried shoving old Samson off so I could see what was wrong with the master, but the bloomin' cat would just jump back on top of him. Cat hates getting his paws wet."

"Why didn't you just give him a good whack to clear him off?" Barnes asked.

"Because Samson knows how to put up a good fight, just ask anyone that works here. A couple of months ago, one of the footman reached down to shove the beast off a footstool in the kitchen, and Samson tore his arm up. He don't just give you a scratch or two, that cat jumps ya with all of his claws out."

"Yet he let you pick him up?" Barnes asked.

"It surprised me, too," Grantham said. "I finally picked him up and took him into the house, just to get shut of him so I could see what was wrong with Sir George."

"Wasn't the house locked?"

"Sir George's bedroom door was wide open. I tossed Samson inside and went running back to the pond. But there were nary I could do, he was dead. So I went back into the house through Sir George's bedroom to rouse the household. Miss Charlotte come runnin' first, and as she went out, I went on to get Mrs. Merryhill."

"Miss Charlotte went outside to see him? She was alone?" Barnes probed. He knew it was going to be important to get the sequence of events correct. He had a feeling it might be the only way they'd solve this case.

"What time was this?" Witherspoon asked. He thought perhaps this case might need a good time line. In previous cases his time lines had been very useful.

"It must have been about half past four or a quarter to five. I don't own a watch, so I can't say for certain."

Betsy stood on the corner and stared at the row of shops spread along Marsh Glen Road. There were people about on the street, but nowhere near as many as you'd see on a London high street. A weak sun peeked through an overcast sky, so it wouldn't be bad weather keeping shoppers at home. This was simply a much quieter neighborhood than the ones in London. She'd have to be a bit more careful here.

Betsy studied the area, trying to determine where she ought to go first. There was a greengrocer's, a butcher's, a chemist's and a baker's. She'd developed a kind of "feel" for which shop to go into and which shop to avoid. She watched as two well-dressed matrons carrying shopping baskets went into the grocer's. That wasn't the place to go, not yet. Next, she saw an elderly woman wearing a heavy green wool cloak shuffle into the chemist's, and a moment later, she saw a young maid dressed in a short, brown plaid jacket hurry into the baker's shop. Betsy headed for the baker's.

As she stepped through the door, she was enveloped by the scent of yeast and cinnamon. On the wall behind the counter, row upon row of breads, cakes, pies, and buns filled the shelves. The maid was at the counter, pointing at a loaf of bread. "Cook needs another loaf, and she wants it put on account, please."

"Certainly, that's one loaf for the Hadley account." The plump, middle-aged woman behind the counter pulled the bread off the shelf and wrapped it in a sheet of brown paper. "Anything else? We've some nice mince pies today, they're always nice this time of year. You might tell Mrs. Hadley we're running a special between now and Christmas."

"I'll tell her. Thank you, Mrs. Bartlett, that will be all for now. But knowing Mrs. Hadley, she'll have forgotten something, so you'll probably see me later this afternoon as well," the girl grinned. "Maybe she'll even order us a mince pie. That would be nice."

"There was a lot of police down your way this morning, Abigail," Mrs. Bartlett continued as she handed the maid the loaf. "I heard there was some trouble."

"It was ever so exciting," Abigail replied eagerly. "Sir George Braxton's got murdered. We weren't supposed to notice, Mrs. Hadley kept chasing us away from windows sayin' it wasn't proper to see such things and murder wasn't supposed to happen in our neighborhood. But Lizzie and I managed a few peeks, and we saw what was what. There were police all over the place, and they were searchin' everywhere." She broke off and giggled. "Mind you, Mrs. Hadley doesn't know it, but Lizzie and I saw her taking more than one peek out the upstairs windows."

"That's terrible." Mrs. Bartlett flicked a quick glance at Betsy, assessed her dress in a split second and then went on talking to Abigail. "Do they have any idea who did it?"

Betsy wasn't offended. She'd worn her old gray jacket and her plain black wool hat for just such a situation as this. She'd found in the past that the lower down you looked to be on the social ladder, the more people were apt to speak freely in front of you. In their past investigations, she'd always learned more when she wore her broadcloth working dresses than when she slipped on one of her "good" outfits.

Abigail shrugged. "The police are still up there, it'll be ages before they find out anything. Mrs. Hadley says she thinks it must be that 'Ripper' feller. But I think that's silly. The Ripper only murdered women. Well, I'd best be off. Mrs. Hadley needs this loaf for luncheon."

Betsy was torn between following the maid and staying where she was. Mrs. Bartlett obviously loved to gossip, but the girl was obviously from a house close to the Braxton home.

"May I help you, miss," said Mrs. Bartlett. "I'm sorry, I didn't mean to ignore you. But we've had a spot of trouble in the neighborhood, and I find it's always best to be well informed about one's community. What can I get for you?"

Betsy made up her mind to stay. She could always try and find Abigail later. "Those buns look wonderful." She pointed at a tray of buns on the shelf under the loaves. "I'd like two, please. I couldn't help overhearing, did you say there had been a murder in the neighborhood? I'm not asking out of idle curiosity."

Mrs. Bartlett pulled two buns off the shelf. "There's nothing wrong with curiosity, idle or not. That's what makes life interesting, that's what I always say. Sir George Braxton was murdered, and I'm not in the least surprised. I don't care if he is a baronet, he's a strange one. Cheap as the day is long, he is, and his household isn't much better. You know, they only buy day-old bread. Can you imagine such a thing? He's as rich as sin, but he's too tightfisted to spend a bit of coin for fresh bread."

"My goodness, that's terrible." She wasn't sure if she was agreeing that the murder was terrible or whether it was terrible that the household only bought day-old bread. But it apparently didn't matter, Mrs. Bartlett didn't stop talking.

"And his three daughters aren't any better. Mind you, I wouldn't be surprised if one of them did the old blighter in." She leaned across the counter. "There's no love lost between any of them. They're all money mad, and that cousin of theirs, Clarence Clark, there's some that say he isn't really a cousin, if you know what I mean."

"Really?" Betsy had no idea what the woman meant, but she was fairly certain she could find out. She prayed no one else would come into the shop. She knew she'd struck gold.

Smythe and Wiggins stood in front of the Kings Road Pub on the Upper Richmond Road. "Good, they're open already," the coachman said, "so I'll nip in and see what I can find out."

Wiggins rubbed his hands together for warmth. "I'll go over to the common and see if anyone's about. Is it a nice common?" he asked. "You know what I mean, the sort of place where people would walk and such?"

"It's cold, lad, so they'll not be many people out and about. But I can't think of anyplace else for you to go, not while the inspector's still at the Braxton house. It's too dangerous for you to go too close to the house."

He didn't think Wiggins would have much luck today, but he didn't want the lad to be stuck at home twiddling his thumbs while they waited for the police to clear out of the Braxton house.

"Don't worry, I'll find someone to talk to me, I always do." Wiggins smiled gamely. "Cor blimey, but I feel so bad about poor Luty and Hatchet bein' left out."

"We'll tell them tomorrow," Smythe promised. "Now get on with you, time is awastin', and we've got to be back for supper or Mrs. Goodge will 'ave our 'eads."

Wiggins laughed and hurried off. Smythe pulled open the door of the pub. The bar was straight ahead. The barman stood behind the counter polishing glasses. He looked up as Smythe stepped inside. A couple of men dressed in working clothes were standing at the bar, two men wearing suits were sitting at a table by the small fireplace, and an old man smoking a clay pipe was sitting on a bench next to the door.

Everyone looked at him. This wasn't good. The place was dead quiet. He'd never get anyone to talk. In his experience, people tended to talk freely when a pub was noisy, crowded, and filled with drunks. But he was here now, he might as well give it a go.

"What can I get for you?" the barman asked as he stepped up the counter.

"A pint, please."

"You a stranger in these parts?" The barman shoved a glass under the keg and pulled the spout. "I've not seen you in here before." His voice was just a tad unfriendly.

"Never been 'ere," Smythe replied. "Why? You only serve locals?"

An embarrassed flush crept up the barman's broad face. "We serve the public," he muttered. He gave Smythe his pint. "No offense was intended. I was just making conversation."

"No offense taken," Smythe said easily. "I expect everyone's a bit nervous, what with murder 'appenin' around these parts," he commented. He was fairly certain that whatever chance he might have had at getting any information was now ruined. He shouldn't have reacted so harshly, the whole neighborhood was probably nervous. People tended to get suspicious of strangers when murder had been done.

The barman grunted in agreement. "Murder's rare

around these parts." He picked up a towel and wiped the end of the tap.

"Wonder if they know who did it?" Smythe watched the barman over the top of his tankard. Maybe it wasn't hopeless after all. The fellow was talking.

The barman looked at Smythe curiously. "When did you hear about it? Is it in the papers?"

"Nah, it only 'appened last night," he replied. He was prepared for the question. "But people were talkin' about it at the train station this morning and at the café next to it. I overheard one fellow say he thought it was that Ripper fellow that did it, the police never caught him."

"It weren't the Ripper," one of the taller of the two men at the other end of the bar said. "It was probably one of the poor sods who worked for him."

"Mind your tongue, Harry," the barman snapped. "You'll not be speaking ill of the dead."

Harry snorted in digust. "Just because he died doesn't make him a saint. He treated his servants worse than a dog, and that's fact. Look how he done our Addie."

"For goodness sakes, Harry, that was two years ago. Addie's married and moved to Brompton now." The barman shook his head. "Give it up, the man's dead."

"Don't like to be speakin' out of turn," Smythe said to Harry. "But what did he do to . . . uh . . ."

"He tried to stop her last quarter's wages when she give notice," Harry replied. His companion nodded his head. "Can you believe it? That bunch had worked her like an animal, and when she'd finally had enough and found another situation, he said he'd not pay her."

"So she left without her wages?" Smythe pressed. That could be a motive for murder.

"Oh, no, he had to pay up, we threatened him with the law, so that toff-nosed daughter of his gave Addie her money. But that's the way he treated everyone, even that cousin of his works like a dogsbody about the place to earn his keep."

"I'm glad the young lady got what was due her," Smythe said. He wanted a few more details.

"With no thanks to that tightfisted sod," he said.

"Harry, let him rest in peace," the barman said softly.

Smythe wondered if the barman would be quite so compassionate if Braxton had died owing him any money.

"Why do you care?" Harry's companion asked accusingly. "You didn't like him any better than we do."

"No, I didn't, but it just don't seem right to talk about the man when he can't defend himself," the publican snapped. He looked at Smythe. "You want another pint?"

"No, thanks, this will do me." Smythe had a feeling that the well had finally gone dry.

Wiggins rubbed his hands together to keep them warm. Sheen Common was a cold, miserable, and ugly patch of ground. Even worse, it was almost empty. A lone man walked slowly up a footpath on the far end, and there was a telegraph boy hurrying across the other end. All in all, the prospects for finding someone to talk to didn't seem very good.

He sighed and wondered what he ought to do. He'd been here for almost an hour, and he was near frozen, but he didn't dare go near the Braxton house. He desperately wanted to have something to report at today's meeting.

Maybe the telegraph boy was a possibility? Maybe he was taking a message of importance to someone that had something to do with the murder. Wiggins turned to see where the lad had got to, but he couldn't see him anywhere. Then he decided it was just as well, telegraph boys were trained not to talk to people about the contents of messages.

Cor blimey, it was getting cold. He'd seen a café just near the railway station; he'd get a cuppa and see if he could find anything useful there. Wiggins headed toward the Upper Richmond Road. Just as he reached the edge of the common, an auburn-haired woman wearing a wool hat and long gray coat entered the common. She walked past Wiggins without a glance, her attention focused on the far side of the common. She wasn't the sort of woman he'd generally try to speak with, but there was something else about her that gave him pause.

He continued walking and then when she'd gone down the footpath a bit, he turned and stared at her. Wiggins watched her as she went farther across the common.

"You're bein' right silly," he told himself. "You'd best get to that café and 'ave a cup of tea before you freeze to death." But just as he turned to go, a man came out from behind a tree and stepped directly in front of the woman. She stopped short. Wiggins stared hard at the two figures. He could see the man speaking, but he was too far away to hear what was being said. He'd no idea if these people had anything to do with the dead man or not, but at least it was something to concentrate on. The man and woman spoke together for a few moments, their heads so close they were almost touching. Wiggins had decided to follow them, when suddenly the man gave the woman his arm and the two of them walked off toward the far end of the common.

"Well, blast a Spaniard, it's just a fellow and his sweetheart, meeting up on the ruddy common so they can 'ave 'em a bit of privacy. Just my bloomin' luck."

Disgusted with himself for getting so carried away over such a small thing, Wiggins turned and headed for the road.

Surely he could find someone in the café to talk about the murder, or failing that, he could at least get a cup of tea and keep warm.

Everyone made it back by half past four for their meeting. Wiggins was the last to come to the table. He looked quite glum as he took his seat. "I 'ope the rest of you 'ad better luck than I did."

"Not to worry, Wiggins." Mrs. Goodge cut an extra-large slice of seed cake, slapped it on a plate, and handed it to the footman. "It's early days yet. You're not to worry about what you have or haven't found out."

"We've only just started, Wiggins," Mrs. Jeffries said briskly. "No one expects you to find out everything on the first day."

"I didn't find out anything at all," he replied.

"Stop frettin', lad," Smythe said kindly. "The only thing I found out is that Sir George Braxton was tightfisted and tried to rob his servants of their wages." He told them everything he'd heard in the pub that afternoon.

"That could be a motive for murder," Betsy speculated. "I mean, maybe this Addie didn't do it, but if Sir George was like that to all his servants, maybe one of them had a fit of rage and killed him."

"That's possible," Smythe agreed.

"You've no idea when this incident took place?" Mrs. Jeffries asked.

"Actually, I do, the barman said something like, 'That was two years ago'." Smythe shook his head. "I can't recall the exact words, but I've got a sense that it was some time ago. The girl seems to have gone off and got married."

"And as Betsy says, it could well be a motive for murder." Mrs. Jeffries said.

"I know it's not much." Smythe took a quick sip of his tea. "But I'll go back out tomorrow and see what's what."

"We'll have a bit more information by then," Mrs. Jeffries said. "That ought to help. Let's hope the inspector has had a very successful day." She looked around the table. "Mrs. Goodge, did you have any luck today?"

Mrs. Goodge pursed her lips. "I only had the laundry boy through here this afternoon, and he was useless. I wasted my last bun on the lad, and he'd never even heard of Sir George Braxton. But not to worry, I've got a goodly number of tradespeople in tomorrow, and I've invited one of my old colleagues over for morning coffee, so I ought to have something to report by tomorrow's meeting." She'd sent Hilda Bradford, an old acquaintance of hers a note as soon as they learned of the murder. Hilda was a notorious gossip and had absolutely no scruples about repeating everything that came her way. Mrs. Goodge couldn't wait for the woman to come into her kitchen.

"Did you find out anything, Betsy?" Mrs. Jeffries asked.

"Actually, I did hear a bit. According to Mrs. Bartlett, she owns the baker's shop, Sir George was very tightfisted with his coin. So much so, that they only bought day-old bread for the household."

Mrs. Goodge snorted. "I'm not surprised. Aristocrats can be the stingiest people on earth. In my younger days, I worked for a countess who was so cheap she reused tea leaves!"

Betsy giggled. "It seems the Braxton family might be cut from the same cloth. Mrs. Bartlett said the daughters are just as miserly."

"The daughters frequent the baker's shop?" Mrs. Goodge asked.

"No, but Mrs. Bartlett is friends with the family's dressmaker. She told Mrs. Bartlett that all three of the daughters find fault with anything the seamstress makes so they can cut a few bob off the price. Mrs. Bartlett said that the seamstress has gotten so fed up, she's decided not to take any more custom from the family. There's not enough profit, and they're not worth the trouble."

"Does the seamstress work out of her home or a shop?" Mrs. Jeffries asked. This could well be a good avenue of information.

"She works out of a shop on the Upper Richmond Road." The maid grinned. "I think I might go in and have a look at some of her patterns, and see if I can get her talking a bit."

Smythe opened his mouth and then clamped it shut just as quickly. He'd almost told Betsy to go in and get fitted for a dress. He could well afford to buy her any dress her heart desired. Just in time, he'd remembered that not everyone in the household knew about his financial situation.

The problem was he was a rich man. He'd made a fortune in Australia. Betsy knew, of course, and he suspected that Mrs. Jeffries had figured it out, but the others hadn't a clue. He wanted to keep it that way.

"That's an excellent idea," Mrs. Jeffries said.

"Oh, and I heard that there's some cousin that lives at the house, and the gossip is that he's not really a cousin at all. But Mrs. Bartlett didn't have any details."

"Did she know anything about the murder?" Wiggins asked.

"Not really, she just said that it was a strange household, and that no one in the neighborhood was as surprised by the murder as they were pretending to be. I wanted to ask her what she meant by that, but wouldn't you know, half a dozen customers came in all of a sudden, and I couldn't keep hanging about. I tried the greengrocer's next, but there was a sour-faced old puritan working there, and she wasn't interested in gossip, thank you."

Everyone laughed. Mrs. Jeffries said, "We've all done quite well today. We'll meet again at breakfast, and I'll tell you what I get out of the inspector tonight. Now, we must decide what to do about Luty and Hatchet."

"It wouldn't be right not to tell them," Mrs. Goodge said.

"But Luty's still so ill, and you know what she's like, she'll not want to stay abed if we're on a case," Betsy warned. "We don't want to risk her health."

"True, but as Mrs. Goodge says, it's not right to keep 'em out of it," Smythe argued. "Besides, I'm thinkin' we're goin' to need Hatchet on this case as soon as possible."

"Maybe we ought to wait another day or two before we tell 'im," Wiggins suggested. "We don't want Luty gettin' upset."

"We can't wait. The victim's an aristocrat," the coachman explained. "We need someone on the case who has access to the rich and powerful. Lady Cannonberry's out of town until next week, so we can't ask her to 'elp."

Lady Ruth Cannonberry was their neighbor and their friend. The inspector was trying to court the woman, but she kept getting called out of town to take care of one or the other of her late husband's sick relatives.

"She'd be useful in this case," the cook agreed. "Let's hope she comes home early."

"She'll definitely be back by Christmas," Mrs. Jeffries said. "She's coming for Christmas dinner with the inspector. Speaking of which, have you ordered the turkey yet?" Mrs. Jeffries had been meaning to ask the cook that very question for two days now, but she'd kept forgetting.

"The butcher's got a nice plump one all picked out for us," Mrs. Goodge replied, "and he's sending along a nice cut of beef for Boxing Day as well. I've ordered an extra-large bird as Luty and Hatchet are having Christmas dinner with us, providin', of course, that Luty's well enough by Christmas."

"Are we goin' to have them crackers as well," Wiggins asked eagerly. "The ones that pop when you pull out the paper? You know, we 'ad them last year, and they were ever so nice."

"Christmas crackers," Mrs. Jeffries laughed. "Of course we are . . . Oh dear, I'm afraid we're getting off the subject. Sorry, Smythe, do go on with what you were saying."

"Hatchet's got some inroads into society," Smythe continued. "And Mrs. Goodge can call on 'er old friends for information, but I've a feelin' this murder is goin' to be a bit 'arder than the others, and I don't think we can risk leavin' Hatchet out of it. Truth be told, we could use Luty's connections as well."

"I suppose you're right," Betsy replied. "But it's important that Luty gets well first."

"I agree," Mrs. Jeffries said softly. "I also think that it's important that we all understand that having a murder case this close to Christmas might be quite distracting."

"Just a tad." Smythe grinned. "But I don't mind a bit of interruption now and then."

"Thank you, Smythe," Mrs. Jeffries laughed. "Let's all remember that the season is the season, and murder or not, it is important to celebrate the birth of the Lord."

"Of course it is," Mrs. Goodge agreed. "Now that that's settled, let's decide what to do about Luty and Hatchet." She glanced at the clock on the pine sideboard. "It's gettin' late, and I've got a few things to do before the inspector gets home and wants his supper."

They discussed the matter for a few more minutes and

decided that Mrs. Jeffries would nip over the next morning and have a quiet word with Hatchet.

Wiggins said nothing as he was too busy wrestling with his conscience to pay much attention to the conversation. But by the time the meeting ended, he knew what he had to do. After all, a promise was a promise.

It was almost half past seven before the inspector's footsteps sounded on the front steps. Mrs. Jeffries met him at the front door. "You look absolutely exhausted, sir," she commented as she took his bowler and hung it on the coat tree.

"It's been a rather difficult day," he replied. He shrugged out of his heavy overcoat. "I do believe I could use a sherry. That won't inconvenience Mrs. Goodge, will it?" The inspector didn't want his servants waiting up half the night to dance attendance on him. They worked hard and needed their rest. On the other hand, he'd so looked forward to having a nice glass of Harvey's and discussing this case with his housekeeper. She was such a good listener. Of course, their neighbor, Ruth Cannonberry, was an excellent listener as well, but for some odd reason, Mrs. Jeffries was just a bit better at asking the sort of questions that got him thinking. Besides, Ruth wasn't due back yet. He sighed. He did miss Ruth very much when she was gone.

"No sir, Mrs. Goodge has made a nice, hot pot for supper and an apple tart for dessert. I'll bring it up anytime you're ready." She took his coat and hung it up next to the bowler. "Let's go into the drawing room, sir. I've already poured you a sherry."

CHAPTER 4

"This has been a very long day," Witherspoon said as he sank into his favorite chair. "What's more, this case is already showing signs that it's going to be very strange."

"In what way, sir?" Mrs. Jeffries picked up the glasses of sherry she'd poured earlier and handed one to him.

"Thank you," he said as he reached for his drink. "You know how, generally, when one deals with a certain class of people, one has trouble getting much information out of them."

"You mean the upper classes don't feel they're under any obligation to speak to a police officer," she replied. It was true, the further up the social ladder one went, the less inclined they were to talk. Some of them even seemed to have the idea they were completely above the law.

"Unfortunate, but true," he took a sip from his glass. "But in this case, everyone in the household seems quite eager to speak to me, unless, of course, they've a meeting with their solicitors." He sighed. "Sir George has three daughters, all of whom were home last night when he was murdered, but I didn't get to speak with them for long at all. They had some sort of meeting with their solicitors."

"They've already hired lawyers?" Mrs. Jeffries sank down into the chair opposite the inspector. "Gracious, are they suspects?"

"No, no, I didn't mean to imply anything like that." He waved his hand dismissively. "The solicitors were already scheduled to come to see the family." He broke off and frowned. "At least I think they were already scheduled to come to the house. I really must ask someone."

"You certainly should, sir," she said quickly. "Solicitors generally meet with people for a reason, and if the appointment had been set some time ago, it could well have something to do with Sir George's murder."

"Yes." He nodded. "I see what you mean. The solicitors might have come to the house expecting to meet with Sir George, not find him dead and gone to the morgue."

"But I'm sure you'd already thought of that," she said easily. "It should be simple to find out when the appointment was set and who the solicitors were actually expecting to meet with."

"True." He took another sip of his sherry. "Everyone, including the servants, speaks quite freely. No one appears to be hiding anything, though it is difficult to get a coherent account out of any of them. As a matter of fact, we've still to interview two of the houseguests and a cousin who lives on the premises." He yawned. "We wanted to have a chat with everyone in the household today, but by the time we'd finished searching the victim's room and getting the gardener's account of finding the body, everyone had left the house. It was the oddest thing, both the houseguests had gone off to the shops to buy Christmas presents, and the cousin had disappeared completely. No one had a clue where he'd gone. I don't understand it, Mrs. Jeffries, it's almost as though none of them thought anything out of the ordinary had occurred. They simply went right on with their daily activities as though finding a corpse with a bashed-in skull was something that happened every day."

"Some people aren't very sensitive," she said softly. Unfortunately, the inspector was quite sensitive, and she could see that he was greatly distressed by the cavalier attitude of the household.

"I suppose not," he agreed. "I just hope I can catch the person who did this. I don't think Sir George Braxton was a particularly nice person, but no one deserves to be murdered."

"You will find the killer," she replied stoutly. "You always do, sir. You're an excellent detective."

"Thank you," he replied. "Another reason we didn't make much progress today was that we had to go back to the Yard."

"That's quite a distance, sir. It must have been very inconvenient." She held her breath, hoping that he'd not gone back to be told that Inspector Nigel Nivens was horning in on the case. The staff hated Inspector Nivens. The man had spent years trying to undermine their inspector.

"It wasn't so much inconvenient as it was alarming. Chief Inspector Barrows asked for an update on the case."

"But you'd just started your investigation."

Witherspoon nodded in agreement. "That's what I told him, and to his credit, he said he understood and that we must conduct a thorough investigation. But he also said the department was under a lot of pressure to solve this murder."

"What does that mean?" she asked. She suspected she knew exactly what it meant.

Witherspoon sighed. "Apparently, the deceased is some sort of distant cousin to the queen and, well, Barrows hinted that it would be a good idea to have it resolved by Christmas."

"That's only a week away," she said softly. "But I'm sure you'll do just fine, sir. I take it you'll be going back to the Braxton house tomorrow?"

"We've no choice. As I said, there are still a number of people in the household we must interview, and I want to have another chance to speak with Sir George's daughters. Though I must admit, getting any sort of sense of who was where and doing what is a bit muddled."

"Muddled?" she repeated. "How so?"

He took another sip of his sherry and told her about his encounters with the dead man's children. "I don't believe those three women are overly fond of one another," he finished.

"You're very perceptive, sir. Was the Home Secretary still there when you arrived?"

"No, his assistant was waiting for us."

"Then what happened, sir?" Mrs. Jeffries wanted to direct the conversation so that his account started from the time he and Barnes had arrived at the Braxton household.

He continued with his recitation of the day's activities, and Mrs. Jeffries listened patiently, occasionally asking a question or making a comment. When it became clear his narrative was taking a good deal longer than usual and that his dinner was in danger of getting cold, she ushered him into the dining room, and they continued their discussion while he ate.

By the time the inspector had finished his last bite of

dessert, he felt much better about the case. "I believe I'll take Fred for a quick walk before I retire." He rose to his feet. "Is he down in the kitchen?"

"Yes, sir, he was lying on the rug earlier." Mrs. Jeffries began to stack his dishes onto a tray. "Do bundle up, sir. It's still very cold outside."

"We'll just do a short walk." The inspector went downstairs and pulled Fred's lead off the hook by the kitchen door. Hearing the familiar voice and the rattle of his lead, Fred leapt to his feet and bounced up and down in anticipation of going out. It took Witherspoon a few moments to get the lead attached to the collar, but he finally got Fred settled enough to complete the task. "We'll be back soon," he said with a laugh as the dog pulled him toward the back door.

The rest of the household cleared up the last of the dinner dishes and by the time Witherspoon and Fred came home, the household was ready for a brief meeting. They waited till Witherspoon was safely up the stairs before taking their places at the table.

Mrs. Jeffries told them everything she'd learned, taking care not to leave out anything. They'd learned from previous cases that even the most insignificant detail could be important. When she'd finished, no one said anything for a moment or two.

Finally, Smythe said, "So it was probably someone in the house that killed him."

"Why would you say that?" Betsy asked. "The door to his bedroom was wide open. Anyone could have gotten inside."

"There weren't no evidence it had been forced," Wiggins pointed out, "so that means he opened the door."

"And from what we've heard of Sir George, he doesn't

sound the sort to open the door to a stranger," Mrs. Goodge added.

Betsy looked doubtful. "I'm not so sure. Something might have lured him outside. He might have heard a noise and gone out to investigate."

"Humph," the cook snorted. "More likely he'd get one of the servants up and make them go out to investigate. I've worked in enough noble houses to know those people would wake a housemaid or a footman rather than put themselves to any trouble."

"Both of you could be correct," Mrs. Jeffries said to the two women. "But it's early days yet, so we've plenty of time to find out what happened."

"I thought the chief inspector told our inspector he wanted the case finished by Christmas," Wiggins said.

"He didn't exactly tell him that," Mrs. Jeffries clarified. "He simply said it would be a good idea."

"And we all know what that means," Smythe snorted. "It means find the killer or else. Not to worry though, I've faith in our inspector and in all of us."

"At least now we've a goodly list of names to start working on," Mrs. Goodge said. "I'll get my sources on it right away. I'm sure there's plenty to be had about Sir George's daughters."

"And the houseguests," Betsy said. "We mustn't forget about them. I wish I knew where Fiona Burleigh came from, she's a Braxton cousin. Maybe she wanted Sir George dead."

"I'll see if I can find that out," Mrs. Goodge said. "And I'll see if I can find out where Raleigh Brent hails from as well."

"Good," Mrs. Jeffries stood up. "Then we know what we're about then."

"There were a lot of people in the house when Sir George was murdered," Wiggins said. "We'll be stretched a bit to try and cover them all."

Luty Belle Crookshank owned a beautiful home in Knightsbridge. Hatchet, Luty's tall, distinguished white-haired butler, let Mrs. Jeffries in the front door. "This is a pleasant surprise. Madam will be delighted you've come to see her," he said as he took her cloak.

"Actually, it's you I've come to see. I don't even want Luty to know I've been here." Mrs. Jeffries replied.

"Let's go into the drawing room," Hatchet said softly. He glanced at the grand staircase leading to the second floor. "The walls have ears."

Generally, a butler would have escorted his visitor to the butler's pantry, but Hatchet had a very unusual relationship with his employer and essentially had the run of the house and the command of the household.

He escorted Mrs. Jeffries into an elegantly furnished drawing room done in pale blue and cream. "Do sit down, Mrs. Jeffries and tell me what's wrong." He motioned her toward an ivory-colored damask settee.

"Nothing is really wrong," she replied as she sat down. "But we've a murder."

"Sir George Braxton?" He sat opposite her on an ivory-and-blue-striped wing chair.

She nodded. "We're going to need your help."

"So the inspector caught that one, did he?" Hatchet pursed his lips.

"I'm afraid so." She told him about the circumstances of the inspector getting the case. "But my real concern isn't the murder, it's Luty. She's far too ill to be out investigating, yet

I'm concerned she'll hear about it and be very upset that she wasn't included."

"She will hear about it, and she will be most upset," Hatchet replied slowly, "but, nonetheless, she's still too ill to be out. Don't worry, Mrs. Jeffries, I'll handle Madam."

"Good," she smiled. "I was hoping you'd say that. We're going to need you on this case, Hatchet. You've so many sources in aristocratic circles, and, frankly, without Luty, we'll have to rely on you."

He shrugged modestly. "I'm pleased to be of service. Now, what else have you learned about the murder?"

Inspector Witherspoon and Constable Barnes made themselves a makeshift office in what was the old butler's pantry. Barnes whipped out his notebook and took a seat at the rickety table. "I've asked Mrs. Merryhill to send the servants in again. They were all in such a state yesterday that I want to reinterview them and see if they've remembered anything else."

"That's an excellent idea. It's odd, isn't it? If you wait too long to take a statement, witnesses may have forgotten all sorts of useful information, but if you interview some people too quickly, they're in such a dither they can't recall anything."

"Are you going to interview the sisters again?" Barnes asked curiously.

"Oh, yes, only this time I'll make sure to speak to each of them privately." He frowned slightly. "They do tend to argue if they're together in the same room."

"I know," Barnes replied. "I heard them last night just before we were leaving. What about the solicitors, sir? Are you going to find out why they were here yesterday?"

"That's on my list of questions to ask," he replied. "I'll be in Sir George's study if you need me."

Mrs. Merryhill waited for the inspector at the top of the stairs. "I'll escort you to Sir George's study," she said solemnly. "Miss Burleigh is waiting for you."

"Thank you, but that's not necessary. I know where the study is located. However, I would appreciate it if you'd tell Sir George's daughters that I'll need to speak with them sometime today."

She nodded briefly. "I'll insure they get the message, Inspector."

He pulled open the door and stepped inside the study. The room was large, poorly lighted, and crammed full of oversized furniture, the centerpiece of which was a huge mahogany desk. A woman was sitting on a chair in front of the desk.

She stared at him coldly. She was a thin woman with brown hair, pale skin, and hazel eyes, and she was wearing a high-collared green dress with lace at the cuffs and neck.

"Good morning, ma'am," Witherspoon said politely. "I'm Inspector Witherspoon."

"I know," she replied. "I'm Fiona Burleigh. But I expect you know that already."

He hesitated for a moment and then went behind the desk and sat down. Sitting in a dead man's spot felt a bit awkward, but as she was already seated, he had no other choice. "I need to ask you a few questions."

"Of course you do," she replied. "That's why I've come. But I don't know what I can tell you. I was asleep when Sir George was killed."

"Did you hear anything in the night?" he asked.

"No, I'm a sound sleeper. The first I knew that Sir George was dead was when I went down to breakfast. Of course, there wasn't any. They didn't think to feed us for hours, can you imagine that? I finally had to find Miss Merryhill and insist she send up food. I mean, really, just because someone's died is no reason to starve your houseguests. Raleigh was quite famished. He gets light-headed when he's hungry."

"Are you sure you heard nothing, ma'am?" Witherspoon wasn't sure what to make of this, especially as Miss Charlotte Braxton had apparently had hysterics in the wee hours of the morning and had been quite noisy.

"Quite sure, Inspector," she sniffed disapprovingly. "I wouldn't have said so if I wasn't."

"Where is your room located?"

"I beg your pardon?"

"Does it face the front or the back of the house?" he asked.

For a moment, she simply stared at him, and he was afraid she wasn't going to answer at all. Finally, she said. "It's at the back of the house, Inspector. I overlook the back garden."

"And you didn't see or hear anything the night Sir George was murdered?" He really found that difficult to believe. But some people did sleep very soundly. Perhaps she was one of them.

"I've already told you I didn't," she said.

"How long have you been a guest in the house?"

"I arrived on Saturday," she said. "Raleigh and I took the train down from London together. We'd been invited to stay over Christmas."

"And once you were here, did you see or hear anything that seemed odd?" The moment the question was out of his mouth, he wished he could take it back. This entire household was strange.

She thought for a moment. "Not really. The household was much as it was the last time I was here."

"You come often for a visit?"

"Yes, Inspector," she said. "We're cousins, and as I've very few relatives, I tend to come occasionally to visit. Family is family."

Witherspoon nodded. "Can you describe what happened on the evening of the murder?" He'd found that was sometimes a useful question to ask. It would be interesting to compare her version of the evening with what he'd heard from the servants and from Lucinda Braxton. Sometimes, people lived through the same moments but saw the events in those minutes very differently.

Her thin face creased in a frown. "I don't really know where to begin. Let's see, Raleigh and Lucinda and I went for a walk late that afternoon."

"You went for a walk? But the weather was dreadful that day. It snowed."

"A little bit of snow never hurt anyone," she snapped. "Besides, it was supposed to just be Raleigh and myself. But of course, Lucinda was dogging his heels, and we couldn't get away without her tagging along. Honestly, some people just don't know when they're not wanted."

"What time was this?"

"Just before dark," she replied. "We didn't go very far because as you've said, it was snowing. It came down hard as well, it was covering the grounds by the time we got back to the house."

"Did you leave the grounds?"

"Yes, we went up the road about a hundred yards."

"Who all was here that night?" He already knew the answer to this one, but it never hurt to get the answer verified from an independent source.

"Myself, of course, and Sir George. Raleigh and the sisters. Clarence was here as well, but then, you knew that, he lives here."

"What did you do after your walk?" Witherspoon pressed.

"I went up to my room to rest before dinner. Raleigh went upstairs to write some letters, and Lucinda went into the drawing room to have a word with her sisters."

"Did anything unusual happen at dinner that night?"

She shrugged. "Not really. It was quite cold, and I recall Charlotte asked her father to put more logs on the fire. But he simply told her to put on another garment. He was in a foul mood, that silly cat of his had gone missing, and he was worried sick about the stupid animal. He blamed the girls."

"The girls?" Witherspoon repeated. He wasn't sure if she meant the servants or the Braxton daughters.

"His daughters," Fiona explained. "He claimed that one of them had run off the cat out of spite. He thought they were jealous of his affection for the beast. Of course, that was nonsense, they loathed the creature."

"So I take it dinner wasn't a very pleasant affair."

"It was miserable, Inspector." Fiona looked him straight in the eye. "The only reason I came was because Raleigh was going to be here. We've become quite fond of one another and, frankly, once I knew that Lucinda had invited him for Christmas, I made sure I was invited as well. The woman will stop at nothing to get her hooks into him. Raleigh is very much the innocent when it comes to dealing with strong-minded people like Lucinda." She sighed. "I don't know what I shall do now."

"What do you mean?"

She shrugged her thin shoulders again. "Isn't it obvious? Now that Sir George is gone, the girls will get their inheritance. That means Lucinda will have quite a bit of money at her disposal."

"I see," he replied. He wondered if the dispersal of Sir George's estate was common knowledge.

"Sir George's death has worked out very well for Lucinda," Fiona said harshly. "Now that she has money, she and Raleigh will be able to marry. I hope she has the good grace to wait a decent interval."

Witherspoon was beginning to understand. "You mean that while Sir George was alive, they couldn't marry. Didn't he think Mr. Brent was a suitable husband for his daughter?"

Fiona laughed harshly. "Oh, Sir George had no objection to the marriage, he liked Raleigh well enough, but he refused to give Lucinda a dowry or a settlement. Lucinda was furious when Sir George told her he wouldn't fund her dowry."

"How do you know this?" Witherspoon asked.

"I heard them quarreling," she replied. "It happened when I first arrived. Raleigh had gone upstairs to freshen up, but I needed to send a quick note to my housekeeper in London. I wanted to borrow some paper from the Sir George's study, so I went down the hall, but before I could go inside, I heard the two of them arguing. Lucinda was shouting at Sir George that he was ruining her life and her one chance at happiness. He shouted back that he didn't care. I'd never heard her talk that way to her father before, that's how I know she was furious. But he wouldn't budge. He was quite cruel. He said to her, " 'Look, old girl, you're simply too old for such nonsense.' " She giggled maliciously. "She was, you know. No matter how hard she tries to pretend, she's well into her forties, and she looks every day of it."

*   *   *

Mrs. Goodge handed her guest a cup of freshly made coffee. "I'm glad you could come, it's been such a long time since we've seen each other, Hilda."

"It has been a long time." Hilda Bradford bobbed her gray head in agreement. She was a few years younger than the cook, but as she was a housekeeper and not a cook, her frame was a good deal thinner than her companion's. "I heard from Ida Leahcock that you're now working for a police detective. Do you like it here?"

"Indeed, I do. He's a very nice master, he treats me and the other servants like human beings, not slaves. The wages are much better, too, and the work is easier. I don't have to do those awful eight-course dinners anymore. How about you? Are you still keeping house for Lord Grimethorpe?"

Hilda made a face. "Yes, and he's still a stingy old sod, too. But it's not for much longer. I'm joining my daughter in America next spring, so I suppose I can put up with him for a few more months"

"Then I'm glad I sent you that note. America's a long way off, and I'd have felt bad if I'd not seen you before you left. You and I worked together a long time."

Hilda laughed. "That we did, and we had a few chuckles along the way. What's it like working for your detective? Do you ever hear about his cases?"

"Oh, yes, he's investigating this one from down in Richmond."

"You mean Sir George Braxton?" Hilda helped herself to one of Mrs. Goodge's buns.

"That's right."

"I've seen the fellow. He'd been to Grimethorpe's for supper a time or two. He wasn't a particularly well-liked person. Even amongst his own kind."

"What do you mean?" Mrs. Goodge leaned forward eagerly.

"He was a miserly sort," she replied. "He gave those daughters of his a pittance for an allowance, and he practically starved his household." She took a quick sip of coffee. "He may have been a baronet, but he couldn't keep servants. These days, people won't put up with bein' poorly fed and worked like plough horses. Not only that, but I've heard his youngest daughter is just like him. She can pinch a penny so tight the copper curdles. Mind you, I also heard she does have a way of making money grow."

"I don't understand," Mrs. Goodge said. "How can she make money grow?"

"Investments," Hilda replied. "She's been handling all the family money for years now. It saved Sir George having to pay fees for financial services. You ought to have heard Lord Grimethorpe ranting and raving when he heard about it." She grinned. "He'd just paid out some huge fees to his brokers for some Brazilian bonds that were no good, so he was looking for something to shout about. Mind you, the girl's done a good job. Unlike a lot of aristocratic families, the Braxtons have got a bit of money. That annoys Lord Grimethorpe as well. His family are a pack of fools, money goes through their hands like water."

Mrs. Goodge shook her head in amazement. "That's really strange, isn't it? Back in our day, no woman would dream of handling money, and now the daughter of a baronet is acting as a financial manager!"

"Good for her, I say," Hilda said stoutly.

"What about Sir George's other children?" Mrs. Goodge asked. The nice thing about Hilda was she loved to gossip so much she never thought it odd that others were equally curious.

"He's got two other daughters, and they're odd ducks as well," she continued. "The middle one supposedly likes to travel so much that she hired herself out as a companion a couple of years back so she could go to Italy. Have you ever heard of such a thing? Scandalous it was, but they say the old man didn't care, that he had a good laugh over it and told the girl to enjoy herself. Not that any of them are girls, they're all in their forties, if they're a day."

"What about the eldest daughter?" Mrs. Goodge asked.

Hilda peered thoughtfully toward the window. "The only gossip I've ever heard about Lucinda Braxton is that she's got a foul temper. I expect she inherited that from her father as well."

"Those no-good pole cats," Luty Belle Crookshank muttered darkly as she crept up the back stairs and down the corridor toward her bedroom. "Think they can tuck me away and leave me out just because of a piddlin' little sniffle, well, I'll show them." She coughed harshly, a deep nasty one that seemed to well out of the pit of her belly and take every ounce of strength she had just to stay on her feet.

"Madam, what on earth are you doing?" Hatchet came up behind her. "You know you're not supposed to be out of bed."

She had to wait a moment to catch her breathe. "I'm fine," she whispered as she struggled to breath. "I just got tired of laying there and wanted to stretch my joints a little."

He put his arm around her shoulders and tugged her gently in the direction of her room. "Really, madam, I don't think dashing up and down the back stairs is an appropriate way to get some exercise."

One of the maids came rushing down the hall. "There you are, ma'am, we've been looking everywhere for you."

"Nells bells, Julie, I only went for a bit of a walk, I'm fine. Stop fussin', now, both of you." She shook Hatchet's arm off her shoulder, straightened her spine, and marched

toward her room. She was madder than a wet hen but determined not to show it. The last thing she wanted was
Hatchet watching her when they had them a murder.

"Are you sure you're all right, ma'am?" Julie asked, her
round face creased in worry. "You gave me such a fright, I
just popped out for a moment to get you that book, and
when I came back, you were gone!"

Luty hurried into her room and headed for her bed. "I'm
fine, Julie, just fine." She smiled at them. "You and
Hatchet go on about your business. I'm going to take a little rest now."

Hatchet stared at his employer suspiciously. He watched
her carefully as the maid helped her into the four-poster bed
and pulled the covers up to her chin. Surely she couldn't
have overheard his conversation with Mrs. Jeffries. Surely
she couldn't possibly know there was a murder afoot. But
Luty was a wily old fox, and he wasn't going to underesti-
mate her abilities. "Why did you go down the back stairs?"

Luty was ready for that one. "I was going to the kitchen
to get me a cup of tea."

"I'd have brought you some tea, ma'am," Julie said de-
fensively. She was quite devoted to Luty.

"Nells bells, will you two quit your fussin'," Luty sighed
loudly. "I wanted a bit of movin' about, that's all. My joints
are achin' from layin' here, and so I took a quick stroll down
toward the kitchen." She didn't mention that the footman,
Jon, had told her that Mrs. Jeffries was downstairs. When
Hatchet hadn't brought her friend upstairs for a visit, she'd
known something was going on and had decided to do a bit
of snooping on her own. "Now get out of here so I can get
me some sleep."

Julie sighed melodramatically and flounced toward the
door. Hatchet gave Luty one last suspicious glance and then

followed the maid. As soon as the door to Luty's bedroom was firmly shut, he turned to Julie and said, "I don't trust her. Keep a close eye on her and make sure she doesn't get out of that bed."

"Yes, sir, I'll do my best. But you know what she's like, once she's made up her mind, there's no stopping her."

"I understand you wished to speak to me," Raleigh Brent said as he stepped into the room.

Witherspoon stared at the fellow and tried to think why Lucinda Braxton and Fiona Burleigh were both so keen on the man. Brent was short and skinny with thin lips, a weak chin, and a disapproving, rather sour expression. "Yes, actually, I would have liked to have spoken to you yesterday, but you left before we could take your statement."

Brent was taken aback. "I beg your pardon? I didn't realize I needed permission from the police to come and go."

"A murder was committed, Mr. Brent," the inspector explained, "and it's important that we interview everyone as soon as possible. Please, sit down." He was generally very polite to people, but he had the sense that this man had deliberately avoided speaking to them, and he wanted to know why.

"I've no idea what you think I can tell you," Brent said as he sat down. "I know absolutely nothing about Sir George's murder."

"You were in the house on the night it happened, weren't you?"

"Yes, but I was sound asleep."

Witherspoon wondered if there was an epidemic of sound sleeping that night. "Did you hear anything, anything at all during the night?"

Brent shook his head. "No, nothing."

"Did you hear or see anything odd or unusual before you retired for the night?" Witherspoon pressed. He was struck by the fact that both guests claimed they'd heard nothing, when he knew very well that Charlotte Braxton had had hysterics and the entire household had been tramping about the back garden in the wee hours of the night.

"Not really," Brent said. "We had dinner, it wasn't particularly festive, but it was decent enough. The conversation was rather muted. Sir George was complaining his cat was still missing, Clarence was talking about his orchids, and Lucinda was trying to get her father to put more logs on the fire. It had gone dreadfully cold."

"What happened then?" Witherspoon asked. He hoped that Barnes was having better luck than he was.

"Nothing." Brent seemed surprised by the question. "We finished dinner and went into the drawing room. Mrs. Merryhill served coffee, and then Sir George retired. Fiona and I played a game of whist."

"Were the other members of the household present?" Witherspoon asked.

"Oh, yes, everyone was present. Charlotte was reading a travel book, Nina was reading the financial news, and Lucinda was helping me play my hand."

"What about Clarence Clark?" the inspector probed. "Was he present?"

"Only for a little while." Brent frowned. "He disappeared right after dinner. I think he and Sir George might have had words."

"Why?"

"Well." Brent looked around the room, as though he expected someone to be hiding behind a chair. "I overheard

Clarence and Sir George having what sounded like an argument just before dinner."

"Did you hear what they were arguing about?" Witherspoon pressed. He began to think he might be getting somewhere. Sir George had argued with both his daughter and his cousin on the evening he died.

Brent shook his head. "Not really, they were trying to keep their voices down. But later, Lucinda told me that Clarence was upset because Sir George was selling the conservatory."

"I'm afraid I don't understand," the inspector said. "Isn't it attached to the house?"

"Apparently, it can be taken off," Brent replied. "And Clarence spends all this time there, he grows the most wonderful orchids. They really are spectacular. He's won lots of prizes and is considered an expert in the field. But then again, it could be that Sir George was haranguing the poor fellow about the cat. God knows he'd harangued the rest of us continually since the wretched beast went missing."

"How long had you known Sir George?" Witherspoon asked.

"Five years," Brent replied.

"And did you like Sir George?"

Brent looked surprised by the question. "I didn't really know him all that well. This is the first time I've ever been invited here."

"I see." The inspector's mind went blank.

"Is there anything else?" Raleigh was already getting to his feet.

"Not at present," Witherspoon replied. "How long will you be staying? We may need to ask you some additional questions."

"Oh, I shan't be leaving for a long while." The man smiled broadly. "Miss Lucinda Braxton has consented to become my wife, and I think it important that I stay on until this matter is sorted out."

"Congratulations," Witherspoon said. "Have you announced your engagement?"

"Not yet, we'll wait a decent interval before we announce it publicly. After all, Lucinda has just lost her father."

"Are you keeping it a secret then?" The inspector had no idea where that question had come from, but to his amazement, he saw a deep flush creep up Brent's face.

"We've not told anyone. I only mentioned it to you because you asked if I was staying on, otherwise I wouldn't have said a word." He glanced at the door. "It doesn't look good, does it, I mean, announcing an engagement so soon after a death in the family?"

"Not just a death in the family, Raleigh." Fiona Burleigh stepped into the room. "It's a murder in the family. Let's be honest here, you wouldn't have given a tinker's damn about marrying Lucinda Braxton as long as her father was alive. But now that he's dead, everything's different, isn't it?"

Smythe hesitated in front of the Dirty Duck Pub. He pulled his heavy coat tighter as a gust of cold wind blew in off the Thames. He knew he should be doing the investigating on his own, but, blast, there was only so much you could find out from cabbies and street urchins. Besides, what was money for if you couldn't use it as you saw fit?

He opened the door of the pub and squinted against the dim light as he stepped inside. It was just after opening hours, and the place was relatively empty. His quarry was sitting at his usual table by the fire.

His quarry spotted him as well. Blimpey Groggins raised

his glass and waved. He was dressed in his usual checked coat, white shirt, and dirty porkpie hat. A bright red scarf was wound around his neck.

Blimpey Groggins bought and sold knowledge. He had an army of bank clerks, street urchins, telegram boys, household servants, and street vendors who kept him supplied with information. If a house had been robbed while its owner was in the country, Blimpey would have a good idea who was behind the theft. If a member of Parliament was leaving the country for a holiday, he'd know what train the fellow was taking. Blimpey had once been a thief, but had discovered that the negative consequences of getting caught weren't to his liking, so he'd taken his phenomenal memory and put it to work for himself. He sold his information to politicians, private inquiry agents, real estate developers, and a whole host of people who were willing to pay to know who was doing what to whom.

Smythe slipped onto the stool across from Blimpey. "Hello. Blimpey. Keepin' warm?"

"Doin' my best, mate. I was wondering how long it would be before you showed up." Blimpey grinned. "What'll you have, mate?"

CHAPTER 5

"I've got a job for ya," Smythe said. "And it's a bit of a rush one."

"Take a minute to catch yer breath," Blimpey replied. "Come on, mate, it's Christmas. What'll you have to drink? It's on me."

Smythe waved him off with an impatient gesture of his hand. "I know what time of year it is and that's why I'm in such a bloomin' rush. Do you want the job or not?"

" 'Course I do, old friend, 'course I do. But there's no reason you can't take five minutes and be sociable, have a bit of Christmas cheer." He gestured to the barmaid. "Now, what'll you 'ave?"

Smythe suddenly felt mean and petty. Blimpey was a decent sort, and they'd known one another a long time. "It's good of you to offer, I'll 'ave a pint. 'Ow's your good wife?"

"She's fine, mate." Blimpey grinned broadly. "She's all in

a state over Christmas, bakin' up a storm and puttin' out pretty paper streamers. She even wants one of them Christmas trees like they 'ave at the palace." He looked at the barmaid and said, "Bring me another one, Agnes, and bring my friend here a pint of your best bitter, please."

"Coming right up, Blimpey," Agnes replied.

Blimpey turned back to Smythe and continued with what he'd been saying. "I told her, I wasn't sure where I could even get one of them trees, let alone all the folderol she wants to put on the thing, but she's insistin' that we 'ave one."

"Don't tell me she believed that," Smythe grinned. "You can get your 'ands on anything."

"That's just what she said," Blimpey laughed. "So I expect I'd best make sure I do what's right to keep the lady 'appy."

"You sound like an old married man," Smythe said. As he'd had a hand in bringing the two of them together, he was pleased with Blimpey's good-natured complaining about his spouse. Smythe hoped he'd be doing some good-natured complaining of his own in the coming years. But first he had to get that ring on Betsy's finger.

"It's costin' me an arm and leg." Blimpey nodded politely as Agnes put their drinks down on the table. "But then again, that's what money is for, inn't it? Speakin' of money, why don't you tell me what it is you're needin', my good fellow."

Smythe almost laughed out loud. "Pull the other one, Blimpey, you know why I'm 'ere." He was certain that Blimpey had already heard about the Braxton murder, and he was equally certain that Blimpey had already sent out some feelers about who might be responsible for the deed. Blimpey survived by knowing things. He'd not want toffs to start dying without him learning what he could about the situation. Knowing what was going on amongst the criminal classes was the man's business.

" 'Course I do, Smythe, I was just bein' polite. So, your inspector caught the Braxton murder. I'm not surprised." Blimpey took a sip of his beer. "They'll want that one solved quickly. It's embarrassin' for the government when a toff gets killed in his own back garden. Makes it seem like we're not a tidy, safe little country."

"We've more or less got until Christmas to get the thing sorted out," Smythe murmured.

"What do you need from me?" Blimpey asked.

"Anything you can find out would be 'elpful."

"I've already got a bit of information about Sir George."

"You goin' to share it?" Smythe took a drink of his beer.

"If the price is right," Blimpey replied with a laugh. "But then again, old mate, you've always paid up. Now, let me tell you what I know about your dead baronet, and then you can tell what else you need me to find out."

Smythe nodded. "That's fair."

"Sir George had a bit of reputation as a bad one," he continued. "He's one of them ponces that thinks because he's got a title that he owns the world. His title, by the way, is an old one, it was created by James the First in 1614."

"Has the estate always been at Richmond?" Smythe asked.

"Nah, the Richmond property was bought by Sir George's father about sixty years ago. Unlike a lot of aristocratic families, this one's managed to hang onto their money."

"How much do they 'ave?"

"Plenty," Blimpey replied. "I don't know exactly what the family is worth, but it's a good deal more than most aristocrats in this country. The Braxtons were smart; they got out of land and started puttin' their money into factories and overseas investments. One of Sir George's ancestors sold off the original estate and used that money to seed his investments. The family has either been clever or lucky ever since, 'cause they've managed not only to 'ang onto their wealth, but to make it grow."

"Money is always a good motive for murder," Smythe mused, "and Sir George obviously wasn't a pauper."

"Far from it," Blimpey continued. "And what's more, the title can go either way."

"Either way?" Smythe raised an eyebrow. "What does that mean?"

"It means it can be inherited by a daughter if there isn't any sons," Blimpey explained.

"Are you sure about that?" Smythe asked. "I've never 'eard of such a thing."

"That doesn't mean it isn't true," Blimpey shot back. "I don't get my facts wrong. The title can go to a female as well as a male, and it did just that about a hundred years ago. It went to Bartholomew Braxton's daughter, Georgina. She was Sir George's grandmother."

"Does it go to the eldest?"

Blimpey shook his head. "Not necessarily. It's a bit complicated."

"But Sir George has three daughters, so if it doesn't go to the oldest, who gets it?"

"In the case of this many females and no males, the title goes into what's called abeyance until there's only one woman left in the direct line. Then she gets the title, and it passes on through her line when she dies. Or in some cases of female inheritance, the crown can step in and give the title to one of the daughters." Blimpey looked a bit embarrassed. "Truth is, Smythe, I'm not really sure which of these situations applies to the Braxton title. My man who sorts out really complicated peerage matters went off on a drunk, fell into the Thames, and drowned. It's not easy findin' people who know this kind of thing, you know."

"Of course it isn't," Smythe agreed.

"It all gets very complicated," Blimpey continued, "but take my word for it, one of Sir George's daughters is going to end up being Lady Braxton in her own right."

"And that might be worth killin' for," Smythe muttered.

"That's right, but then again, titles don't mean what they used to, do they?"

"I don't know, seems to me that there's plenty that would still kill to get one. Maybe one of his daughters did."

"Anything's possible, I suppose," Blimpey said. "But the ladies in question are all a bit long in the tooth, if you get my meanin'. Now, who else was there the night he was killed?"

"Gracious, this is place is huge," Witherspoon said as he stepped into the conservatory. "And very warm."

"Of course it's warm, I'm growing orchids." A tall, thin man dressed in a brown jacket, mud-splattered trousers, and high black boots stared at Witherspoon. "I'm Clarence Clark."

"Yes, I know. I've been trying to have a word with you for quite some time now," Witherspoon replied. He stared at his surroundings as he moved farther inside the greenhouse. There were plants everywhere. Rows upon rows of seedlings, flowers, cuttings, green plants, and flowering orchids. Along the side of the conservatory was a worktable that stretched the length of the long building. Underneath it, he could see stacks of pots, buckets, baskets, and even bundles of newspapers. Next to the door was a large glass cabinet filled with bottles, tins, and different-colored boxes.

"I've been busy, the flowers require a great deal of work and effort. I can't leave them on their own."

"Mr. Clark, your cousin has been murdered. I really do need to speak to you, is there somewhere we can sit down?" Witherspoon's day had just started, and he was already getting tired.

"I know perfectly well that Sir George has been murdered. But that doesn't mean that life completely stops for the rest of us. We can talk here." Clark dashed to the worktable. "I really have too much to do to waste my time sitting and chatting."

"I'm sure you do, sir, but as you're admitted, there has been a murder, and I must ask you some questions."

Clark didn't appear to hear. He'd stopped in front of a pale purple flower that the inspector assumed was an orchid. He was staring at the plant with a worried frown. "Oh, dear, she's turning brown about the edges. That shouldn't be happening, she only came to blossom two days ago. I knew I shouldn't have used that soil mixture."

"Mr. Clark," Witherspoon snapped. "I must have your attention."

Clark reluctantly drew away from the plant and looked at the inspector. "What is it you want to know?"

For a moment, Witherspoon's mind went completely blank. Then he caught himself. For goodness sakes, he knew what he needed to do here. "Did you happen to see or hear anything unusual on the day Sir George was murdered?"

Clark's thin eyebrows creased in thought. "What do you mean by unusual?" He glanced back down at the flower.

Witherspoon sighed inwardly. Keeping the fellow's attention was going to be difficult. "Did anything happen that was out of the ordinary? Did Sir George receive any visitors or correspondence that upset him?"

"He was always upset about something," Clark replied without looking at the inspector. He whipped a pair of tweezers out of his pocket and gently peeled back something on the bottom part of the flower. "He liked being upset. It was his nature."

"Mr. Clark, did you have words with Sir George on the day he died?"

Clark went still, and Witherspoon realized he finally had the man's full attention. "Who told you that?"

"That doesn't matter, sir. Please answer the question. Did you and Sir George have an argument on the day he was murdered?"

"Yes," Clark replied. He put the tweezers back in his pocket.

"What did you quarrel about?"

Clark hesitated. "It was nothing, really. George was upset because I'd ordered some extra fuel without consulting him."

"Fuel?" Witherspoon repeated. "You mean for the house?" He would have thought that was Mrs. Merryhill's domain, but perhaps not.

"Of course not for the house, for here." Clark waved his arm in a half circle. "For the conservatory. It's been a dreadfully cold winter, and I'd got through my allocation of heating fuel quicker than I expected, so I ordered more. George was not pleased. Honestly, you'd think even a fool would understand that when it was colder than normal, more fuel would be required. But did he? Certainly not."

"So you had words," the inspector pressed.

"That's right, but the argument was no worse than any other we've had." Clark pulled a pair of gloves out of his pocket and slipped them on his long, bony hands. He started down the closest row of cuttings.

"Do you argue frequently with your cousin?" Witherspoon asked as he followed after the man. Drat, these questions weren't going at all as he'd planned.

"No more than anyone else in the household," Clark replied. He stopped in front of a wooden tray of seedlings, leaned down, and studied the soil. "George quarreled with everyone. As I said, it was his nature, he wasn't a nice person. The only pleasure he got out of life was tormenting others. He was quite good at it, he seemed to get better at it with each passing year."

"Exactly how long have you lived in his household?" Witherspoon asked.

Clark straightened up and looked at the inspector. "That's an odd question. Why does it matter?"

"In a murder investigation, anything could be pertinent," Witherspoon replied. But in truth, he'd no idea why he'd asked the question. It had simply popped into his head. But he recalled a conversation he'd had with Mrs. Jeffries about homicide investigations. "Trust your instincts, sir," she'd said. "Trust that inner voice that has led you to so many correct conclusions." Sometimes he couldn't quite see how his "inner voice" or his instincts had done such a thing, but on the other hand, he'd solved a good number of murders, so she must be right.

Clark sighed and took off down the aisle, his attention once again on his precious flowers. "I've lived here since Sir George's father died, and he inherited the title. That was thirty years ago."

"And you're a cousin, is that correct?" the inspector pressed. He wanted to make sure he understood all the details correctly. Small things often turned out to be quite important.

Clark nodded, bent down, and pulled a small wooden tray of dirt out from under the seedling table. "Is there anything else? I've quite a lot of work to do." He shoved the tray onto an empty spot next to the seedlings and began to examine it closely.

"I'd like you to describe your movements on the night of the murder."

"After dinner, I came out here and worked for a while, then I went to bed. I was awakened in the wee hours and told that George was dead. That's all I know about it."

"Did you hear anything that night?"

"No, I'm a sound sleeper."

"Where is your room? The front or the back of the house?"

"Neither, Inspector." He pointed toward the front of the conservatory. "My room is on the side of the house, directly over the conservatory. I can look out and see the place from my study. I've a small study and a bedroom."

"I see. Did you see anything unusual when you went outside that night?"

"The entire event was unusual, Inspector. One doesn't generally expect to see one's cousin face down in a frozen pond."

"But did you notice anything untoward, anything that struck you as odd?" He wasn't sure what he was trying to find out, but surely someone must have seen or heard something out of the ordinary that night.

"Like what, Inspector? I didn't notice anyone lurking about the grounds or scampering off in the distance," Clark replied. He was speaking to the inspector, but his attention was focused on something over Witherspoon's shoulder.

Clark gasped suddenly and then took off running down the aisle. "Good God, this is awful, it looks positively dreadful. This is terrible. It's the last one I've got. None of the others survived. I'll be the laughingstock of the orchid society if it dies. This simply cannot be happening."

Witherspoon turned to see what he was going on about, but by that time Clark had stopped and was staring at a bloom of pale purple flowers. The blossoms were facing downward and appeared to be mounted on a large piece of tree bark.

The inspector hurried after him. Clark was gazing at the plant with a stricken look of horror on his face.

"It looks fine to me," Witherspoon said kindly. He knew some gardeners were inordinately attached to their plants. Constable Barnes had complained that Mrs. Barnes got a tad testy when their neighbor's dog got into her flower beds. But Clark seemed unduly upset. The poor fellow had gone shockingly pale.

"It's hardly all right," Clark snapped. "This is a *Leptotes unicolor* and it's one of the finest orchids in the world. Ye Gods, man, this is a disaster, an absolute disaster. Maybe I can save it. I'll try that new soil mixture that came in from Brazil." He was speaking more to himself than the inspector.

"Er, Mr. Clark, I'm sorry about your plant—"

"It's not just a plant, Inspector," Clark cried. "It's part of my life's work. Now I must take care of this, you'll have to ask any more questions you might have at another time." With that, he turned on his heel and stalked toward a row of long cabinets at the far end of the conservatory.

Witherspoon was of two minds. One part of him wanted to follow the fellow and insist that he continue the interview, while another part was rather relieved to be rid of him. He decided to let the man alone; Clark did appear to be genuinely distressed, so he'd not get Clark's full attention. Perhaps he ought to go and have a word with Constable Barnes. Perhaps he was having better luck with the servants.

For once, Witherspoon was correct. Barnes was indeed having a better day than his inspector. He'd caught the cook at just the right moment, and they were alone in the kitchen. Mrs. Merryhill was upstairs writing the grocery list, the scullery maid was having a day out, and the second kitchen maid was scrubbing down the shelves in the dry larder. Mrs. Cobb, the small, slender gray-haired cook, was sitting across from him at the kitchen table and chattering like a magpie.

"Well, I says." Mrs. Cobb took a quick sip of tea. "It's no wonder someone's killed the old fellow, he was meaner than two snakes in a Turkish bathhouse."

"So you weren't surprised by Sir George's sudden death?" Barnes prodded.

"No one was surprised," she replied, "no matter how much they like to pretend they was. His own kinfolk couldn't abide him."

"Are you referring to his daughters?" the constable asked.

"And Mr. Clark," she added. "He couldn't stand him, either. They'll all go the funeral and wear black, plunge the whole ruddy house in mourning, but it's worked out well for all of them."

Barnes nodded. "You mean they'll inherit his money."

"Now that he's gone, Miss Charlotte won't have to hire herself out as a paid companion just to do a bit of traveling."

"Charlotte Braxton is a paid traveling companion?" Barnes wanted to make sure he got that right. If true, it was genuinely strange. The daughters of baronets didn't do such things.

"Oh, yes, she loves to travel, she does. Sir George gave her one trip to the continent when she was a girl, but she wanted more, so he told her to pay for it herself." She shrugged. "I know it's awful, but she hired on with Lady Celia Cavendish. Every time Lady Cavendish goes abroad, she pays Miss Charlotte's way as well, but Miss Charlotte has to do all the fetching and carrying and taking care of the tickets and the hotels. It's shocking, it is, especially as Celia Cavendish is just the daughter of a businessman and married the title rather than being born to it. Mind you, they all think no one outside the family knows about it, but things like that get out, don't they?" She laughed. "Even Sir George was a bit embarrassed, but not so embarrassed that he opened his wallet and gave her any traveling money."

Barnes nodded. He wondered if a desire to see the world was a sufficient reason for murder. But as soon as the idea entered his head he realized he was being foolish; he'd seen murder done for a lot less reason than someone wanting a trip to Italy.

"Will Sir George's other daughters benefit as much as Miss Charlotte?" he asked. He made a mental note to be sure and verify any information he got from Mrs. Cobb with the family solicitor.

"They'll all get their fair share," Mrs. Cobb replied. "Mind you, there's some that think Miss Nina will get a bit more, seeing as how she's been managing the money for the past ten years."

"But Sir George does have a will?" he pressed.

"Oh, yes, but it'll make no difference, Miss Charlotte and Miss Lucinda will still think that Miss Nina is hoodwinking them somehow. They had a fit when the master handed over the investment accounts to her. But he was a lazy old sod, and as soon as he realized that Miss Nina knew as much about finances as them fancy financial advisers that was chargin' him an arm and a leg, he handed it all to her. Matter of fact, his banker and his broker were both due here that day. For some reason, the lawyers showed up instead."

"Perhaps with Sir George's death, someone cancelled the appointment," Barnes suggested.

Mrs. Cobb shrugged. "I suppose so. Is there anything else you're needin' to ask me? I've got to get the funeral baking started."

Barnes shook his head. "We may have more questions for you later, Mrs. Cobb, but for now, you can go on about your business."

"Inspector, Inspector Witherspoon!" Lucinda Braxton's shrill voice stopped him in his tracks as he came out of the conservatory.

He looked up and saw her frantically waving at him from an open window on the second floor. "Do hurry," she called, "I've not much time, and I must have a word with you."

"Er, yes, ma'am." He started for the door, wondering if the woman was in her room and did she expect him to meet her there. He supposed he ought to be glad for the chance to speak to her at all, as neither she nor her sisters had been available when he and Constable Barnes had arrived this morning. He opened the door and stepped into the darkened hallway. A second later, he heard footsteps coming down the stairs, and then Lucinda Braxton came flying around the corner and almost knocked him down. "Ye Gods, man, watch where you're going. Now listen, I've not much time, and I must tell you something."

Witherspoon was far too much of a gentleman to tell the woman she'd bumped into him. "Yes, ma'am, what is it?"

Lucinda looked around, her expression furtive. "Charlotte hadn't been to bed on the night that father was killed," she hissed softly. "She'd been out of the house."

"How do you know that?" he asked. He remembered that Sir George's middle daughter had been fully dressed when the alarm was raised. He'd been planning on asking her to explain why.

"Because I saw her coming home," Lucinda replied. "It was an hour or so before the alarm was raised. Something woke me up, and I got up and looked out the window. My room faces the front of the house, Inspector, and I saw Charlotte coming down the drive. She went around to the side of the house. I expect she came in this door." She pointed in the direction he'd just come. "Which means she might have been outside near the time father was being murdered. I think you ought to ask her what she was doing out there, don't you?"

"Are you absolutely certain of this?" he pressed. He hoped she wasn't making up tales to inconvenience her sister.

"Of course I am." Lucinda sounded offended. "I'm not in the habit of lying."

"No, ma'am, I'm sure you're not. Why didn't you tell me this earlier?" Witherspoon asked. "You claimed you slept soundly that night."

"I did, Inspector," she snapped. "And I went right back to bed. Seeing Charlotte slip into the house wasn't anything unusual. She did it all the time." With that, she stuck her nose in the air and flounced off down the hall. Witherspoon was so surprised by her departure that he simply stood there with his mouth agape. After a moment, he shook his head and went off in search of Constable Barnes. He'd reached the top of the back stairs, when he heard a distinct hissing sound. Suddenly, a large orange-colored cat leapt out of the shadows and landed on top of a walnut table. The cat pinned back its ears and hissed at the inspector.

"Oh, dear, you don't look as if you're in a very cheerful state," he muttered. The cat glared at him.

"Samson, get down from there." Charlotte Braxton appeared in the hallway.

"He doesn't seem in a very good mood," the inspector said. Perhaps this might be a good time to ask this Miss Braxton a few questions, he then thought.

"He's never in a good mood," Charlotte replied. She continued past the inspector to the staircase. "I expect he's hungry. I doubt anyone's fed the beast since father died."

"Gracious, that's awful." The inspector hurried after her. "The poor thing is probably half-starved. No wonder he's in a terrible temper. Er, Miss Braxton, I'd like to ask you a few questions."

"It'll have to wait, Inspector, I've an appointment, and I can't be late." She'd reached the bottom of the staircase, turned to her right, and disappeared.

"I must insist, Miss Braxton. I've just heard something that is very important, and I must speak with you. Also, we need to find out about when your solicitors were called to the house, and what the bankers wanted with your father." Witherspoon charged down the stairs after her, but by the time he got to the bottom, she'd gone.

Wiggins walked slowly across the railway station. His day seemed to be going from bad to worse. He'd gone along to Luty's this morning, hoping to see her and keep his promise to tell her about the murder. But once there, he'd had to hide behind a letter box as Mrs. Jeffries had shown up right on his heels. He didn't dare try and see Luty then. He'd just have to go there again this evening and try to sneak in and have a word with her.

He glanced over and saw the clerk watching him. Blast a

Spaniard, this was getting dangerous. He'd been here for an hour now pretending to be meeting someone off the train. Lurking about was easy if it was one of the big London terminals like Liverpool Street or Victoria, but in a small station like this, he was making a spectacle of himself. He heard a train pull in, so he went to the archway and looked out, scanning the few passengers that got off.

A tall well-dressed woman with a cane got out of one of the first-class carriages, but she obviously wasn't a servant, so talking to her would be useless. Then he flicked his gaze to a middle-aged man wearing a black overcoat walking toward the end of the platform, but Wiggins didn't think he looked like a likely prospect, either. Finally, a young woman wearing a gray jacket, a brown wool bonnet, and with a bandage wrapped around her hand got out of the third-class carriage at the end of the train and hurried toward the exit. Wiggins made up his mind: the pickings were slim, but if he was going to speak to someone, it would have to be her.

Knowing that the ticket clerk was still watching him, he made a point of sighing and shaking his head as he left the station, trying to convey the impression that whoever he'd been waiting for hadn't shown up. He hoped his charade worked; with a murder in the neighborhood, he didn't want the clerk running off to the police and giving out his description.

Wiggins stepped out of the station and saw the girl from the train standing in front of the café, staring in the window. He went toward her, taking off his hat respectfully as he spoke. "Excuse me, miss, but may I speak to you?" He had a good story at the ready.

She turned and looked at him, her expression surprised. She was a short, chubby girl with thick black eyebrows, blue eyes, a rosebud mouth, and slightly protruding front teeth. Her features were such that she ought to have been homely, but oddly enough, she was quite attractive. "Why do you want to speak to me?" She smiled brightly.

"Please don't be offended, miss, but I was wonderin' if there was any positions at the place you work?"

Her smile faded. "Do I look like I'm in service?"

"Not really, miss," he said quickly, "but I noticed the color of your skirt peekin' out beneath your jacket, and it's the same color as the one my sister wore when she was in service." He made a quick bow and stuck his cap back onto his head. "No offense was meant, miss, it's just my sister and I 'ave been out of work for a long time, and I'm desperate enough to try anything to get a position. You've got a lovely, kindhearted face, and I didn't think you'd mind me askin'." He turned and started to walk away.

"Wait," she cried. "Don't go. I might be able to help."

Wiggins felt like a worm. His speech had been calculated to play on her conscience, and apparently it had worked. "You can?"

"There's nothing goin' where I'm at now, but there might be a position soon." She frowned slightly. "But you must have references. Do you?"

"We've both got references," he said quickly. "Please, miss, let me buy you a cup of tea, and you can tell me all about the place."

She hesitated, and he quickly added. "Please, miss, this is very important. We need jobs."

"It's not that," she replied with a smile. "It's just that it don't seem right for you to spend what little money you have on buyin' me a cup of tea. I've got some coins, I'll only go in if you let me pay for it."

Now he really felt like a worm. But he could think of no good reason to argue with her. If he insisted on doing the

gentlemanly thing and not letting her pay, she might suspect he was lying. "All right, miss, but if we get a position,
you must promise to let me pay you back out of my first
quarter's wages."

She laughed and took his arm. "You can make sure I will.
My name is Alicia, what's yours?"

"Jon," he lied. "My name is Jon Upton, and my sister's
name is Betsy." He pulled open the door and the two of
them stepped inside the small café.

"What did you do to your hand?" he asked, jerking his
chin toward the bandage.

"I got scratched by a cat. It's a dreadful old beast of a
thing, too. But when the master died, no one thought to
feed the animal. Well, even if it's a nasty creature, you still
don't want to see it starve to death, do you?"

"It scratched you when you were feeding it?" he asked.
Cor blimey, he thought, she really is a nice girl.

"No, it scratched me afterwards, I got too close to its
food dish," she laughed. "As I said, the household where I
work is a bit strange."

They went to the counter, and Alicia ordered two cups of
tea. Wiggins felt miserable when she drew a tattered blue
coin purse out of her pocket and handed the counter boy a
sixpence. He vowed he'd find a way to get the money back
to her. It was only a few pence, but to someone in her position, that was a lot. She was so poor she wasn't even wearing
gloves, yet she was willing to pay for his tea. He decided
he'd not only pay her back, but he'd secretly send her a new
coin purse. He had plenty of money himself. He didn't understand it, but every time he went to the old Cadbury's tin
where he kept his supply of coins, there seemed to be more
than he remembered. He'd mentioned it to Mrs. Jeffries,
but she simply shrugged and said he must have forgotten

how much he'd put in the tin in the first place. But he didn't, he was sure of it. It was almost as if someone was filling the ruddy thing for him. Not that he was complaining, but it was a mystery.

The counter boy handed them their cups, and they made their way to a table by the window. Wiggins had a good view of the train station.

"Thanks, very much," he said as they sat down. "What did you mean when you said there might be some positions soon?"

She took a quick sip and then grinned at him. "You don't scare easy, do you?"

"I don't think so." He contrived to look puzzled, though he was fairly sure he knew what she was going to say. "Why? Is there a ghost walkin' the back stairs?"

She looked amused. "Not yet."

That did surprise him. "What?"

"I mean, I don't know if he'll be comin' back to haunt the place or not. In any case, if he did, it wouldn't be the back stairs he'd be haunting, it'd be the little pond out in the back garden. That's where he was murdered."

"Murdered!" Wiggins yelped. "You mean you've had a murder where you work?"

She nodded eagerly. "Oh, yes, someone coshed the master on the head and then stuck him in the fountain. That's why we're goin' to have some positions available. The upstairs maid has already given notice, and I'm fairly sure the gardener is goin' to leave. Mind you, they'll probably not hire anyone for his position. The master was goin' to sell the conservatory, so Mr. Clark will probably take on doin' the grounds."

Wiggins wasn't sure which bit to inquire about first. "Goodness, sounds like there's dozens of things happening all at once." He took a drink of his tea to give himself a moment to think. He wanted to get her to slow down. She was giving him a lot of information, and he'd no idea if it was or wasn't important. They'd all learned that lesson in their other investigations.

"How come the upstairs maid is leavin'?" Wiggins asked. He decided to ask the questions in the same order as she'd spoke. "Is she afraid?"

"Not really, it's just that now that the master's gone we don't know which of the daughters will be running the house, and Maisie is afraid it'll be Miss Nina. She's even stingier than the old master was. Besides, Maisie's fellow is comin' home from Canada, and they'll probably be getting married soon. She's goin' back home to Earl Shilton to spend time with her family before he takes her off to Canada."

"That's good, I mean, it'd be strange to work someplace where people was scared of bein' murdered in their beds," he replied.

"No one's really scared," she added. "We're pretty sure whoever did it was out the get the master, not one of us."

"Then 'ow come the gardener's leavin'?" he asked, delighted with the way her comments were leading right into his questions.

She shrugged. "He's not a proper gardener at all."

" 'E's not a gardener?"

"Maisie said she overheard Mrs. Merryhill talkin' to the master when Grantham, that's the gardener's name, first come there," she explained. "Mrs. Merryhill told the master that having someone like Grantham on the property was askin' for trouble."

" 'Ow could 'e be trouble?" Wiggins muttered. "Even if 'e weren't a proper gardener, maybe 'e's just a workin' man.

That's what I am. There's plenty of us about. Just 'cause you don't 'ave proper trainin' don't mean you can't do the job. Especially for somethin' like gardenin'. Seems to me that all it takes is a strong back and a willingness to dig and weed and prune."

He hoped he wasn't going too far in his attempt to convince her he was just a bloke looking for work, and he hoped she wouldn't stop talking.

"There's nothing wrong with wanting to do an honest day's work," Alicia replied. "But there's nothin' honest about the reasons Grantham come to work for Sir George."

"Wouldn't 'e be workin' for the same reasons as any of us?"

Alicia shook her head. "Not him. He was workin' there because he didn't have a choice. It was either work for the old master or go to prison."

CHAPTER 6

"Do you know where Constable Barnes might be?" Witherspoon asked the maid who was coming out of the dry larder. She was carrying a scrub brush and bucket.

"He was in the kitchen talking to Mrs. Cobb," the girl replied. "But I heard him go outside a few minutes ago."

"Thank you." Witherspoon smiled at her. He noticed her hands were cracked, and blood was seeping out of one of her knuckles. "Er, excuse me, miss, but did you realize your hand is bleeding?"

"It's the soap, sir, it's hard on the skin." she smiled brightly. "But Mrs. Cobb's got an ointment for us to use. So it'll be fine."

"Mind you take care of it," he said gently. He suddenly felt so very sorry for the girl. She was young and pretty and would no doubt spend the rest of her days fetching and carrying for people like the Braxtons. It didn't seem right, yet at the same time, he couldn't quite decide what was wrong. He hated it when these kind of thoughts crept into his head. It never did him any good at all. Besides, he knew it was his duty to find out who killed Sir George Braxton, whether the man was a decent human being or not. "You don't want infection to set in."

"I will, sir." She bobbed a little curtsey, smiled, and started back toward the kitchen.

"Excuse me, but do you happen to know if anyone's feeding the cat?" He'd no idea why he blurted out the question, especially as it was a cat that probably wouldn't be grateful for his interest, but the words had slipped out before he could stop them.

"One of the maids has been making sure the monster's been fed," she replied with a grin. "We'll not let the animal starve, sir"—she glanced toward the front of the house—"no matter what some say."

"Did the Misses Braxton forbid you to feed the animal?" he asked.

She hesitated.

"Don't worry, I'll not tell anyone I've spoken with you," he assured her.

"They don't like Samson, sir, who does? Miss Lucinda told Mrs. Merryhill not to waste any more food on the cat. That's not right, sir. The animal doesn't know how to fend for itself. We don't know how it survived those few days it was lost before the master died. I think someone around here was feeding it."

"Really?"

"Yes, sir, someone must have been. Samson wasn't that hungry when he got home. Turned his nose up at Mrs. Cobb's leftover fish stew, he did."

"Inspector, is that you?" Constable Barnes voice came from the doorway.

"Excuse me, miss." Witherspoon nodded politely at the maid, who smiled shyly and went off toward the kitchen. "Yes, Constable," he called out. "I'm coming." He went back down the hall to the side door and stuck his head out.

"I think you'd best take a look at this, sir," Constable Barnes was standing in the doorway of the conservatory.

Perplexed, the inspector stared at Barnes. "When did you come out here? I was just in there a few minutes ago. I interviewed Clarence Clark."

"I was looking for you, sir, and one of the maids told me the last place she'd seen you was in the conservatory, so I popped inside." He gestured for the inspector to follow. "I found something."

"Found something?" Witherspoon repeated as he stepped inside behind the constable. "But wasn't this place already searched?" He surveyed the area, looking for Clark, but the man was nowhere to be seen.

"It was, sir." Barnes turned and walked down the first aisle in front of the row of plants up against the conservatory windows. "And it was searched properly. But this was easy to miss." He stopped about a quarter of the way down the aisle and bent down. "Take a look, sir."

Witherspoon squatted next to Barnes and peered under the wooden table. There on the gray paving stone was a dried pool of dark red. A tiny mass of what looked like hair and tissue rested in the center of the stain. "Oh, dear, is this what I think it is?"

"I don't know, sir." Barnes reached past him and gently picked up the tiny bundle. "But I thought you ought to see this for yourself." He stood up, holding the object between his thumb and forefinger so that it dangled at eye level. "I'll warrant that this hair came from the victim, sir. But for the life of me, I can't see how it got under the table in here. There's no sign of a murder weapon in here."

"And the lads checked all the gardening tools?"

"We did that straight away on the first search, sir. There was nothing on anything, no blood, no tissue, no hair. We checked every spade, shovel, and hoe on the whole place, sir, and found nothing. P.C. Baggers was in charge of it, and he's very thorough."

"I'm sure that he is, constable. I was simply double-checking." He frowned. "How did you happen to see it? It's quite small."

Barnes grinned. "When I stepped inside and saw that the place was empty, I thought I'd have a good look around and see if I couldn't pick up some growing ideas for the missus. You know, see how the seedbeds was planted and that sort of thing. You know how the wife loves her gardening, and she's always wanted to grow her own orchids. But she's never had much luck, sir. So I had a gander down the rows, and I happened to drop my notebook just here," he pointed down at spot near their feet. "I saw it when I bent down to get the notebook."

"I see." Witherspoon was very confused. He'd no doubt the place had been thoroughly searched, especially given the manner in which the victim had been murdered. Gardening tools like shovels and spades were the sort of object that could have easily been used as the murder weapon, and even the most inexperienced of constables would have had a good look at them. This was a puzzle. But then again, this entire murder was a mystery. He'd no idea what the motive might be, he'd no idea who might have killed the fellow, and they hadn't come close to finding the murder weapon. This case wasn't going very well at all.

"What on earth is going on here?" Clarence Clark closed the conservatory door and glared at the two policemen.

"I'm glad you're here, Mr. Clark," Witherspoon said. "We've something we'd like to show you." He pointed at the stain. "Do you have any idea what this might be?"

Barnes stepped to one side to give Clark a better view. He also tucked the tiny bundle of tissue and hair neatly into his palm and out of sight.

"What what is?" Clark asked impatiently. "Why are you in here? How did you get in anyway? The door is always locked."

"It wasn't locked, Mr. Clark," Barnes said easily. "And I came in looking for the inspector. Could you please answer our question?"

"You and I were just in here a few minutes ago," Witherspoon reminded him. "Perhaps you forgot to lock it when you left. Now, sir, will you please answer the constable's question?"

Clark knelt down and stared at the pavement. "It looks like a stain," he said irritably. "It's probably from one of my fertilizer mixtures. I do a lot of experimenting."

"We're fairly certain it's blood," Witherspoon said softly. "And we'd like to know if you have any idea how it got there."

"I've no idea how it got there, if, indeed, it's blood. Oh, wait, it could be that wretched cat." Clark stood up and smiled slyly. "Sometimes he catches vermin and brings them in here. He doesn't eat them, of course. He simply tortures them and plays with them till they die of fright, then he mangles them up and puts them in Sir George's room. It's quite fitting, I should think."

Wiggins didn't have much time. He looked up and down the quiet Knightsbridge street, but he saw no one. Thank goodness it was still so cold—it kept people indoors. He found a handhold in the ivy that covered the wall, and in a few seconds he was up, over, and inside the communal garden of Luty's elegant house. He dodged behind a tree trunk and then stuck his head out, making sure there was no one outside. But his luck seemed to be holding, as the garden was empty save for a few birds that darted from tree branch to branch. He hurried toward Luty's house and then dodged behind another tree trunk when he got close. He looked up at the balcony protruding from the second floor. Those were Luty's rooms, but he had no way of getting up to them. He pulled out a pebble he'd stuck in his pocket earlier, took a deep breath, prayed that Luty was in her room, and took aim. He heard the pebble strike stone and knew he'd missed the window, so he tried again. This time, he heard the soft ping as the pebble hit the glass. He waited and waited and waited. Finally, when he was getting ready to try a third time, he heard a door open. But it was the door down here, the one that led from the kitchen to the garden. Blast a Spaniard, now he was done for, he turned, intending to sprint for the wall, when a soft voice hissed, "Wiggins? Is that you?"

Wiggins whirled around and saw Luty standing in the back door, waving him over. She was wearing a bright red dressing gown over which she'd thrown a green-and-gold striped mantle. "You'll catch your death out 'ere," he said softly as he ran toward her. "It's bloomin' cold. Get back inside."

"Don't be silly." She looked over her shoulder toward the kitchen. "I'm fit as a fiddle, but hurry, we don't have much time. Come on." She motioned for him to follow her.

Wiggins wasn't sure going into the house was such a good idea, but he did as she instructed. As soon as he stepped inside the hallway, she closed the door softly and then shoved him through another door into the wet larder. It was almost as cold in there as it had been outside.

"Hurry up and tell me what's goin' on," she demanded, "and be quick about it. They're goin' to come looking for me soon, so don't waste time arguing."

"The inspector caught the Braxton case," Wiggins whispered, "and we've got to get it solved by Christmas. I tried to get in to see you this morning, but it was impossible."

"Don't worry about that." She pulled a handkerchief out of her pocket and blew her nose. "I know you did yer best. Just tell me what we know so far."

"Are you sure you're up to it? I'd feel terrible if you got ill again," he said.

"Don't let these sniffles fool you, boy. I'm strong as a horse. Besides, I can do like Mrs. Goodge and do plenty of investigating right from inside this house. Now tell me what's what."

Wiggins gave her a quick, concise, and well-ordered report on what they'd learned so far. "I'm just on my way back for our afternoon meetin'," he finished, "so I can get you another report tomorrow."

"That'll be tricky," she replied. "But we can manage. Come around nine o'clock. Hatchet will be gone by then, and I can send Julie over to the chemist's. I can keep the others busy on some pretense or another. I'll make sure this door is unlocked, you stick your head in and make sure it's all clear before ya come upstairs. You're a smart boy, that oughn't to be a problem for ya."

"You've got a lot of faith in me." Wiggins looked uncertain. "Won't your kitchen staff be comin' in and out?"

"Nah, there ain't that many of 'em here. I let most of

them have a few days off for Christmas, so there's just a few of us here in the house."

"All right," he promised. She pulled the door open, stuck her head out, and then stepped into the hall. He followed her out.

"Thanks for keeping your promise," she said as he stepped out into the garden. "I knew I could count on you."

"Don't be angry at the others," he replied. "They just didn't want to do anything that would hurt your health, that's why the didn't tell ya."

"Humph," she sniffed disapprovingly and then flashed him a quick grin. "Don't fret, lad. I know that. Here," she pulled a large brass key out of her pocket and handed it to him. "Unlock the gate at the corner. It'll save you having to climb over it."

Everyone arrived at Upper Edmonton Gardens in time for their afternoon meeting. Mrs. Goodge put a plate of brown bread next to the butter pot on the table as Mrs. Jeffries poured out the tea.

"Who would like to go first?" the housekeeper asked as she began handing round the mugs.

"I hope the rest of you have done better than me," Betsy said glumly. "I've talked to every shopkeeper in Richmond, and the only thing I heard was the butcher complaining that Braxton accused him of shorting him on their meat order last week. Honestly, the way the man went on about a few missing chicken livers, you'd have thought he'd been accused of high treason."

"Anyone can make a mistake, maybe the butcher forgot to include them in the order. That happened to us just last week, they left out a rasher of bacon," Mrs. Goodge said.

"Mind you, they sent it round straight away when they realized it'd not been sent."

Betsy shook her head. "He claims it's just the household trying to avoid paying the full amount. He says it's happened before."

"That sounds about right," Smythe said. "I didn't 'ear much, but I did 'ear more than one tradesman say that getting money out of that lot was like pullin' wax out of a pig's ear."

"The family does seem rather miserly," Mrs. Jeffries murmured.

"But you'll have to admit, they've managed to hang onto their money," Mrs. Goodge added.

"I think they're mean," Wiggins said. "Wait till I tell you what I found out."

"Why don't we let Betsy finish first?" Mrs. Jeffries suggested.

Betsy gave a self-deprecating laugh. "I really didn't hear much of anything else. The best part of my day was listening to the butcher complain. No one else seemed to know anything except what we already know, that all the Braxtons are miserly, mean-spirited and not well liked. But not to worry, I'll be out and about again tomorrow."

"Can I go now?" Wiggins asked. Mrs. Jeffries nodded, so he plunged straight ahead. "Well, like I was sayin', aristocrats or not, they are a mean bunch. They're not even feedin' Sir George's cat." He told them about his meeting with Alicia. He took care not to leave out any details, including her bandaged hand and the information she'd shared with him about the Braxton gardener.

"Are you certain of this?" Hatchet asked softly.

"She's got no reason to lie," he replied. "Mind you, she

was just repeatin' gossip, but from what we've 'eard of Sir George Braxton, it don't seem wrong."

"Did she have any idea what Grantham had done to Sir George?" Mrs. Jeffries pressed.

"Alicia didn't know for certain," Wiggins said eagerly. "But she thinks he must have been caught thievin' by the old gent. Only instead of calling the police, Sir George made him work for nothin' and live out in the garden shed."

"Why does she think it was thieving?" Betsy took a sip of her tea.

"I asked her that, and she said she didn't rightly know why she had that idea, it's just that she had it. Maybe she 'eard somethin' and she don't remember exactly what she 'eard, but it was enough to leave an idea in her mind, if you know what I mean."

Mrs. Jeffries nodded knowingly. "That seems very likely. We often find we know things without recalling precisely how or when we obtained the information."

"Did Alicia know anything else?" Hatchet asked.

"Only the usual bits and pieces we've already 'eard," he replied. "You know, just what Betsy said she'd 'eard, them bein' a miserly, mean-spirited lot. But I'm sure there's more to find out, and tomorrow I'll see if I can find out for sure what it was that Grantham did."

"Yes, that seems very appropriate," Mrs. Jeffries muttered.

"So that means at least one of the servants 'ad a good reason to want Sir George dead," Smythe mused.

"Maybe more than one," Mrs. Goodge said. "Not that I've heard anything specific, but my source told me that the housekeeper had a long history with the family, and that there'd been some gossip a number of years back about her relationship with Sir George." She was annoyed with Hilda, who'd dropped that tidbit just as she was getting into a hansom cab this afternoon. Naturally, there hadn't been time to get any decent details out of the woman. But now that Mrs. Goodge had the scent, so to speak, she'd be able to follow the trail.

"What kind of relationship?" Wiggins asked curiously.

"I'm not sure," the cook replied. "But I suspect it's of a nature that isn't fit for some ears, if you get my meaning."

"You mean the old blighter had his way with the poor woman," Betsy muttered. "That's a sad but common enough old story."

"I'll find out more details about it later," Mrs. Goodge promised. "I've a couple of good sources I can tap. But this isn't all I found out today." She told them the remainder of the gossip she's gotten from Hilda that afternoon. "I wasn't able to find out anything about Fiona Burleigh or Raleigh Brent, my friend hadn't heard of either of them, but I'll keep at it, I've a number of people coming in tomorrow. Someone's bound to know something about them."

"You've all found out rather more than I have." Hatchet sighed heavily. "Unfortunately, most of my sources were unavailable in the short time I had to be out today. But never fear, I've a number of people to see tomorrow."

"Does Luty 'ave any idea of what you're up to?" Wiggins asked. He crossed his fingers under the table, asking the question almost seemed like lying.

"I don't think so," Hatchet replied slowly. "She was taking a nap when I left today. But I've got one of the maids keeping a close eye on her. Being dishonest with her doesn't really feel right, but I don't know what else to do. Madam's health must be my first concern, and if she knew about the case, she'd refuse to stay inside."

"If she continues to improve, perhaps you can tell her about the murder in a day or two," Mrs. Jeffries suggested.

She glanced at the clock on the sideboard and noted that it was getting late.

Smythe caught her eye. "Before we leave, there is one thing I forgot to mention." He told them what he'd heard from Blimpey. When he'd finished, they all stared at him.

"Cor blimey, that could be a motive for murder," Wiggins exclaimed.

"It could be," Smythe said slowly, "but then again, all the daughters in that household is a bit long in the tooth. What good would 'avin' a title do any of them if they couldn't pass it on to their children? Whoever inherits it has to wait until the other two sisters are dead, and unless one of them is a killer, the deaths of the other two might take years."

"Unless the crown gives one of the surviving daughters the title," Hatchet said softly. "If it's not a title that goes into abeyance, then the daughter that has some influence in court circles might get it."

"I wish we knew which kind of title it was," Mrs. Jeffries said. "That might make a huge difference in ascertaining motive."

"I think you can leave that up to me," Hatchet said. "I happen to have a good friend that's an expert in peerage matters."

As Mrs. Jeffries had expected, Inspector Witherspoon arrived home quite late and utterly exhausted. "You do look tired, sir," she said as she helped him off with his hat and coat. "Would you like a sherry to relax, or would you prefer to go straight in to dinner?"

"I should love a sherry," he replied.

They went into the drawing room, and Witherspoon settled into his favorite chair as Mrs. Jeffries poured both of them a sherry. "Here you are, sir," she said as she handed him the small crystal glass.

"Thank you, Mrs. Jeffries." He took a sip and closed his eyes briefly as he relaxed. "Has there been any word on when Lady Cannonberry might be returning?"

"Her butler mentioned to Wiggins that she hopes to be home a day or two before Christmas," she replied. "As we discussed last month, sir, I invited her for Christmas dinner."

"That's excellent." A blush crept up his cheeks. "I've bought her a present, I do hope she likes it. It's difficult buying presents for ladies, isn't it? One never knows what they'll like, what their tastes might be."

"I'm sure your gift is lovely," she said quickly. She didn't want to waste their time discussing the inspector's relationship with their neighbor. That could wait till they didn't have a murder. "You have such excellent taste."

"Thank you, Mrs. Jeffries." He took another sip of his drink.

"How is the investigation going, sir?"

"It's a bit of a muddle," he sighed. "But I'm hoping it will all sort itself out."

"I'm sure it will, sir," she said calmly. She wondered if he needed a bit of confidence boosting. Sometimes he didn't feel he was up to the task at hand. "But you'll find the killer. You always do. Did the house-to-house turn up anything?"

"Not really. None of the neighbors saw or heard anything that night. But as the murder happened at such an unusual hour, I'm not surprised. Most people are sound asleep in the middle of the night." He told her everything he and Constable Barnes had learned that day.

Mrs. Jeffries listened carefully, storing all the information in the back of her mind and hoping that when the time

was right, it would all make sense or fall into some sort of
pattern.

"But at least I managed to find out about the solicitors,"
he said. "Miss Nina Braxton sent for them as soon as she
found out her father was dead. She said she had to speak
with them about the funeral arrangements, but I'm not sure
I believe her. Generally, the lawyers don't show up until after the funeral."

"They don't sound as if they are a very conventional family, sir," she said. "What about the broker and the banker,
sir? Did Miss Braxton have any idea why they'd been called
to the house."

He frowned as he recalled his short conversation with
Nina Braxton. "She said she didn't know, that it was odd because she took care of the finances." He sighed again. "They
are a most unusual family."

"Indeed they are, sir," Mrs. Jeffries agreed, "and obviously,
their eccentricities are well known. As soon as the neighborhood found out you had this case, I've been accosted half a
dozen times today with gossip about the Braxtons."

"Gracious, I do hope it isn't distasteful for you."

"Not at all, sir. As a matter of fact, I picked up a few tid-
bits that might be helpful to you." She told him, in the
most roundabout way, most of the information the household had learned in the past two days. "I know it's just gossip, sir," she finished, "but as you've always said, oftentimes
a word here or there can point to the right direction."

He nodded thoughtfully, and she could see he was thinking about much of what she'd just told him. Good. She
wasn't sure herself where they ought to be looking in this
case, but it never hurt to have all of them going in every direction for answers.

"I must say the most puzzling thing is the blood and tissue in the greenhouse," he frowned. "We've no idea how it could have gotten there."

"Blood and tissue?" she repeated.

"Oh, dear, I forgot to mention it, didn't I?" He told her about Constable Barnes' discovery.

"And you had searched the entire conservatory for the murder weapon?" she pressed.

He nodded. "Twice. It was given a good going-over the first day we were there, and I had the lads go over it again today after we found the bloodstain. Frankly, I'm a bit concerned about us missing the stain in the first place."

"You said it was under a table," she clarified. She wanted to make sure she understood the entire circumstance in her own mind. She had a feeling this might be an important clue.

"More like a whole row of wooden slats, you know the sort of thing I mean. They're used to hold seedbeds and potted plants. I think the reason we missed it the first time is because it was so wet that day, I suspect that when the greenhouse was searched, the lads simply saw anything pooled under the rows as water."

"That's possible. I expect when they were in the greenhouse they were concentrating on looking at the gardening tools. The spades and shovels, that sort of thing. Which reminds me, sir, you never said if you'd found anything in Randall Grantham's room."

"There was nothing suspicious in his shed," he replied. "All he had was an old carpetbag that held his personal belongings. Actually, I'm going to speak to him again tomorrow," he said. "Like the gossip you heard today, there's some sort of mystery as to how he obtained his position. According to the other servants, one day he was simply brought into the servants' dining room and introduced as the new gardener. Mrs. Merryhill seemed to be as surprised at the rest of the staff when Sir George brought the fellow down-stairs. That means she wasn't expecting any staff additions, and let's face it, Mrs. Jeffries. The housekeeper would be the first to know when a household needed more staff."

"That's true, sir, and as you've often said in the past, sometimes it's a good idea to thoroughly investigate the newest person in the victim's life."

"Really? I said that?" He looked genuinely puzzled. But then again, he often said things and possibly did things that he couldn't recall.

"Now don't tease me, sir," she laughed softly. "You know good and well it's one of your 'methods.'"

"Oh, yes, my methods." He smiled faintly.

"You should be very proud, sir. Your methods are becoming quite widespread in the force. Why just look at this case. As soon as the Home Secretary arrived, he immediately made them put the body back where it was originally found. That's because other policemen have learned that your methods solve cases. Everyone uses them now."

Witherspoon beamed. "Well, one does what one can, and of course we're going to look at Mr. Grantham again." He drained his glass and set it on the table next to his chair. "Tomorrow should be a better day."

Mrs. Jeffries finished the last of the chores and then went up to her room. As she got ready for bed, her mind raced, going over and over every little bit of information they'd learned so far.

She knew she wouldn't be able to sleep, so instead of getting into bed, she turned out the lamp and sat down in her chair by the window. She stared out into the night, her eyes on the gas lamp across the street, and let her mind wander. She'd found that by doing this, by letting the thoughts and ideas come as they would, she'd eventually find the way to the truth. Mrs. Jeffries had no idea why such a random, undisciplined way of thinking seemed to work, but it did.

Sir George Braxton wasn't a very nice man, but then again, that was often the case with murder victims. Not all of them, of course. Sometimes perfectly nice people happened to be at the wrong place at the wrong time or simply standing in the way of someone who wanted something badly enough to kill for it. She shifted slightly into a more comfortable postion.

But Sir George wasn't just murdered; he was humiliated in the process. Whoever killed him went to the trouble of dragging him to that pond, chipping a hole in the ice, and then shoving his head into it. That seemed a bit excessive. Whoever killed him, hated him. She was certain of that. Then again, perhaps the killer was simply very clever and had deliberately manufactured the circumstances to make it appear the murder was the result of hatred. She shook her head. Most people were simply too mentally lazy to come up with such an elaborate scenario to give a false impression. No, she was fairly sure that the killer had genuinely wanted to humiliate rather than just murder. She sighed and pulled her shawl tighter against the cold seeping into her bones. There were so many suspects. The entire household seemed to have disliked the victim, and that included his own children.

He'd been murdered outside the house, she reminded herself. That meant it didn't necessarily have to be someone from the household. It could have been a stranger, someone that they'd never even considered as the killer, someone from Braxton's past who'd nursed a grudge and then finally worked up the nerve to murder the man. But how did they get him outside that night? It had been dreadfully cold.

What would make an elderly man get up out of his bed and go outside in the snow? Someone he knew must have come to his door that night—either that, or the killer got inside and marched him out using a weapon of some kind. But that didn't seem likely. From what they knew of Sir George's character, he'd have bellowed like an enraged bull if he'd been accosted in his own room. And how did that bit of blood and tissue get under a row of seedlings in the greenhouse? Was it even Sir George's hair and blood?

The questions drifted in and out of her mind, one after the other. She didn't try to come to any conclusions or find any answers. She simply let the thoughts move in and out as they would.

She got up from her chair and climbed into bed. But she didn't sleep. Again, she simply let her mind drift where it would. Charlotte Braxton had been fully dressed that night. Why? She loved to travel so much that she'd even hired herself out as a paid companion. Was that motive enough? What about Lucinda Braxton, who desperate to marry? Now that Sir George was gone, she'd get her share of his estate, and she could marry Raleigh Brent. Nina Braxton had to be considered as well; she was the one who'd sent for the solicitors as soon as she'd realized her father was dead. Mrs. Jeffries caught herself. She mustn't focus on just the immediate family. There were plenty of others who hated him.

Early the next morning Smythe cornered Betsy on the first-floor landing. Everyone else had gone down to breakfast, so he felt it was permissible to sneak a quick kiss.

"Stop that," she whispered even as she kissed him back. "Someone will see us."

"They're all downstairs, and so what if they did. We're

engaged. Now, lass, what do you want for Christmas? You've been avoidin' tellin' me for days now."

Betsy's smile faded. This was a bit of a sore subject to her mind. "I've already told you, a pair of gloves or a nice scarf will do just fine." She looked away as she spoke, not wanting to see the hurt or disappointment in his eyes. But he simply didn't understand. He might be rich as sin, but she wasn't, and she didn't want him getting her an expensive present when she could only afford to get him something modest. She'd not bought his present as yet; she hadn't been able to decide what to give him.

"Now, lass, we can do better than that," he protested.

Betsy stepped out of the circle of his arms. "Smythe, I'll not have you spending a fortune on me when I can't do the same for you."

"Don't be silly." He pulled her close again and stared into her eyes. "Once we're married, what's mine is yours."

"But we're not married yet," she pointed out, "and if you go getting me something that costs the world, everyone in the household will think you've gone daft."

"Half of them already do," he replied. He knew that Mrs. Jeffries had a fairly good idea of his financial resources. He'd never meant to deceive the rest of them, it had simply happened.

When he'd come back from Australia, he'd only planned on stopping in to say hello to his former employer, Euphemia Witherspoon. But when he'd arrived, she'd been deathly ill and at the mercy of her servants. Wiggins had been there, but he'd just been a boy then and much too confused to see what was happening in the household. Smythe had sent all the servants but Wiggins packing, hired a nurse, and the three of them had taken care of the dying woman. Euphemia made him promise to watch over her nephew, Gerald Witherspoon. But once Witherspoon had come, everything had happened so fast. Before he knew it, Mrs. Goodge and Mrs. Jeffries had come, then Betsy, starving and ill, had collapsed on their doorstep, and he'd taken one look at her and known he couldn't leave until she was better. By that time, Mrs. Jeffries had them out following up clues on those horrible Kensington High Street murders, and well, what was a man to do? Rich or not, this was where he belonged. Australia had been good to him. He'd used his brains and his muscle, and he'd carved out a fortune for himself.

He could buy and sell half of London's toffs several times over, but he had to hide it. The others wouldn't take kindly to the idea he'd deceived them. Neither he nor Betsy were ready to give up their investigations as yet, and the truth was, the minute he got that ring on her finger, he'd want to give her the world. "Now stop worryin,' lass, we'll 'ave a wonderful Christmas together."

"You won't spend too much money?" she asked.

" 'Course not," he grinned. "But if you think my present is too grand, you can hide it until after our wedding. It's not long now, is it?"

"Six months," she replied with a wide smile. "The time has passed so quickly. June will be here before we know it."

"After Christmas we ought to start thinking about where we're going to live," he said softly. He knew he was treading on thin ice. She loved him, but she didn't want anything to get in the way of their investigations. Truth be told, neither did he.

She shrugged. "We've plenty of time for that. We might even think about staying on here."

Smythe knew that was what they should do if they

wanted everything to stay as it was, but he couldn't stand the thought of the two of them setting up housekeeping in the small attic room upstairs. "I don't think that's a good idea," he said. "But we'll find a way to have both a decent home and our investigations."

"I hope so." She sighed, pulled away, and started for the stairs. "But you're a proud man, and I don't want you letting your pride get in the way of our work. A lot of killers have been brought to justice because of us, and that's important. We're good at what we do, Smythe, and I don't want to give it up."

"Neither do I," he insisted. "We'll find a way, Betsy, I promise you."

"I'd best get downstairs. They'll be waiting for me." She wasn't angry with him; she knew he loved her more than his own life. But she also knew that once they were married, he'd not want her fetching and carrying in someone else's household, even for someone as good and decent as Inspector Witherspoon. "Come on," she called over her shoulder, "get a move on. They'll be waiting for you too. We've a lot to do today if we're going to find out who murdered Sir George Braxton."

Mrs. Jeffries was laying the table as they came into the kitchen. She glanced up and smiled at them. "Good morning. There's tea in the pot."

"I'll pour," Betsy said. "Where's Wiggins?"

"He's taken Fred for a walk," Mrs. Goodge answered. She was at the stove, cooking breakfast.

"We've much to do today," Mrs. Jeffries said.

"What are you going to do?" Betsy asked the housekeeper as she poured out the tea into mugs.

Mrs. Jeffries hesitated. "I was thinking about going to Richmond to a domestic agency."

"What's that?" Wiggins asked as he and Fred came into the room. "One of them places that fixes up 'irin' servants?"

"That's right," Mrs. Jeffries went to the stove and picked up the platter of eggs the cook had just taken out of the pan.

"Do you think they'd tell ya anything?" Smythe asked as he took his seat at the table.

"They're supposed to be discreet." Mrs. Goodge picked up the platter of bacon and came to the table. "But I'll warrant Mrs. Jeffries can get a few bits out of them. She's good at that sort of thing."

"So you don't think it's a silly idea?" Mrs. Jeffries asked quickly.

"I think it's a grand idea," the cook replied. "But I'd use a different name if I was you."

CHAPTER 7

Mrs. Jeffries changed from her plain brown bombazine dress, which clearly marked her as a housekeeper, into a walking dress of gray-blue cloth. The outfit consisted of a bell skirt edged with navy blue cording and the merest hint of a train, coupled with a gray blouse trimmed in navy at the collar and cuffs. With this, she wore her new calf-kid shoes and her good gray mantle with the matching hat. Mrs. Jeffries wanted to look as rich as possible.

She stepped outside and went toward Shepherds Bush Station. The day was clear, bright, and quite cold. Some of the shops had put holly wreaths and ribbons in their windows, reminding Mrs. Jeffries that Christmas was less than a week away and that they were running out of time.

She entered the station, bought a return ticket, and then walked out to the platform to wait for the train. Within half an hour, she was in Richmond and walking briskly down

Kew Road. She knew exactly where to go; she'd gotten the name of the domestic agency from the local newspaper.

The Saunders Domestic Agency was housed on the second floor of a narrow brick building. Mrs. Jeffries pulled open the outer door and stepped inside. She went up the wide staircase to the second floor, found the office door, and stood outside for a moment taking a long, deep breath. She kept reminding herself their work for the inspector was very important and one had to do what one had to do to get information.

She opened the door, stepped inside, and then came to a full stop, blinking hard to insure she wasn't seeing things. It wasn't the office itself that was the source of her amazement, for it was quite an ordinary office with a large desk in the center of the room and two high desks over by the windows. She blinked again making sure she wasn't mistaken. At each of the high desks there sat a woman. They were dressed much the same, both of them wearing dark skirts and white blouses with stiff, high collars. The third woman, dressed in much the same fashion but with a matching jacket over her blouse, was sitting at the center desk writing in a ledger.

Mrs. Jeffries knew that women sometimes ran domestic agencies, but generally all the clerks were male, and the female owners frequently went to great pains to stay in the background.

"Good day, madam." The woman at the center desk rose to her feet and closed the ledger in one smooth movement. She was a middle-aged woman with light brown hair, a longish nose, and a wide mouth. "May I be of service?"

Mrs. Jeffries remembered who she was supposed to be and stopped gaping. She nodded regally. "Yes, thank you. I've come to inquire about obtaining some staff."

"Of course, madam, I'm sure we can accommodate you. We have a full range of domestic help for all sizes of households." She waved at one of the two elegantly upholstered parlor chairs chairs opposite the desk. "Please have a seat, madam. I'm Mrs. Saunders, the proprietress of this establishment."

"How do you do, I'm Mrs. Edwin Roberts," Mrs. Jeffries replied as she settled herself in the chair.

Mrs. Saunders sank into her own seat and pulled a sheet of paper out of the top drawer. "Now, how can I be of service?"

"My husband and I are moving our household to Richmond and most of our servants are unwilling to come. We're currently living in Yorkshire, and most of the servants don't want to leave their families to come this far south," she explained. "I'm going to need a full staff, a cook, a housekeeper, three housemaids, two scullery maids, and a gardener."

Mrs. Saunders nodded. "Will you be needing a footman or a coachman?"

"No. We've gotten rid of our carriage. These days it simply isn't necessary. We'll be moving into a house on Derby Hill Road—" She broke off as one of the other women gasped.

Mrs. Saunders glared at the offender. "I'm sorry," she said softly. "Do please continue."

Mrs. Jeffries said nothing for a moment. So far, things were going precisely as she'd planned. "Is there something wrong with Derby Hill Road?"

"No, of course not," Mrs. Saunders replied. "It's a delightful neighborhood."

"But I think there is something amiss," Mrs. Jeffries pressed, "and I'd be most grateful if you could tell me what it is. My husband and I are new here, and we'd appreciate being told if there is something wrong with our new community. We've been told we'll be moving into an excellent neighborhood. There's a knight that lives right down the road from our new home."

Mrs. Saunders hesitated. Mrs. Jeffries could tell she was torn between wanting to acquire Mrs. Edwin Roberts' business while at the same time not wanting to anger her new customer by hiding something important from the woman. "Well, there has been a bit of a problem recently," she admitted. "I'm afraid the knight you mentioned has died."

"Died?" Mrs. Jeffries shrugged. "How unfortunate for the poor man. Was it a sudden death?"

The woman who'd gasped now snickered. Mrs. Saunders threw her another glare and hissed, "Pauline, please." Then she turned to Mrs. Jeffries and smiled weakly. "You must excuse us, please. I'm afraid my sister-in-law has an odd sense of decorum."

"Meaning the death was sudden?" Mrs. Jeffries inquired. "Please, I would appreciate knowing anything I can about this community. We've already purchased our home and frankly, I don't care for surprises."

Mrs. Saunders hesitated again. Finally, she said, "Sir George Braxton was murdered."

"Ye Gods, there's a maniac in the neighborhood," Mrs. Jeffries cried. "That's dreadful."

"Oh, no, ma'am." Pauline leapt down from her high stool and scurried over. "It's nothing like that, everyone's sure the murder was done by one of his own people. You're quite safe as long as you're not a relation to Sir George. Leastways, that's what everyone's saying."

Mrs. Saunders sighed. "Thank you, Pauline. Now, if you don't mind, I'm sure Mrs. Roberts' time is very valuable, and we must attend to her business." She smiled again at Mrs. Jeffries. "I'm sorry, this sort of gossip must be most upsetting—"

"Nonsense," Mrs. Jeffries said briskly. "If anything, hearing that the murderer is one of the dead man's relatives or friends makes me feel much better. I don't fancy moving into a neighborhood where there's a killer running loose. But why does everyone think the murderer is from his own household?"

"Because he's not a pleasant person," Pauline said quickly, "and his three daughters are unpleasant as well."

"Oh, dear, I do believe they're my neighbors." Mrs. Jeffries clucked her tongue. "That's not very good."

"This had been a bit of shock for you, Mrs. Roberts," Mrs. Saunders said softly. "I'm sure things won't be quite as bleak as they appear. Derby Hill Road really is a wonderful place to live."

"I don't know," Mrs. Jeffries murmured. "I did so want congenial neighbors."

"And most of the people in that neighborhood are very congenial. Look, you've had a shock. I'm sure you could do with a nice hot cup of tea."

That invitation was precisely what Mrs. Jeffries had been waiting to hear. "That would be very nice. But I must insist that you ladies will have one with me."

Wiggins popped his head into Luty's room and saw that she was sitting up in bed, apparently waiting for him. "Can I come in?" he asked in a loud whisper.

" 'Course you can," she replied. "I've been watchin' the clock, waitin' for you. No one saw you, did they? I did my best to keep 'em busy upstairs. I've got everyone up there polishin' silver and cleanin' out the linen cupboards."

He grinned proudly. "No one saw me. I was quiet as a mouse and nimble as a cat."

"Good. Sit yourself down then. Before I forget, I want you to take these notes to some people for me. One's to a friend of mine, she's wonderful, she loves to gossip more than a fat man loves to eat, and the other's to my lawyer." She reached under her pillow, pulled out two cream-colored envelopes and handed them to Wiggins. "I figured I might as well git the two of them helpin' us."

"Do you think your solicitor will know somethin'?" Wiggins asked as he sat down. He'd met the man on one of their previous cases and rather liked the fellow.

"He ought to, he's a right nosy feller." Luty grinned slyly. "Once I put a flea in his ear that I'm interested in the murder, he'll do what he needs to do to find out what's what. I think he gits a bit bored bein' a solicitor. But that's by the by. Now, tell me what you learned at the meetin' yesterday afternoon." She waved at the parlor chair next to her bed.

Wiggins studied her closely, hoping he wasn't taxing her health by doing her bidding. But her eyes were bright, her expression cheerful, and her skin seemed just the right color. She wasn't coughing or gasping for breath, either. Besides, she wasn't going to be out and about in this weather, she was going to do her share of the investigating right from the comfort of her own room.

"Has the cat got yer tongue?" she demanded. "Now go on, start talkin', and don't be leavin' out any details. Sometimes it's them little things that set us on the right track."

"Sorry, I'm woolgatherin'." He reached into his jacket pocket for a small brown notebook, a twin to the one he'd seen Constable Barnes use. "I wrote most of it down so I wouldn't forget anything."

*   *   *

The dressmaker's shop was located on the ground floor of a commercial building around the corner from the railway station. Betsy stood outside and stared through the small front window into the shop. She wanted to make sure there were no other customers before she went inside. Sometimes it was easier to get tradespeople to chat a bit if they were alone. She was in luck: all she could see was one young girl sitting on a straight bench next to row of sewing machines.

Betsy grasped the brass handle, turned the knob, and stepped inside. The girl looked up and smiled in welcome. "Good day, miss. May I be of service?"

Betsy smiled in return. The lass couldn't be more than seventeen. Her red hair was pulled back into a knot at the nape of her neck, she wore a plain dress of pale gray that fitted beautifully over her thin frame, and there was a half-inch gap in her front teeth. "Good day, I'd like to speak to the proprietress, if possible. I'll be needing a wedding dress soon," she paused momentarily as the truth of the words struck home, "and I'd like to see what patterns you've got to offer."

"Mrs. Tortelli isn't here, miss." The girl laid the white lace to one side and got to her feet. "But I'm a full dressmaker, and I'd be pleased to show you our pattern books."

"That would be lovely, thank you. My name is Elizabeth Ann Berry," she replied, giving the girl her name. Betsy generally never gave out her real name when they were gathering clues, but this time, she had a legitimate reason for visiting a dressmaker, so even if it got back to the inspector, he'd think nothing of it. He might wonder why she went all the way to Richmond to find a dressmaker, but she could easily explain that she'd heard the shop was both inexpensive and did excellent work.

The girl bobbed a quick curtsey and then pointed to a

pattern book on a round table by the window. "If you'll step over and take a seat, Miss Berry, I'd be pleased to serve you."

"What's your name?" Betsy asked as she took a seat.

"I'm Sophia, miss." She smiled broadly and took the chair next to Betsy. Reaching for the pattern book, she flipped the pages to a section toward the back. "These are all our wedding-dress patterns, miss. They're quite lovely but if there's nothing here that pleases you, we can get Mrs. Tortelli, she's the owner, to come up with something you'll like."

Betsy stifled a gasp as she stared at the lovely gown on the page. The dress was done in a rich ivory satin with a tight bodice, scoop neckline, high sleeves, and a short train. An orange-blossom wreath with a diaphanous veil was also on the page. Betsy blinked, trying to tear her gaze away from the gorgeous dress. "It's beautiful," she murmured.

"It's very much like one done for the Countess de Parma," Sophia replied proudly. "Not exactly like it, of course, but very close."

Betsy forced herself to look away from the beautiful dress. She had to keep her mind on why she was here. "The countess must have looked lovely. You must have a lot of posh customers. Are any of them aristocrats?"

Sophia said nothing for a moment, and Betsy was sure she'd made her move too soon. Then Sophia grinned. "Not that many, and, frankly, they're a lot more trouble than they're worth. But Mrs. Tortelli likes doin' for them because they bring us business."

"Truth to tell, that's why I came," Betsy laughed. She was relieved the girl hadn't gone all toff-nosed and proper on her. "I do need a dress, and I can afford a nice one"—that was true, she could—"and I heard that Sir George Braxton's daughters come here for their clothes. Mind you, I don't know them or anything like that, it's just that one of my acquaintances mentioned you did their dresses."

"Not anymore," Sophia said with a shake of her head. "Mrs. Tortelli stopped taking their custom when Miss Charlotte Braxton wouldn't pay for a very expensive traveling dress we did for her last year. She still owes us, and do you know what? Just the other day, they sent a boy here wanting to know did we have any funeral clothes for hire." She pursed her lips and shook her head, clearly disgusted. "We couldn't believe it. Have you ever heard of such a thing, wanting to hire mourning clothes. For goodness sakes, it's not like you're only going to wear them once. Proper mourning lasts for a year."

"That's terrible." Betsy clucked her tongue. "But if they've had a death in the family, perhaps they're not thinking clearly. Shock does that sort of thing to some people."

"Shock, my foot," Sophia snorted. "Nothing could shock that family. Aristocrats or not, when they don't pay their bills, they're nothing more than thieves."

"How dreadful. Why don't you take them to court?" Betsy asked.

"Mrs. Tortelli was going to, but yesterday Charlotte Braxton came in and paid part of what she owed. She claimed she'd pay the rest as soon as the estate was settled. I was quite shocked. Can you imagine? She's already talking about her inheritance, even Mrs. Tortelli was surprised. Mind you, she was glad to see part of her money." Sophia seemed to catch herself. "Oh, dear, this is terrible, I'm supposed to be showing you wedding-dress patterns, not sitting here chattering like a half-wit."

"Oh, but chatting is so much more interesting," Betsy said eagerly. She had a feeling the girl didn't often get to talk to young women her own age. "Especially when it's about people like the Braxtons. Who would have thought they didn't pay their bills?"

"That's not the worst of it," Sophia sniffed. "I'm surprised you haven't heard, it's been in all of the papers."

"What has?" Betsy asked.

"The reason they needed mourning clothes," Sophia replied. "It wasn't just a death in the family. It was a murder, and it was Sir George got done in. Of course, everyone's pretending to be so surprised, but no one really is, if you get my meaning."

"Really?"

"Oh, yes, considering all the things they say about that family, it's no wonder one of them ended up dead. First of all, Sir George was playing with fire by hiring that man who does the gardening, and then, of course, there's that talk about Miss Charlotte."

Betsy already knew about Randall Grantham and that Charlotte Braxton loved to travel. But just in case there was something else, she said, "Miss Charlotte, the one who owed you money for a long time?"

"That's right." Sophia nodded eagerly. "Mrs. Tortelli heard from Mr. Parnell, he's a cabbie that works out of the stand over near the train station that he's taken Miss Charlotte across the river on more than one occasion."

"Across the river?" Betsy repeated. She hadn't a clue what that meant, but she had a feeling it didn't have anything to do with a trip to the continent.

"For card games," Sophia's voice dropped to a whisper. "That's where they have them, at private houses across the river."

"You mean—"

"That's right," Sophia exclaimed, "Miss Charlotte likes to gamble."

*   *   *

Inspector Witherspoon stared at Nina Braxton in exasperation. "Miss Braxton," he said. "The question is very simple. Please tell us what you were doing on the day your father died."

"I've already told you that." She folded her arms over her chest. "And I don't care to repeat myself."

"You've told us where you were on the evening your father was murdered," Barnes clarified. "What we'd like to know now is what you did the afternoon of that day."

Barnes had been somewhat surprised when Witherspoon had initiated this line of inquiry, but he'd learned long ago that no matter how irrelevant some questions might seem, there was generally a good reason to be asking them. Besides, he suspected that Mrs. Jeffries might have put a flea in the inspector's ear about finding out what everyone was doing on the day of the murder.

She stared at them for a long moment. "I spent the greater part of the afternoon going over some financial papers, and then at four o'clock, I met with the builder."

"The builder?" Witherspoon pressed. "Would you explain that, please?"

"My father was getting estimates on having the conservatory dismantled so it could be sold."

"Your father had you deal with such matters?" Witherspoon probed.

"He wasn't particularly interested in dealing with tradespeople," she replied. "So he asked me to take care of it."

"What's the name of the builders?" Barnes looked up from his notebook.

"Curriers, they're in Twickenham," she said. "I dealt with Neil Currier."

"What time did Mr. Currier arrive?" Witherspoon asked.

He'd no idea if any of this information was going to be useful, but for some reason after he'd finished his breakfast this morning, he'd found himself wondering if perhaps it might have been something that happened early in the day that precipitated the murder.

"Four o'clock. I met with him and his assistant in my father's study," she replied.

"How long were you with them?" Barnes asked.

"It was close to five o'clock when they left," she said. "After that, I went up to my room to take care of some correspondence. I didn't come down until dinner." She rose from the couch and started for the door. "If you'd like to confirm the time, you might have a word with Clarence, he was hovering about in the hall when the builders left. Now if you'll excuse me, I've a number of things to take care of before the funeral."

"Miss Braxton," Witherspoon called. "Have you any idea why your father's brokers were coming to see him?"

She stopped and turned to look at them. "Inspector, I believe you've already asked me this question. I've no idea why Father wished to see them. You'll have to ask them."

"May we have their names?" Barnes asked quietly.

"Hopkins and Flannerty," she replied. "They're in Fenchurch Street."

"I understand you sent them a message telling them not to come," Witherspoon said.

"I've already told you I did. As soon as I knew that Father was dead, I canceled the appointment and sent for his solicitors instead."

"His solicitors." The inspector nodded encouragingly, hoping she'd continue.

"For the funeral arrangements, Inspector," she sighed. "I told you all this yesterday afternoon."

"All you mentioned yesterday was that the solicitors were coming about the funeral arrangements," Barnes said softly. "But you never told us why they couldn't have just sent a clerk over with that information. That's what most firms would have done." He wasn't in the least sure this was true.

"They didn't send a clerk, Constable, because my father was a baronet," she replied, her tone caustic. "He was rich and important. Father had very specific requirements about his funeral arrangements. He had them with his solicitors, so I sent for them so we could make the arrangements according to his wishes."

"Thank you, Miss Braxton," Witherspoon said. He made a mental note to find out if there were any Judges' Rules that precluded the Braxton solicitors from confirming her story.

She turned and walked out of the drawing room. Witherspoon sighed heavily. "Honestly, Constable, getting information out of these people is very difficult."

"I think you're doing quite well, sir," Barnes replied as he flipped through his notebook. "We might have a hard time getting anything useful out of the solicitors, they never like to talk unless they have to, but Braxton's brokers and bankers aren't bound by Judges' Rules or client privilege."

"Let's go and see them as soon as possible," Witherspoon said.

"Yes, sir." Barnes continued, "The servants confirm most of what has Miss Braxton has told us, but none of them mention Mr. Clark being in the vicinity of the study or even in the house that afternoon."

"Yes, well, he does live here, so I don't think it makes a great deal of difference." He shook his head. "It's getting quite late, Constable, let's interview the other sisters again and then see if we've time to get to the Yard."

"Is the chief inspector pressing you, sir?" Barnes asked. "We're doin' the best we can."

"I'm sure he's well aware of our efforts, but he's probably being pressed himself about the matter." Witherspoon cocked his head to one side. "I don't know why, either. It's not as if this family is particularly well thought of in aristocratic circles. From what we've learned, the entire family is universally disliked. They don't pay their bills, they're not sociable, they're nasty to all and sundry, and they've never been involved in any sort of government or community service. Honestly, I don't understand why Whitehall is putting pressure on the chief."

Barnes stared at Witherspoon sympathetically. The poor man just didn't understand how society really worked. "Sir George was a distant cousin to the queen," he reminded the inspector. "And having his murderer walk around free is an embarrassment to the crown and therefore, to the government. It doesn't matter what sort of character the man had, all that matters is how it looks, sir."

"Yes, I suppose you're right, not that I was saying it wasn't important that we catch the killer, it most assuredly is important. But I am at a loss to see why we have to get it done so quickly. I don't want to rush this investigation and arrest the wrong person, Constable."

"You won't, sir." He knew the inspector had a horror of sending an innocent person to the gallows. "Now, sir, I'll go and see if I can find Miss Charlotte Braxton."

"There's no need of that. I'm right here." Charlotte Braxton flung open the door and stalked into the room. The heavy door barely missed the constable.

Barnes leapt back, stumbling slightly as he tried to get out of the way.

"Are you all right, Constable?" Witherspoon asked, his

expression concerned. "That door could have done you great harm."

"I'm fine, sir." He straightened and pulled out his notebook.

"Really, Miss Braxton," Witherspoon chided. "You really should be more careful."

"Why? It's my house, Inspector, and I wasn't to know the constable would be lurking about the door, was I?" She sat down on the settee.

The inspector contented himself with a disapproving look and then said, "Can you please tell us what you were doing the day your father was killed?"

"What's that got to do with anything?" she asked.

"Miss Braxton, please, it's a simple enough question," Barnes snapped. He'd just about had enough of the Braxton sisters.

"Unless, of course, there's a reason you don't want us to know what you were doing that day," Witherspoon pressed. He was still annoyed at the woman's horrid behavior toward the constable.

"Don't be ridiculous." Charlotte's eyes narrowed. "Of course there's no reason you shouldn't know what I was doing. I was sorting through the attic. Father wanted me to have a look at all the things stored up there and sort out what was to be worth selling."

"What time did you go up to the attic?" Witherspoon asked. He was fairly sure this line of inquiry was useless, but as he'd started along this road, he couldn't very well turn back.

She leaned back against the back of the settee. "I went up straight after lunch and spent most of the afternoon sorting through it all. After that I went for a walk to clear my head."

"What time did you go outside?" Barnes asked. He didn't look up from his notebook.

"I'm not certain."

"How long were you gone?" he shot back.

"Quite a while, my head ached from being up in that dusty attic."

"Were you back in time for tea?" Witherspoon asked.

"No, but I do recall the wind was howling horribly by the time I got back, and it had started to snow." She got up from the settee, smoothing the skirt of her dark gray dress as she rose. "Now, if there's nothing else, I'm very busy."

"But there is something else," the inspector said quickly. He was afraid she'd run off again. "We've had a report that you were seen coming in the side door of the house approximately an hour before the alarm was raised on the night your father died. Is this true?"

Seemingly unsurprised by the question, she shrugged her shoulders. "Yes, it's true. I'd been out that night."

"Where were you?" Barnes asked.

"I had a social engagement."

"An engagement," the inspector repeated. "We will need to speak with your friends to confirm your movements, Miss Braxton. You do realize that you were outside very near the time your father was being murdered."

"Of course I realize that, Inspector, that's one of the reasons I didn't mention this earlier." She smiled nastily. "And the people I was with weren't my friends. They're acquaintances that I occasionally meet with for a friendly card game."

"You were playing cards?" Witherspoon looked surprised.

"Was it just a friendly game?" Barnes studied her carefully.

"No, it wasn't friendly at all," she sighed heavily. "As a

matter of fact, I owe some of them a great deal of money. But now that father's dead, that shouldn't be a problem." Her eyes narrowed. "Which of my sisters gave you this little tidbit, Inspector? I'll bet it was Nina, she always did love to tell tales."

"Miss Braxton, when you came in that night, did you see or hear anything unusual?" Witherspoon asked. "I know this isn't the first time I've ask you this question, but that was before I knew you were outside the house and near the murder scene close to the time it actually happened."

She shook her head. "I saw and heard nothing. That's God's truth. When I came home that night, I was so worried about how I was going to pay my gambling debts that I didn't notice anything. Honestly, I'm telling the truth. The driver let me off at the end of the drive at half past two. I came around and went in the side door because I had the key. But I heard nothing and saw nothing."

"Where did you play cards?" Barnes asked.

"At a house in Teddington. Number fifteen Barnaby Way. They'll vouch for my story." She smiled bitterly. "They're not going to thank me for sending the police along to see them, but they don't want any trouble. Now, if there's nothing else, I must go."

"Thank you, Miss Braxton," Witherspoon replied wearily. "That'll be all for the moment."

As soon as she'd left, the door on the far side of the room flew open, and Lucinda Braxton flounced into the room. "Honestly, Inspector, you don't really believe that nonsense she was spouting, do you?"

"I beg your pardon," Witherspoon replied. His head was beginning to ache.

"Oh, she spent the afternoon in the attic all right, because Father made her do it. But you should have asked her what else she was doing up there." Lucinda smiled maliciously. "Go ahead, call her back and ask her if she found something valuable up there, something for her to sell. Ask her where she went on her walk and where she got the money to play her precious cards. Go ahead, fetch her back and ask her."

"Miss Braxton, I'm not sure I understand," Witherspoon said softly. "Perhaps you could sit down and explain—"

"Oh, don't be so dense, man," Lucinda snapped. "She steals. She found something up in the attic that she could sell, and that's where she went that afternoon. Father had finally figured it out. He was going to do something about it as well. I know because he told me he was going to put a stop to it."

"A stop to what?" Witherspoon asked.

"To Charlotte's thieving!" Lucinda cried. "She sells things to pay her gambling debts."

"We know about her gambling," Barnes said softly.

"But you didn't know about her thieving, did you?" she cried. "Charlotte was furious when Father told her to clean out the attic, until she found something she could sell, then she was out of here like a shot. Honestly, Inspector, that's probably why she killed Father. She knew he was going to toss her out of the house for her constant thieving."

Smythe was tired, but not too tired to give up and go home. So far, he'd had no luck at all today. Blimpey hadn't sent him word that he had anything for him, he'd talked to every cabbie he could find, and he'd visited half a dozen pubs in the neighborhood, but he'd found out nothing he didn't already know.

He stood in front of a stable and knew he was grasping at straws. It wasn't likely he'd find out anything here, but he felt he had to try. The stable was located half a mile off Derby Hill Road in Richmond, the closest one to the Braxton household, and Smythe had reasoned that if the family ever hired coaches, they'd probably do it from one in the neighborhood.

He opened a tall wooden gate and stepped into a cobblestone courtyard. A burly bearded fellow was leading a black horse out the double doors of the stable proper. "Good day, sir. Can I be of service to ya?"

"That depends, sir. Are you the owner of this establishment?" The answer he got would determine how he handled himself.

"No, sir, that'd be Mr. Carpenter. He's not 'ere at the moment. He's showin' 'orses to a customer."

"You buy and sell horses here?"

"A few, sir." The man and the horse had reached him and had stopped a few feet away.

"This one's a beauty, is he for sale?" Smythe moved closer and stroked the horses nose.

"No, sir, she belongs to Mr. Craig, and he's right fond of her."

"Pity."

"I'm John Blackston," the man said. "Er, uh, what can I do for you?"

Smythe fingered the roll of bills he'd stuffed in his pocket. He hesitated before taking the money out and flashing it about. Not everyone was the sort of bloke that sold information. "I'm wonderin' if you could help me," he began, his mind working furiously as he tried to come up with a plausible story this fellow would believe. "My mistress left somethin' important in a 'ired coach the other night, and she needs it back right quick."

Blackston shook his head. "We've not hired out any coaches at night for nigh onto a week now. Are you sure the coach was one of ours?"

"Now that's just it," Smythe replied. "She was picked up around nine o'clock on the night of the eighteenth from the end of Derby Hill Road by friends, and she just assumed the coach came from here."

Blackston patted the horse's nose. "It weren't one of ours, sorry. I can't help you."

"Do you 'ave any idea where it might be from?" he asked. He'd started asking these questions just to get the man talking, he'd no idea if anyone had been picked up near the Braxton house or not that night, but he'd considered it worth a try. After all, if the killer wasn't someone in the household, he or she had to get there that night some way. "I mean, it's real important I find out if any hired coaches came or went from there that night."

Blackston looked at him sharply, his eyes narrowing. "You're wanting to find out if anyone hired a coach from here on the night Sir George Braxton was killed, don't ya? Don't waste your time, man, the constables have already been around here askin' questions, and I'll tell you the same thing I told them. We stopped having anything to do with Sir George's household years ago, and we've not hired out a carriage for more than a week, now get on with you. I've got work to do."

"Sorry, I don't mean to delay ya, but can ya tell me why you stopped 'avin' anything to do with the Braxton 'ouse-hold?" He figured he might as well ask.

Blackston gave an exasperated sigh. "What's it to ya, man?"

"It's not just idle curiosity," Smythe said quickly. "I'm workin' with a private inquiry agent to 'elp find the killer."

He felt he was staying close enough to the truth here. In one sense, they were private inquiry agents.

Blackston gave him a long hard stare and then said, "We stopped dealin' with them after Sir George ruined our best carriage and then wouldn't pay for the damage he'd done. It was a good few years back, so if someone hired a carriage to drive over and kill him that night, they didn't hire it from us. Now, get on with you, man, I've work to do."

"Inspector, I know you're doing your best, but you really must try harder," Chief Inspector Barrows said. He was seated behind his desk with the inspector's latest report spread out in front of him.

Witherspoon was seated directly across from him. "Yes, sir, I certainly will." In truth, he didn't see how he could try any harder.

"Have you any idea who committed the murder?" Barrows asked.

"Not as yet, sir, but we're making progress on the case."

"Yes, yes, I'm sure you are. But could you hurry it up a bit? We're getting a great deal of pressure from the Home Office, and they're getting a great deal of pressure from the—" He broke off and looked down at the report on his desk. "Oh, never mind, suffice to say we must put this to rest quickly, Inspector. That's the reason I assigned you to this case, now I trust you'll not disappoint me."

"I'll do my best, sir."

"They want this case solved by Christmas," Barrows muttered harshly. "I don't know what they expect us to do. We can't pull a suspect out of a hat. We're not magicians, we're detectives." He looked at Witherspoon, his expression almost pleading. "Are you quite certain you've no really good suspects?"

"I've a goodly number of suspects, sir," he replied. "Yet there isn't one that stands out as the killer. But we're doing our very best, sir. We really are." He couldn't promise to catch the killer by Christmas, and he wasn't going to arrest someone just for show. "As a matter of fact, I'm going to have a word with Mr. Venable again. I understand he was there right after the body was discovered." He'd no idea why that idea popped into his head, but it had, and he was desperate enough to latch onto anything that appeared useful.

"Who?"

"Darwin Venable, the Home Secretary's assistant."

"Oh, yes, that's right. He was with the H.S. the night the body was discovered," Barrows murmured.

"I hope to ask him a few questions," Witherspoon said. "He might be quite useful. Unless, of course, you think I ought to speak to the H.S. directly."

"He's already made a statement," Barrows sighed, "and I think it unlikely he'll want to give another one. Besides, I believe he's gone to Scotland. You have a word with the assistant, and let's hope for both our sakes that he remembers something useful."

CHAPTER 8

"It's gone cold again," Mrs. Goodge commented as she put a pot of tea in the center of the table. "Mark my words, we'll have more snow for Christmas."

"I hope it holds off till then." Betsy put a plate of seed cake next to the teapot. "Bad weather makes it hard to get about quickly. The trains are always late, the omnibus doesn't show up half the time, and I hear the lifts on those new tube stations don't work properly in the wet. I'd hate for our investigation to be slowed by the weather."

"Humph, seems to me it's going slowly all on its own," the cook grumbled. She'd not had a good day. Half of her sources hadn't shown up, and those few that had trooped through her kitchen hadn't known much of anything. She had very little to contribute to their meeting.

"I don't know," Wiggins said as he and Fred ambled into the kitchen. "I think we're doin' just fine." He'd not found out much himself, but helping Luty be a part of the investigation had restored his usual optimism.

"As do I, Wiggins," Hatchet nodded at the footman. "The information is coming in slowly, but I've no doubt we'll get to the right conclusion in the end."

"I'm sorry to be late." Mrs. Jeffries burst into the kitchen behind the footman. She took off her jacket as she headed to the coat tree, pausing just long enough to reach down and give Fred a friendly pat on his back. "Naturally, the train got held up, that always happens when you're in a rush." She hung up her garments and surveyed the room. "Where's Smythe?"

"He's late as well," Betsy said. "But I'm sure he'll be here soon."

Mrs. Jeffries hurried to the table and took her seat just as they heard the back door open. "I expect that's him now," she commented as she reached for the teapot.

But Smythe wasn't alone—he had a guest with him. "Look who I found out in the garden."

Ruth Cannonberry laughed. "I was trying to decide whether or not to barge in on you," she said.

"But then I made the decision for 'er," Smythe grinned broadly, "by takin' her arm and insistin' she come inside for a visit."

"Ruth, it's so very good to see you again," Mrs. Jeffries leapt to her feet. "We're delighted you've come back. You must have tea with us."

"Only if you promise I'm not interrupting something important," she said. "I heard that the inspector got the Braxton murder, so I know you're all very busy. I'd not like to intrude."

Lady Cannonberry was a tall, blonde woman of late middle years. She was the widow of a lord, but as the daughter of a very progressive vicar, she had a well-developed social conscience. She worked hard for women's rights and didn't believe in the separation of people by social status. She also loved to help the household with the inspector's murders, and, like them, knew enough to keep her investigations very discreet. She and the inspector were doing their best to develop their friendship, but it was most difficult for her. She was constantly being called out of town. When her husband had died, she inherited his relatives, most of whom were elderly and of a nervous nature. Even the slightest sniffle could convince one and all of them they were at death's door. Lady Cannonberry had privately speculated there must be something quite odd in the way the family reared its children, as all of them, including her late husband, had had the same character trait. But as she had both a kind heart and a social conscience, she considered it her duty to go and take care of them whether they were genuinely ill or not. Most of them, she'd discovered, were simply lonely and that, of course, was a malady they could only cure for themselves.

"You never intrude," Wiggins said easily. "Matter of fact, it's good that you're 'ere. This case is a bit jumbled, and if you know anything about Sir George Braxton, it's bound to 'elp."

She laughed and slipped into the empty chair next to the footman. "Actually, I got away as quickly as I could when I heard about the murder. Cousin Harry was a bit annoyed, but he'll manage quite well without me."

"Do you know anything about the Braxton family?" Mrs. Goodge asked eagerly.

"I know his daughters," Ruth replied as she accepted a cup of tea from the cook. "I've met them several times, but I wouldn't say we were well acquainted."

"Did you know Sir George?" Hatchet asked.

"I met him once. He was on some committee or other with my late husband. But I don't think he ever came to any of their meetings, and I know that he wasn't particularly well liked. I can remember there was quite a bit of complaining from the other members that he'd got his name on the committee papers without doing any of the work." She frowned thoughtfully and took a quick sip of tea. "As a matter of fact, all in all, I'd say they're considered a very peculiar family."

"Yes, that's our conclusion as well," Mrs. Jeffries agreed. "But let me tell you what we've learned so far. Once you hear a few more details of the case and the names of the people who were on the property that night, you might recall something about one or more of them." She gave their guest a thorough yet concise narrative of the case. She took care to explain the circumstances under which the body had been found. When she'd finished, she leaned back in her chair and looked hopefully at Ruth. "I don't suppose you've heard anything about any of the principals in the case that might be useful?"

"At this point, anything you knew about 'em might 'elp." Wiggins added.

Ruth thought for a moment before she answered. "I don't know if this is the sort of information that you need, but I do know that Raleigh Brent was desperate to marry money."

"That's right useful," Smythe muttered. "Now that Sir George is dead, he'll get his chance. From what we've heard, Lucinda Braxton is keen to marry him, and now that she's got money, they'll both get what they want."

"But I don't think that could possibly be a motive for murder," Ruth said earnestly. "I mean, I don't think Brent would have committed murder to free up Lucinda Braxton to marry him. The gossip I heard was that he was going to marry Fiona Burleigh, and she's got plenty of money."

"But she's not an aristocrat, is she?" Mrs. Jeffries commented. "Maybe Mr. Brent likes the idea of marrying the daughter of a baronet."

"Especially as the title can pass to a daughter," Mrs. Goodge added.

"But we don't know that the title would go to her," Betsy argued, "and even if it did, she'd be Lady Braxton in her own right, and he'd be just her husband. He'd not get the title."

"But perhaps their children might," Wiggins added. "Mind you, she might be a bit past it." He broke off, a horrified expression on his face as he realized he'd spoken so indelicately. "I'm so sorry," he stuttered. "I don't know what come over me, speakin' as I did."

Betsy snickered, Hatchet looked amused, Smythe laughed, Mrs. Goodge tried to look disapproving but couldn't because she was trying not to smile, and Ruth Cannonberry had put her hand over her mouth to hold back a giggle.

"It's quite all right, Wiggins," Mrs. Jeffries said. "Your words were rather blunt but did rather get to the heart of the matter. The question is, why would Raleigh Brent risk murdering his host just to marry a rich wife, when he had another candidate who was equally rich waiting in the wings?"

"Unless, of course, he wanted entry into aristocratic circles," Hatchet suggested. "In which case, murdering Sir George made perfect sense as it meant he could then marry Lucinda Braxton. Even if Lucinda Braxton inherited the title in her own right, he'd still be the husband of a baroness, and that, my friends, could well be motive enough for him."

Mrs. Jeffries nodded thoughtfully and then looked at Ruth. "Do you know if Brent's from a socially ambitious family?"

"I'm afraid I don't know anything about his background. The first I ever heard of him was when he escorted both Fiona Burleigh and Lucinda Braxton to the Waifs and Strays luncheon at Lambeth Palace. I remember the incident because the lady sitting beside me pointed at Lucinda Braxton and commented that the woman had nerve showing her face, that she'd not given so much as a shilling to the charity, nor had she helped raise any money for it."

"How long ago was this?" Smythe asked.

"It was last November," Ruth replied.

"Maybe Fiona Burleigh isn't as rich as the Braxtons," Mrs. Goodge suggested. She rather liked the idea of Raleigh Brent as the killer. She didn't have much respect for men who married for money, nor women, either.

"She's richer," Hatchet said. "Her family owns Burleigh Ironworks as well as a substantial amount of London property. My source wasn't certain how rich the family actually is, but he knew they had plenty. Of course," he smiled slightly, "Miss Burleigh does have a bit of a reputation as a shrew, but then again, so does Lucinda Braxton."

"Maybe 'e's in love with Miss Braxton," Wiggins suggested. "I know it sounds daft, but maybe it's true."

"The lad's right." Smythe helped himself to another slice of cake. "The 'earts a powerful thing. Maybe Lucinda Braxton is the one he wants to be with, and 'e figured out a way to 'ave both 'er and a nice income."

"We can speculate like this for hours," Mrs. Jeffries said. "And it is actually quite useful. But I think that as we're a bit pressed for time, we'd better get on with our meeting and report on what we've learned today." She gave Ruth a quick smile. "You don't mind sitting through more details, do you?"

"Not at all, you know I'm always delighted if I can actually help, and I think in this case, I might be able to contribute something worthwhile. I do have some rather good connections."

"Excellent," Mrs. Jeffries replied. "I, for one, had a rather good day. Luckily for us, the domestic agency in Richmond had no qualms about discussing the murder case and the entire Braxton clan."

"Not exactly discreet, eh," Smythe chuckled.

"No discretion whatsoever," she agreed. "I heard the usual that we've all heard about the family, about what a mean, miserly bunch they are, but eventually, I got a tidbit we'd not heard before. It was about Clarence Clark. The gossip is that he's Sir George's illegitimate half brother, not his cousin."

"I heard that as well," Betsy added. "The dressmaker wasn't very discreet, either."

"I wonder if he's going to inherit any part of Sir George's estate?" Hatchet mused.

"I wasn't able to find out anything along those lines," Mrs. Jeffries admitted, "but I did find it interesting that no one in the Braxton household had thought to tell the inspector about Clark's true relationship to the deceased."

"Maybe they don't know," Mrs. Goodge suggested. "Sometimes the family is completely in the dark about that sort of thing."

"I wonder if the daughters are fond of him?" Ruth asked.

"I don't think they're particularly fond of anyone," Mrs. Jeffries replied. "At least we've seen no evidence of kindness from any of them. We've heard nothing but negative accounts of their characters."

"Seems to me the only way that Clarence Clark would want Sir George dead is if 'e was standin' to inherit somethin' from 'im," Wiggins said. "From what we've learned of the daughters, they'd be just as like to toss the fellow out into the street as to let him stay on in the 'ousehold."

"Perhaps we ought to determine if Mr. Clark is an heir," Hatchet said. "Otherwise, as Wiggins has pointed out, Sir George's daughters don't appear to be the kind of women to let him stay on at the house out of the goodness of their hearts."

"That's not going to be easy." Mrs. Jeffries pulled the teapot closer and poured herself another cup.

"Perhaps you'd best put a flea in the inspector's ear," Mrs. Goodge suggested. "None of us have the resources to find out the contents of Sir George's will before it's made public."

Wiggins wondered if Luty's note to her solicitor might have had something to do with learning the contents of Sir George's will. He bit his lip and looked down at his plate. Blast, he couldn't say anything about it. Keeping secrets was blooming hard.

"I'll make sure I mention it to him this evening, though I know he was already planning to interview Sir George's solicitors." She looked around the table. "Who would like to go next?"

"I've not got anything to report," Smythe sighed. "I didn't find out a bloomin' thing except that the Braxtons can't hire from their local livery. Apparently, they damaged a carriage a few years back and wouldn't pay to put it right. But that's 'ardly news. None of the tradespeople wanted to do business with that bunch."

"And that includes the local dressmaker," Betsy said cheerfully. She patted his arm. "Don't worry, Smythe, you'll do better tomorrow. Besides, I've found out enough for both of us." She told them everything she'd heard from Sophia. "So now we know that Charlotte Braxton didn't just like to travel, she liked to gamble, too."

Mrs. Goodge clucked her tongue. "Can you believe it? Gambling! How shameful! That woman had every advantage in life. How could she do something like that. Apparently it wasn't enough that she hire herself out as a paid companion. How on earth did Sir George stand the shame of it?"

"Maybe he didn't," Smythe said softly. "And maybe that's why he's dead."

"You think she killed him that night?" Hatchet asked sharply.

The coachman shrugged. "It's possible. We know he opened the door to someone he knew. Maybe he waited till he heard her come home and then confronted her about her behavior. They had words, and it got more and more heated. He turned his back on her, and she bashed him in the head, drug him outside, and dumped him in the pond. Let's face it, she was fully dressed when the alarm was raised, she was supposedly hysterical when she went to wake her sisters, and she has a real motive."

"Why is her motive any greater than her sisters?" Betsy asked.

"Because people you owe gambling debts to aren't very nice. Sometimes, they can get real nasty, even to women like Charlotte Braxton. They might 'ave been threatening her pretty 'ard."

Mrs. Jeffries nodded thoughtfully. "What you've described is certainly possible. But why would she drag him outside? More to the point, would she have the strength to do it?"

"She would," Mrs. Goodge said flatly. "All the girls were

strong, that's one of the few things I've learned today. The
Braxton daughters are all short, stocky, and strong, just like
their mother."

"But why take him outside at all?" Ruth asked. "Why
not just leave him where she'd killed him?"

"By taking him outside, the killer widened the circle of
suspects," Mrs. Jeffries explained. "If he'd been found dead
in a house with all the doors and windows locked, then suspicion would naturally fall on the family or possibly the servants. As it stands now, anyone could have killed him."

"We might be dealing with a very clever killer," Hatchet
said quietly. "If the murderer set up the situation to throw
suspicion on people outside the house, do you think he or
she could possibly be trying to implicate the gardener?"

"Why 'im?" Wiggins asked.

"Because I think the killer thought Grantham was the
most likely person the police would see as a suspect."

"That's true," Smythe agreed. "If it 'adn't been our inspector on this case, the local lads would 'ave already 'ad
Grantham in to 'elp with their inquiries, if you get my
meaning."

Mrs. Jeffries hadn't thought of it in this way before, but
now she began to see things in a very different light. "You
know, you could be absolutely correct. Of course, why
didn't I see this before? The killer probably expected the police to focus on someone exactly like Grantham."

"He's the one that found the body," Betsy pointed out.

"And if we found out Grantham was workin' as a gardener to avoid prison, it'd not 'ave been 'ard for the police to
learn that little fact as well," Smythe added.

"And it could be something the killer knew as well,"
Hatchet continued. "What the murderer didn't count on

was Inspector Witherspoon getting the case and not naturally grabbing the first suspect that appears tailor-made for the crime."

"You think the killer began to plan the crime when Grantham came to the household?" Mrs. Jeffries asked cautiously. She was a bit leery of this kind of discussion, they'd learned on other cases that getting too closely allied to a set of circumstances or an idea could be very detrimental to finding out the truth. But on the other hand, they couldn't afford not to look at everything.

"It's possible, he's only been there three months," Hatchet replied. "It could well be that the killer needed someone to lay the blame on, so he or she waited until they had a likely candidate, bided their time, and then committed the murder when the house was full of people. That would muddy the waters even more."

"That's true, but let's not jump to conclusions," Mrs. Goodge warned. "We've been fooled before."

"Indeed we have," Hatchet smiled to show he didn't take umbrage. "You're right, we should wait until all the facts are in before we speculate further."

"Of course we should," Mrs. Jeffries said quickly. "But I do think your idea is worth thinking about. Now, who would like to go next?"

"I didn't learn anything," Wiggins said cheerfully. "I was all over Sheen Common, but I couldn't find anyone who'd stand still long enough for a bit of a chat."

"Did you hear anything else, Hatchet?" Mrs. Jeffries asked.

He thought for a moment. "Only what I've already told you about the Burleigh family . . . wait, I tell a lie. I did hear something, though I don't think it's got anything to do with the murder. The conservatory at the Braxton house had been designed by Oswald Pellinger, which I think is the reason Sir George was going to sell the structure."

"Who's 'e?" Wiggins asked.

"An American architect," Hatchet continued. "He designed a number of structures in his early days in London and Paris before he moved back to America. I believe he's become quite famous. Perhaps an American is buying the structure and having it moved there."

"Moving a greenhouse?" Mrs. Goodge snorted. "What nonsense. Those Americans will buy anything."

"Mrs. Goodge, did you hear anything else today?" Mrs. Jeffries asked. She really didn't want the cook to feel left out.

"Not really," Mrs. Goodge sighed. "Just what we already know. Most of the tradespeople want their money paid before they'll do any work for the Braxton's. But then, that's not surprising, is it?"

Darwin Venable was quite delighted to see the inspector and Constable Barnes. "I was so hoping you'd come along and have another chat with me," he said, gesturing at a group of chairs by the window. They were in the small office next to the Home Secretary's. "I do hope it's me you've come to see," Venable continued as the men took a seat. "The H.S. has gone to Aberdeen and won't be back till Christmas Eve."

"We should have liked to have a word with him, Mr. Venable, but we were already informed he was out of London. I'm hoping you'll be able to help us. We've some questions on what he or you saw on the night of the murder."

"Then I ought to be able to help you." Venable nodded eagerly. "I was with him. I saw everything that he did that night."

"Did you go into the back garden?" Barnes asked.

"Yes. The H.S. woke me up to come along and take notes when he saw the constables coming to Sir George's house."

"You took notes?" Barnes repeated. He couldn't believe this.

"Oh, yes, indeed." Venable beamed broadly. "The Home Secretary wants to write his memoirs one day, part of my job is to constantly take notes on his daily activities."

"Do you have your notebook from that day," the inspector asked, "and if so, do you mind letting us have a look at it?"

"Of course," Venable who was quite formally dressed in an old-fashioned frock coat, cravat, and stiff tie, reached inside his coat and pulled out a flat, maroon-colored notebook three times the size of Constable Barnes little brown book. "I'm afraid I'll have to read it to you, if you don't mind. After all, most of these notes are for the Home Secretary and are confidential."

Witherspoon hesitated for a moment, then nodded his agreement. He'd no idea if the law allowed him to take the private writings of a Home Secretary into evidence. Perhaps it was best to see what those writings might be. After all, if there was something useful, he was certain there would be a way to enter it into evidence if it became necessary.

Venable grinned and flipped open the book. "I'll read the entry from the eighteenth. I shan't bother with the mundane work details but shall begin at the part where he awakens me to come with him to the Braxton household.

Monday, December 18th, 1893

H.S. woke me at 3:40 A.M. and bade me get dressed and come downstairs right away. I did as instructed and met H.S. in the foyer. He bade me follow him, and the two of us went outside to the house across the road, the home of Sir George Braxton. When I asked H.S. what we were doing, he told me he'd seen several constables enter the premises of Sir George Braxton, and that we'd best find out what was happening. When I asked H.S. why he was up and staring out the window at this hour of the morning, he bade me mind my own business and do what I was told."

Venable looked up, a blush staining his cheeks. "Sorry, I meant to cross that bit out. But honestly, it was a reasonable enough question considering the circumstances. I mean, after all, it was the middle of the night."

"Yes, I'm sure you're absolutely correct," Witherspoon assured him. "Please, do continue with your narrative."

Venable cleared his throat and started again:

"H.S. and I went across the road and up the drive to the Braxton house. H.S. shouted at a constable who'd stuck his head around the corner of the house, identified himself, and asked what was wrong. The constable stated that Sir George Braxton appeared to have been murdered. H.S. immediately demanded to see the body. The constable escorted us around the side of the house to the back garden. We saw a large group of people huddled in a circle by the pond. The constable announced our presence and H.S. demanded everyone step back so he could have a look at the situation."

"Excuse me," Witherspoon interrupted, "but why don't you tell us in your own words what happened next?" This was taking far too long and wasn't particularly useful. The inspector wanted details, the kind of small details that might turn out to be important, that might point the way toward the killer, because at this juncture, he didn't have a clue as to who was guilty.

Venable brightened immediately. "Oh, jolly good. Well,

they were all standing around the corpse and H.S. went over and asked what had happened. Everyone started talking at once, so he shouted at them to be quiet—he rather likes to shout, I think—and then asked who was in charge."

"And who replied?" Barnes asked curiously. He wondered which of the three sisters had stepped forward.

"That was the problem, you see," Venable said. "Virtually everyone claimed to be in charge, but finally, one lady in particular, I believe it might have been Sir George's eldest daughter, managed to out-shout the rest of them and got the H.S.'s attention. She told him her father had been murdered, and that they'd best find out who did it straight away."

"She wanted justice for her father," Witherspoon murmured.

"Oh, no, she said she didn't want her fiancé's holiday ruined." Venable shrugged. "Even the H.S. was a bit taken aback. But being a gentleman, he said nothing."

"Then what happened?" Witherspoon prodded. He was getting very tired. This had been an exceedingly long day.

"The H.S. asked if they'd moved the body, and then another lady, I believe she was the housekeeper, said that they had."

"Who exactly had touched the victim?" the inspector asked. He'd no idea why this might be important. "I mean, who'd pulled the fellow out?"

Venable thought for a moment. "I don't believe the H.S. asked that question. I do know that he insisted they put Sir George back the way he'd been found." He grinned at the inspector. "Apparently, he'd already made up his mind to send for you. As a matter of fact, I know he'd made up his mind to send for you because he sent me to do it."

"So you left at that point?" Barnes asked.

"That's right."

Witherspoon frowned. "What time was this?"

He thought for a moment. "It must have been close to four o'clock."

The inspector nodded. "Can you tell me what you saw as you were leaving?"

"What do you mean? I saw nothing, it was still dark." Venable looked confused by the question. "There were a great number of people in the garden, they were all milling about. But I can't say that I saw anything in particular."

Barnes knew the man had seen more than he realized. "Did you notice if the lights were on in the room directly off the terrace?"

"I don't think so," Venable murmured. "But there was a light in the side hall, I remember seeing that as I walked past to the front of the house."

"How about in the front of the house, any lights there?" Witherspoon asked.

"I'm not sure . . . wait, yes, there must have been, because I noticed a set of footprints running along the side of the greenhouse, and I wouldn't have been able to see them if there hadn't been some light spilling out of the house through the windows. I don't know that it came directly from the front of the building, but there was light enough to see."

"Where did these footprints lead?" the inspector asked. They were probably made by either the police or someone from the household, but it never hurt to ask.

"I've no idea, Inspector," Venable admitted. "I'm sorry, is it important? Well, of course it is or you wouldn't be asking about them. But I was in such a hurry to get to the station, I really didn't notice. I knew we needed to get you to the Braxton house as soon as possible."

"I see," Witherspoon replied. "You certainly did a good job of that."

"I had a bit of luck," Venable shrugged. "The first train of the morning had just pulled into the platform when I got to the station, so I got into London straight away."

"Things did rather happen quickly," Witherspoon murmured. Something took root in the back of his mind. He frowned, trying to grasp the thought before it disappeared, but, as is often the case, the harder he tried to hang on to the idea, the faster it seemed to fall out of his head.

"Thank goodness for modern conveniences," Venable replied eagerly. "I don't know what we did before the telegraph and the messenger services."

"Did you notice anything else?" Barnes asked.

"Not really." Venable scratched his chin. "It was a very strange night, Constable. I must say, seeing that dead body was a bit of a shock. I know I oughtn't to admit it, but I remember feeling as though I were moving very slowly, it's difficult to describe, but the whole experience has taken on a rather peculiar aspect in my recollection."

"Violent death can have that effect on all of us," Witherspoon said sympathetically. "You mustn't let it bother you, but rest assured none of us ever get immune to the sights associated with a murder."

Venable looked out the window, his eyes unfocused. "You're very understanding, Inspector. It's not something I've been able to speak about with anyone. Certainly not the H.S., but I recall such odd details about that night. I shan't ever forget the way our breath frosted on the air, the sight of the trees looking skeletal against the sky, the icicles hanging like jagged teeth off the eaves of the buildings. Icicles are quite sinister really, there was even a great gaping hole in the row hanging off of the shed, it looked like some giant hand had reached down and yanked it off just to make the scene even more frightening." He paused, then shook himself gently. "You must forgive me, gentlemen, I'm normally a very cheerful sort of person, but I don't think I'll ever forget the sight of that poor man lying there in the snow."

"There's nothing to forgive, Mr. Venable," Witherspoon said kindly. He stood up, and the constable followed suit. "Thank you for all your help in this matter. If you can think of anything else, then please contact us immediately."

"Rest assured I will, Inspector," Venable smiled faintly and escorted them to the door. "I'll have a word with the H.S. as soon as he returns. Perhaps he'll be able to add something to what I've told you."

"Now, if Hatchet comes bargin' in, you're not to let on that I sent you a note askin' you to come around," Luty instructed her guest. "You're to say you jest happened to drop by because you heard I was feelin' poorly."

"Well, of course that's why I dropped by," Hilda Ryker grinned impishly. She was a tall woman with salt-and-pepper colored hair and a long nose. "And had I known you were ill, I would have come by. But I've been out of town for two weeks, and I only just returned yesterday. Neville and I decided we wanted to be in London for Christmas. It's so much jollier here than in the country. I do hate to miss the lovely way the shops are done up and the carol singing. Besides, I've still a few gifts I need to get for Neville's brother and his wife. They're dreadfully particular about what they like and what they don't like, I shall be hours in the shops tomorrow trying to find just the right item for them. And do you think that wretched husband of mine will have any sympathy for my plight? He will not—"

"Hilda," Luty hated to interrupt so rudely, but she knew if she didn't, her guest would go on forever. "I'm sure that you'll do just fine in getting the gifts, you've got such good taste."

Hilda studied Luty speculatively, trying to decide whether to be insulted or complimented. "Why, thank you. One does try."

"By the way, I heard that Sir George Braxton had got himself murdered. Isn't he the guest of honor at your New Year's Ball?" Luty knew he wasn't, but she wanted to get the conversation worked around to where it would do her some good.

"George Braxton at my home? Certainly not." Hilda sniffed disapprovingly. "He might be a baronet, but he certainly is no friend of ours. Why on earth would you think he was our guest of honor? I wouldn't ride in the same train carriage with the man, let alone invite him to my home."

"Gosh, what'd he do to get you so het up?" Luty asked eagerly. She glanced at the door, praying that Hatchet would stay gone and out of her way for a few more minutes. She knew he'd gone to Upper Edmonton Gardens for the afternoon meeting, and she hoped that everyone had a lot to report.

"One mustn't speak ill of the dead," Hilda replied. "But in his case, I don't think the Almighty would object. Besides, it's simply the truth. Sir George Braxton was a bounder and a cad." She leaned toward Luty. "The entire family is peculiar. They do the oddest things you can imagine. The eldest daughter is such a shrew, the middle girl hires herself out as a paid companion, and the youngest daughter hangs about the financial district."

"What's so bad about that?" Luty demanded. "I've gone to the City more than once to take care of my business."

"Yes, but you're an American. You can get away with such behavior, and everyone will think it eccentric or charming, but when the daughter of a baronet hangs about the stock exchange watching the share prices, it's considered most unseemly." She waved her hand impatiently, "But that's not why people dislike them so much, they're simply obnoxious bores. Especially Sir George. Do you know he not only seduced his housekeeper, but as the price for letting her keep her position when he got her with child, he made her send the child away the moment it was born. Can you imagine such a thing?" Her eyes narrowed angrily. "It's one thing to dismiss a servant that gets herself in that condition, but it's quite another to keep the woman on, why it's a bad example for the rest of the staff."

Luty stared at her incredulously. "Are you tellin' me you think he was a cad for lettin' the woman keep her job?"

Hilda looked annoyed. "Of course not, he was a cad for seducing the poor woman in the first place. The honorable thing to have done in the circumstances would have been to send her off with a settlement so she could have a least kept her child. Gracious, Luty, what sort of heartless monster do you think I am?"

"You're not a monster." Luty grinned. "But you do have a peculiar way of describin' things. How long ago was all this?"

"Oh, it was back when I was much younger, a good thirty years ago."

"What happened to the child?"

"I've no idea." She shrugged. "It was sent off as soon as it was born."

"Sent off where?" Luty asked.

Hilda pursed her lips in thought. "I don't know, I expect the boy was sent to a foundling home or to one of the woman's relatives. But I honestly don't remember."

CHAPTER 9

Inspector Witherspoon climbed the stairs to Upper Edmonton Gardens and stepped inside. He was so glad to finally be home. "Good evening, Mrs. Jeffries. I believe it's going to snow again."

"I do hope not, sir. We've far too much to do before Christmas, and bad weather makes everything twice as difficult. Gracious, you look exhausted." Mrs. Jeffries helped him off with his bowler and heavy black overcoat.

"I am tired," he admitted. "It's been a very busy day and I'm not sure we're any closer to discovering who murdered Sir George Braxton," he sighed. "This might be the one that defeats me, Mrs. Jeffries."

"Nonsense, sir," she said briskly. "You'll do just fine, you always do. Just you wait, sir, at the very last minute, all the clues with come together in your mind, and you'll know the identity of the killer."

"I do hope you're right. We had another meeting with the chief inspector this afternoon. He wasn't pleased with the progress we've made on the case."

"Not to worry, sir, you'll solve it soon. I've every faith in your abilities, and I'm quite sure the chief inspector does as well. Would you like a sherry, sir?" she asked.

He smiled wearily and started for the dining room. "Not tonight. I think I'll have my dinner and retire."

"That's a pity, sir," she hurried after him. "Lady Cannonberry came home today and stopped in to say hello. She was hoping you'd feel up to going over to see her this evening. But if you're too tired, I'll send Wiggins to convey your regrets."

He skidded to a halt and whirled to face her. "Lady Cannonberry is home, and she wants to see me? Tonight?"

"Indeed she does, sir," Mrs. Jeffries replied. "She was hoping you'd come by before dinner."

He grabbed his bowler and his coat. "Would you ask Mrs. Goodge to hold dinner for a little while? I'll just pop along and say a quick hello."

Mrs. Jeffries regretted that she'd have to wait to get today's information out of him, but it was worth it. A sad inspector wasn't of any use to anyone, least of all himself. "Of course, sir. Dinner will be served when you return. You'd better take your umbrella, sir. It's starting to rain."

But as he'd already dashed out the front door and down the steps, he didn't hear her warning. Mrs. Jeffries laughed softly and went down to the kitchen. "He's gone to Lady Cannonberry's," she told the others, "so we're going to have to wait until later to find out what he learned today."

"Let's hope he's not too tired to talk about it later," the cook muttered as she covered a plate of buns with a towel.

"We don't want him retiring to his bed without telling us what's what."

"Not to worry," Betsy said as she dried the last of their supper plates, "we can always find out what we need tomorrow morning."

Mrs. Goodge snorted, "That's easy for you to say, you've been able to find out what you needed to know. I've not had such an easy time of it." She broke off and frowned. "Where's Wiggins? I wanted him to lift that sausage maker off the top shelf in the dry larder."

"I'll get it for you," Smythe offered. "The lad's taken Fred for a walk. He said for us not to worry if he was gone for a while. 'E said poor Fred needed a bit of a romp. I think 'e was goin' to take the animal to Holland Park."

Wiggins did take Fred to Holland Park, but not because he needed a romp. "Come on, boy, hurry up. It should be around 'ere somewhere. Luty said 'e lived off the 'ere somewhere. Blast, I 'ope 'e's in tonight. It's cold, and I don't fancy doin' this again." He put his mittened hand into his jacket pocket and made sure the note Luty had entrusted to him was still there. He came to the corner and sighed in relief. "There it is, Bastion Street, come on, boy, let's scarper." Picking up his pace, he ran around the corner. Fred, thinking this was a wonderful game, trotted along happily at his feet. They made their way up the road, Wiggins squinting in the darkening night at the house numbers. "Cor blimey, looks like we're in luck, they've got lights on. Now you be a good fellow and stay put." He wound the dog's lead around a lamppost. "I'll be back in two shakes of a lamb's tail."

He dashed up the short walkway to a narrow, three-story redbrick home, lifted the brass knocker, and let it bang against the wood. A moment later, a young red-haired maid answered the door. She looked at Wiggins suspiciously. "Yes, what do you want?"

"I'd like to see Mr. Josiah Williams. I've a note for him from Mrs. Luty Belle Crookshank."

"Who's there, Matilda?" A deep male voice came from inside the house.

"It's a lad, sir," Matilda called back, "and he's brought his dog. He claims to have a note from Mrs. Crookshank."

"I do 'ave a note," Wiggins protested. "It's right 'ere, and it's right important, and I've left my dog by the lamppost, so I don't see 'ow it's any 'arm to you."

He was rather offended by the young maid's manner. He couldn't see her all that closely in the gloom, but he had the feeling she was younger than he was, so he didn't think she ought to be calling him a "lad."

"Invite him in, Matilda," the voice came again.

Grudgingly, she opened the door and jerked her head at him. "Come along, then. It's cold with the door open."

Wiggins hesitated. "I've only just looped the dog's lead around the post—"

"Then bring the dog inside." Josiah Williams appeared behind the maid. He was a tall man with dark brown hair and hazel eyes. He grinned at Wiggins. "He doesn't bite, does he?"

"No sir, 'e's a right good dog. But there's no need to invite me inside, I can just give ya the note." He started to reach into his pocket.

"Please, if Mrs. Crookshank has sent you, I'd like to have a word with you. Bring your dog and come inside where it's warm."

"Yes, sir." Wiggins hoped this wouldn't make him too late getting home. The women of the household always got worried when he got in too late. He retrieved Fred and hurried back to the house.

As he stepped inside he saw that Matilda was quite a pretty girl. He thought she'd be even prettier if she smiled a bit. "Go on in there." She pointed to a door just inside the hall. "He's waiting for you."

"Thank you, miss," Wiggins bobbed his head politely. She had lovely blue eyes.

She snorted faintly, reached down and petted Fred, and then flounced off toward the back of the house.

"Have a seat, please," Williams invited.

"That's kind of you, sir," he replied. Williams obviously didn't recall that they'd met, but there was no reason he should, as it had only been for a few moments on one of their other cases. He noticed Fred's tail was wagging, and that was a good sign. The dog was an excellent judge of character. "But I can't stay long, sir. We've got to get back." He reached into his jacket, pulled out the envelope, and handed it to the solicitor.

"Have we met before?" Williams looked at him closely. "Do you work for Mrs. Crookshank?" He pulled the letter out and unfolded it.

"I've seen ya at Mrs. Crookshank's, but I work for Inspector Witherspoon," Wiggins blurted before he could stop himself. Perhaps Luty hadn't wanted her lawyer to know how closely she was involved in the inspector's cases. Drat, he thought, he wasn't cut out for all this skulking about and keeping secrets. He'd felt bad enough this evening telling them he was taking Fred for a long walk. Deliberately misleading Mrs. Goodge hadn't felt right. On the other hand, he'd promised Luty to take her note to her solicitor.

Williams looked up from reading the note and stared at Wiggins. He said nothing.

"I'm just a footman," Wiggins stammered. This wasn't going well at all.

"Oh, I suspect you're more than just a footman. This is a rather unusual note, but then again, it's from one of my more unusual clients." He gestured toward a chair by the fire. "If you'll take a seat, I'll send her a reply."

Wiggins didn't know what to do now. He'd not counted on having to go back to Luty's with an answer. Drat. At this rate, it'd be midnight before he and Fred got home. He'd best have a good reason for being out so late, or the ladies of the household would have his guts for garters. None of them took kindly to spending their evenings worrying about him. "Do you need to do that?" he blurted. "I mean, I thought Luty, er . . . Mrs. Crookshank expected you to go along and see her."

Williams smiled kindly. "Unfortunately, I've another engagement this evening. An engagement that I should like to keep, as it will actually help me find the information Mrs. Crookshank seeks."

"Oh, right then, I'd best wait." He gave Fred's lead a tug and settled in the chair. The only sound in the room was the crackle of the flames and the scratch of the solicitor's pen.

Finally, after what seemed like ages, Williams put the pen back in the stand, folded the paper, put it in an envelope, and stood up. Wiggins leapt up as well. Fred, who'd settled rather comfortably in front of the fire, got to his feet a tad more reluctantly.

"I would be most grateful if you could get this to Mrs. Crookshank this evening," Williams instructed. "It's rather important."

"I'll get it to her as soon as I can," he said evasively. He'd do his best to give it to her without being spotted tonight, but that might be impossible. If he was too late getting home, even Smythe would be worried. Maybe he could pretend he'd gotten lost.

Williams reached into his pocket, and Wiggins heard the jingle of coin. He raised his hand. "There's no need for coin," he said quickly. "What I do for Mrs. Crookshank, I do because I want to, not for any other reason. I'll take this note along to her."

"I'm sorry, I didn't wish to cause you offense," he apologized.

"None taken," Wiggins said easily. "Come along, Fred, we'd best be on our way."

"How long is he going to be over there?" Mrs. Goodge glared at the back door. "He's going to be so tired by the time he gets home, he'll retire straight away, and you'll not get anything about the case out of him."

Mrs. Jeffries glanced at the clock and saw that it was almost nine o'clock. "It is getting quite late. But I imagine he'll be here anytime now. Let's be patient."

"We've not got much choice," the cook grumbled. "And where's that Wiggins got to? He's been gone for ages. It's a cold night, and if he doesn't get inside soon, he'll be frozen to his bones."

Smythe came into the kitchen carrying a large burlap bundle on his back. Branches of holly thrust out of the open top. "Where do you want this?" he asked Mrs. Jeffries.

"Put it on the table," she instructed. "We might as well do something useful and get the boughs cleaned and ready to be put out."

"Are we going to put the candles out as well?" Betsy asked eagerly. "It looks so lovely when it's all done up properly."

"Did we get enough?" Mrs. Goodge asked anxiously. "We must have enough to do both the dining room and the drawing room, especially as Lady Cannonberry is coming for Christmas dinner."

"And we need some for down here as well," Betsy added. "We need our bits as well." She loved decorating for Christmas. Once she and Smythe were married, she was going to be sure to do something special every year.

"We've plenty," Mrs. Jeffries assured the cook. She looked at Betsy. "The candles are in the dry larder, and we need to clean the lamps, so you might as well bring them out as well." She broke off as she heard knocking on the back door.

"I'll go see who it is," Smythe offered. "But it's probably the inspector or Wiggins."

"They'd have walked straight in," Mrs. Goodge said darkly.

A moment later, they heard the door creak open and then a low murmur of voices. Smythe came back to the kitchen alone. "That was Lady Cannonberry's butler. He said the inspector was having supper with her and for us to put his dinner away."

Mrs. Jeffries was torn between annoyance and delight. She knew how lonely the inspector had been lately, but with him eating his meal with Ruth, it meant they couldn't get any information until tomorrow morning. "We can save his supper for Wiggins."

"We've already got the lad's supper saved," Mrs. Goodge reminded her.

"If he doesn't get home soon, he'll be hungry enough to eat them both," she replied. "I do wish he'd come along, I'm getting a bit worried about him."

"He'll be fine," Smythe went back to the table and continued pulling holly out of the burlap bundle. "Let the lad have a bit of privacy. 'E might be running a special errand."

"What kind of special errand?" Betsy demanded. She looked at her beloved. "What do you know that you're not telling us?"

"I don't know anythin'," he protested. "I'm just thinkin' that maybe Wiggins is doing something he doesn't want to share with the rest of us. It's Christmas. Maybe the lad's out gettin' presents for us."

"The shops are all closed," Betsy persisted.

"Not all of them," Smythe shot back. "There's a few that are open late this week. Sometimes a man needs to be on his own for a while, buyin' presents for people isn't easy you know." He was bluffing about the shops: as far as he knew, every single one of them was shut tighter than a bank vault at this time of night. But Wiggins was a grown man, and sometimes these ladies could get just a bit smothering. Mind you, if Wiggins didn't show up soon, Smythe would have a sharp word or two for the lad.

Betsy didn't look convinced, but she stopped arguing and went to the dry larder to get the lamps and the candles. She was on her way back when the back door opened, and Fred, followed by a red-cheeked Wiggins came charging inside.

"I'm ever so sorry to be late," he gasped. "But it's all Fred's fault. He got away from me in the park, and it took ages to find him."

Fred wagged his tail and bounced up and down, hoping that the maid would give him a bit of attention. Betsy was one of his special friends.

"You bad boy," Betsy scolded the dog. "You mustn't go running off that way. We've been ever so worried about you and Wiggins."

Fred's tail went still, and then he tucked it under his

backside and hung his head. Wiggins, watching his beloved friend go from happy to miserable, and knowing it was his fault, felt lower than a snake. He silently vowed he'd never do this sort of thing again. Who would have thought keeping a promise to Luty would be so difficult? But at least he'd had a bit of luck when he went back with the solicitor's note. She'd seen him coming across the garden and nipped down to the back door to meet him.

Betsy looked at Wiggins. "You'd best get in and eat your supper. Mind you, you'll have to eat on a tray, we've got the table covered in holly."

"I'd eat off the floor if I had to, I'm that hungry," he replied, as he raced toward the kitchen. "My belly's touching my backbone."

"Where on earth have you been?" Mrs. Goodge asked as he hurtled into the kitchen.

"Sounds like he'd been at Luty's," Smythe said. "That's one of her sayins'."

"Fred ran off from him," Betsy explained as she came into the kitchen behind him.

"It took ages to find 'im," Wiggins said quickly.

"Humph, why didn't you have him on the lead?" Mrs. Goodge picked up a thick pot holder.

He was ready for that question. "It got all tangled up in a bush," he explained. "The only way to get the bloomin' thing straightened out was to take it off 'im. But the minute Fred was free, 'e took off running."

"It's not like Fred to run off," Smythe commented.

"I know," Wiggins agreed quickly. "And generally 'e doesn't. But he spotted a cat, and it took off runnin'. You know Fred, he can't resist that." He went to the sink and washed his hands.

"Silly dog," Mrs. Goodge muttered as she got his supper from the warming oven.

Wiggins slipped into a spot at the far end of the table as the cook put down a tray with his dinner on it in front of him. Despite his conscience bothering him something fierce, his mouth watered. "Thanks, Mrs. Goodge."

"Mind you eat all of it," she ordered. "A growing lad needs his food."

Fred whined softly and looked up at him. Wiggins slipped him a huge bite of roast beef. He felt it was the least he could do considering that poor Fred had taken all the blame.

"Supper was utterly delightful," the inspector said. He took a bite of his eggs. "We had such a lovely chat. She's so very intelligent, mind you, I do think some of her ideas are quite modern, more so, of course, than mine. But that doesn't mean I think she's wrong in her thinking."

"Of course not, sir," Mrs. Jeffries replied. "You're each entitled to your own opinions."

"I do hope my coming in so late didn't inconvenience you. I don't mean for you to wait up for me. I'm quite capable of locking the house and putting everything to rights before I go up."

Mrs. Jeffries smiled over the top of her tea cup. "Thank you, sir. I'll remember that for the future. Do you have a busy day planned?" She wanted to find out what he learned yesterday, and to do that, she had to get him talking about the case and not Ruth Cannonberry.

Witherspoon's shoulders drooped just a bit. "I'm sure it'll be busy, but as to whether or not it'll be useful, that's another matter entirely. I don't know what we're going to do.

We're running out of time. Christmas is in just a few days, and frankly, I've no idea who killed Sir George Braxton."

"I take it you didn't learn much yesterday?" She took another sip of tea.

"That all depends," he said, his expression uncertain. "We heard quite a bit of new information about the principals in the Braxton household, but I'm not sure what it all means, or if it has anything to do with Sir George's murder."

"You mustn't get discouraged, sir. This is always what happens with your cases."

"It is?"

"Yes, it is. You're always in a bit of a muddle until right before the very end, and then it all comes together in your mind and you catch the killer."

"Really?" He stared at her with hopeful expression.

She could tell he desperately wanted to believe her, and in one sense, her words were true. They were generally in a muddle until the very end.

"Why don't you tell me what you learned yesterday, sir," she coaxed. "You've always said that discussing your cases helps put all the bits and pieces together."

He brightened considerably. "That's a jolly good idea. Well, now, let's see, where did I go first yesterday? Oh, yes, now I remember."

Mrs. Jeffries listened carefully, occasionally making a short comment or asking a question. By the time Betsy had come up for the breakfast dishes, he'd finished.

"Where are you going this morning, sir, if you don't mind my asking?" Betsy picked up his empty plate and put it on the tray. She'd been hovering in the doorway and had caught most of his narrative. "We're all ever so curious about your cases."

"I don't mind you asking in the least," he said eagerly.

"This morning I'm going along to have a chat with the victim's banker, and then we're going into the city to speak to his brokers. I'm hoping they can shed some light on why they'd been scheduled to come and see him the day he died."

"What about his solicitor?" Mrs. Jeffries asked. She picked up the empty toast rack and put it on the tray next to the dirty plates.

"Oh, yes, we'll be seeing him as well." Witherspoon finished his tea just as a knock sounded on the front door. "That'll be Constable Barnes," he said as he got to his feet. "I shall see you all this evening. There's no need to see me out, Mrs. Jeffries, I can see you're busy."

Smythe banged on the back door of the Dirty Duck. The pub couldn't open for a couple of hours yet, but he'd had a message from Blimpey to come straightaway.

The door creaked open and Agnes, the barmaid, waved him inside. "Blimpey's at his usual spot," she said. "Will you be wantin' something to drink?"

"No, thank ya, Agnes, it's a bit too early in the day for me." He went down a dim hallway and around the bar into the pub proper. "Mornin', Blimpey, I got 'ere as soon as I could."

"That's right thoughtful of ya, mate. I've a full day ahead of me. Have a seat, and let's get crackin'."

"What 'ave ya got for me?" Smythe slid onto the stool across from Blimpey.

"I wanted to get ya here right quick because one of yer suspects might be thinkin' of leaving our fair shores," Blimpey replied. "Charlotte Braxton bought a third class ticket on the *Valiant Sky* on December fifteenth. She's pullin' out of the Liverpool docks tomorrow morning with the tide, and she's bound for New Zealand. You might want to 'ave a word with your inspector."

"You think she's running?" Smythe had a great deal of respect for Blimpey's knowledge of the criminal mind.

"No, she bought the ticket three days before the old blighter was murdered. Unless she's the killer, I think she bought it to escape them that's pressing her about her gambling debts. They're not a nice bunch of people, even her bein' an aristocrat wouldn't 'elp her much if they'd decided to get real nasty."

"You think they might have roughed 'er up a bit?" Smythe asked, his expression incredulous.

Blimpey hesitated. "She's in pretty deep to Horace Quigley's boys, but I don't think they'd have 'armed her person. More like they'd 'ave made sure her father found out about how much she owed 'em, and they'd not be shy about makin' it public."

"And they've got lots of ways they could 'ave done it," Smythe said. "Even someone as 'ard as Sir George wouldn't 'ave liked everyone and 'is brother knowin' 'is daughter wouldn't pay 'er debts."

"True," Blimpey replied. "I've not much more for ya except for a few bits and pieces I expect you've already heard. My sources have been seriously remiss in getting back to me with anything useful. I think they're all slacking off a bit because of Christmas."

Luty was at the back door when Wiggins arrived the next day. "Be real quiet, I got rid of Hatchet, but Julie's upstairs mending one of my gowns, and I don't want her sneakin' in on us." She motioned for him to follow her, and they crept down the hall, past the abnormally quiet kitchen and into the butler's pantry. Luty closed the door and motioned for him to take a seat at the empty table.

He flopped down, wincing as the old cane-backed chair creaked loud enough to wake the dead. "Sorry."

"Don't fret, boy." Luty sat down opposite him. "Josiah Williams stopped by here early this morning, and Hatchet saw him. Josiah's a smart one, though. He said he'd just stopped by to give me some documents I'd asked for a while back. He had the papers with him, too."

"Did Hatchet believe him?" Wiggins didn't want Hatchet getting suspicious about her activities.

"My lawyers are always stoppin' by with something or other for me to read or sign." She grinned. "So he probably didn't think anything of it. Now, let me tell you what I found out."

"Uh, Luty, I've got a question. 'Ow am I supposed to get this information you give me to the others?"

Luty grinned again. "Oh, I've got that all figured out, you just say you dropped by to say hello and see how I was feelin',' and that I happened to mention my lawyer had been here and told me all sorts of good stuff about that murder in Richmond."

He was afraid that was what she was going to suggest. "But Luty, if I do that, they'll be on to us. Mark my words, they'll know I told you about the inspector gettin' the case."

"You really think so?" Luty asked curiously. "Hmm, you're probably right. Well, don't fret, I'm sure you'll come up with some story or other about how you found out."

"Me? But I'm not much good at that sort of thing," he protested.

"Sure ya are. You do it all the time," she shot back. "Now

quit complainin' and listen. Julie is going come lookin' for me any minute."

"All right," he muttered.

"Josiah told me that, accordin' to the terms of Sir George's will, the daughters share the estate equally."

"That's it?"

"He said it was real straightforward. God knows how the man found out in such a small amount of time, but he did. Except for a few bequests to his housekeeper, it all goes to his three daughters."

"What about Clarence Clark? He's family as well, doesn't 'e get anything?"

Luty shook her head. "No, but that's probably because Sir George didn't think he needed anything from him. Clark got his bit when Sir George's father died."

"What do ya mean?"

"Clark was given a small allowance and granted the use of his rooms in the family home for his lifetime."

Wiggins brightened. "That means the daughters can't toss 'im out. That's good."

"Mrs. Crookshank, where are you?" Julie's voice could be heard coming from the kitchen.

"Nells bells, she's come lookin' for me already." Luty peeked out into the hall and then frantically motioned at Wiggins.

"Mrs. Crookshank!" Julie called again.

"Hurry." Luty shoved him out into the hall. "Once she's finished looking in the front storage rooms, she'll head this way. Git goin'."

Hopkins and Flannerty were in the ground-floor offices of a nicely appointed building on Fenchurch Street. The inspector and Barnes were standing in a small foyer in the outer office, waiting to speak to one of the partners.

"This is a busy place," Barnes muttered. Clerks carrying bits of paper and notebooks dashed in and out of the double doors, two men in old-fashioned frock coats were conversing in low tones near the windows, and at each of the many desks, young men were frantically scribbling.

From one of the offices down the hall a door opened, a clerk hurried out and came toward them. "Mr. Flannerty can see you now," he said.

As they stepped into the office, a tall, black-haired man with blue eyes rose to his feet. "I'm Ian Flannerty."

"Good day, sir. I'm Inspector Witherspoon, and this is Constable Barnes. We'll try not to take up too much of your time, Mr. Flannerty, but we'd like to ask you a few questions.

He nodded in acknowledgement of the introductions and pointed to two chairs front of his desk. "I've been expecting you. Please have a seat."

They sat, and Witherspoon waited until Barnes pulled out his notebook and his pencil. Then he said, "I'm sure you know why we've come."

"You're here about Sir George Braxton," Flannerty replied. "I know he was murdered, Inspector. What do you want to ask me, sir?"

"You had an appointment to see Sir George on the eighteenth, is that correct?"

"We were supposed to be at his home at ten o'clock that morning," he said softly. "I was just getting ready to leave for the station when I got the message that he'd died."

"Did a messenger bring you the news?" Barnes asked.

"No, we received a telegram from Nina Braxton. Naturally, I immediately sent her a reply. We sent our condolences to her and the rest of the family."

Witherspoon thought for a moment, and then he asked, "Did the telegram say that he'd been murdered, or simply that he'd died?"

"It said he'd been murdered." Flannerty looked amused by the question. "Miss Braxton is well known for her bluntness, Inspector. She wasn't one to mince words about any subject. However, we were still very shocked, of course."

"Yes, I suppose you must have been," Witherspoon said. "Why were you going to see him?"

Flannerty sighed. "I wanted to speak to him about some of Miss Nina's investment choices. She's been handling all their financial matters for several years now."

"We knew that, Mr. Flannerty," the inspector said quickly.

"Did you object to taking financial orders from a woman?" Barnes asked bluntly. He watched Flannerty as he spoke, wanting to see his face as he answered the question. There were a number of men who would have bitterly resented a woman like Nina Braxton. He and the inspector had discussed the problem in the cab on the ride here, and they'd decided to get it out of the way immediately.

"Not at all, Constable," Flannerty laughed. "Believe it or not, the Braxtons aren't our only clients where the woman handles the family money. I've a great deal of respect for the female mind."

"But you were going to see Sir George about Miss Nina's investments. So even if you respected her mind, you thought something was wrong, correct?" Barnes asked.

"I did." Flannerty put his elbows on the desk and entwined his fingers together. "Nina Braxton has done an excellent job of handling all the Braxton investments since Sir

George handed her the reins several years ago. But this past year, she's made some choices that I thought were wildly speculative."

"Wildly speculative," Witherspoon repeated. "I don't quite understand." He knew very little about finances. His investments were handled by a nice firm just up the road from here that sent him a statement every quarter and rarely asked him to make any decisions whatsoever.

"Nina Braxton was buying into enterprises that could make a great deal of money if they were successful," he explained, "but they were highly risky and, therefore, quite likely to lose money if they failed."

"I see. So you were going to see Sir George and tell him of your concerns?"

"That's right," Flannerty said. He glanced out the window and then looked back at the two policemen. "I didn't relish the idea of running to Sir George telling tales, but I did think I had a responsibility to him the truth. Miss Nina was simply risking far too much of their available capital in enterprises that could be ruinous."

"Ruinous?" Witherspoon asked. "Are you saying she could have sent the family into bankruptcy?"

He shook his head. "Not bankruptcy, Inspector, but she was close to losing almost all the amounts she was authorized to use."

"So Sir George limited her authority," Barnes commented. "We didn't know that."

Witherspoon looked puzzled. "You mean she had a set amount of money she was allowed to invest? But I had the impression she handled all the family finances."

"To all intents and purposes she does," Flannerty replied. "Most of the family money is tied up in non-cash assets that could only be spent if they were sold. Sir George never authorized Miss Nina to have access to any of those assets. But he did give her complete authority over the investment account." He shrugged. "It's not surprising, since financial matters bored him to tears. He simply didn't have a head for it at all."

"And your firm didn't advise him?" Witherspoon queried.

"We charge a fee for that," Flannerty admitted, "and frankly, there were times in the past where our advice wasn't very good."

"He lost money?" Barnes guessed.

"I'm afraid so." Flannerty leaned back in his chair. "Sometimes, even the soundest-looking investments go bad. Sir George wasn't one to overlook the fact that our firm had made recommendations and then charged him for the privilege of losing several thousand pounds."

"Did Sir George have any idea why you were coming to see him?" Witherspoon asked.

"Actually, he did. I'd run into him in front of the Corn Exchange last week, and we spoke for a moment. I mentioned that I'd written to him requesting an appointment. He said he'd received my letter and replied with one of his own, specifying Monday at ten o'clock as a convenient appointment time."

"Is that all he said?" Barnes asked.

"No. I was going to speak to the poor man about business, but I also knew that I was going to be talking about his child, his daughter. Sir George wasn't a very nice person, he certainly wasn't sentimental by any means, yet I know he was like any of us, he loved his children." Flannerty smiled sadly. "I wanted to give him a bit of hint so he wouldn't be totally surprised when I told him of my concerns. I don't think some surprises are good for men his age. So I told him

I needed to discuss the matter of the investment account, but he held up his hand and told me not to worry, that he knew why I was coming and that we'd discuss the matter then."

"How could he have known why you were coming to see him?" Witherspoon asked. "Had you mentioned it in your note?"

"No." He shook his head. "But he knew. He told me that Nina had already spoken to him, and that he knew the investment account was almost empty."

CHAPTER 10

"Are you sure about that?" Mrs. Goodge stared hard at the delivery boy. Generally, she considered him as useless as the lad who picked up the laundry, but he'd just given her a genuinely useful tidbit, and she wanted to make sure it was true.

"I got it from my Uncle Ennis, and he were right there when it happened," Neville Shuster declared. He was a red-haired lad of thirteen with long legs and dozens of freckles. He shoved another bite of custard tart into his mouth and reached for his tea. "Uncle Ennis is the ticket taker at Richmond. He saw the whole thing."

"How did he know it was Sir George Braxton?" Mrs. Goodge asked.

"'Cause he knows who Sir George is, or was," Neville said. "Everyone knew the old blighter, he was a right nasty fellow. Uncle Ennis says he was always complainin' about something or other."

"That sounds like Sir George," she muttered, more to herself than the lad.

" 'Course it were him," the lad stated. "I told ya, my uncle knows him."

"Your uncle saw the whole incident?" she pressed. "He didn't just hear about it from someone else?" Not that that would have made any difference to her, she'd have passed it onto the others whether it was hearsay gossip or not.

"He saw it with his own two eyes," Neville retorted. "This bloke bumped into him and before you could say Milly's-got-a-billy-goat, the old blighter had grabbed the feller and shoved him up against a post. Then he told the feller, he'd better give him his purse back if he didn't want to go to prison."

"What happened then?"

"Uncle Ennis said the fellow tried to run, but the old man just stuck his leg out and tripped him good. Sir George looked at the man and said something like, give it to me before I call the law. The bloke reached into his jacket and handed over the purse, nice as you please. Then he got up, he tried to run off, but Braxton caught him by the arm and said fer him to stand still and listen if he knew what was good for him."

"What did he say to him?" Mrs. Goodge demanded.

Neville shrugged. "Dunno. Uncle Ennis said he was talkin' too soft fer him to hear. When he'd finished speaking, they walked off together like nothin' had happened, and the man took to workin' at the Braxton house. I think he was the gardener."

"How do you know it was the same man?" Mrs. Goodge shoved the plate of tarts closer to the lad.

"Uncle Ennis saw him down at the pub a few days later, he was cadging a pint of beer off one of the porters. He was complainin' to everyone that they worked him like a dog at the Braxton house."

There was one thing that bothered Mrs. Goodge about the tale. Braxton had been an old man. Surely someone on the platform would have tried to intervene when the altercation started. "Didn't someone try to help Sir George when the scuffle started?"

"Why should they?" Neville asked. "No one liked Sir George, and he was one old man that could take care of himself. Besides, Uncle Ennis said it were over real quick."

"What an odd man he must have been," Mrs. Goodge mused. "Taking in someone right off the street like that, it simply doesn't make any sense at all."

"The whole family is crazy," Neville replied. "That cousin of Sir George's cuffed a porter once just because the fellow dropped a tray of flowers. Uncle Ennis saw that one, too."

"Shall we try and see his banker?" Barnes asked Witherspoon as they came out of the law offices of Trent, Steel, and Burnum on Bleeker Street. The two policemen had been to see Oliver Trent and Theodore Burnum, solicitors to the late Sir George Baxter.

"We might as well," Witherspoon said glumly. "Maybe they'll be able to give us something more useful than we've heard so far today."

Barnes stepped to the curb and waved at a passing hansom. The cab pulled over, and the two men got in and settled back in the seat. "Uxbridge Station," the constable yelled at the driver. He looked at the inspector, "After we see the bank manager, should we go back to the Braxton house?"

"As we'll already be in Richmond, we might as well." Witherspoon grabbed the handhold as the cab bounced over a hole in the road. "I was so disappointed by the solicitors. There certainly wasn't any motive there that I could see."

"You were hoping that Sir George had been planning to change his will." Barnes nodded in agreement. "So was I, sir. That's often a good motive for murder. Someone gets wind they're being cut out of the estate, and so they decide to take matters into their own hands. They commit murder before the will can be changed."

"Yes," the inspector sighed. "But according to Mr. Trent, Sir George had no plans to make any changes to his will, and the division of his estate was known to all the heirs and had been for years."

Witherspoon closed his eyes briefly. He'd no idea what to do next. Perhaps they'd get very lucky and Sir George's banker would have information that was useful to the case.

"At least the solicitors confirmed Miss Nina's statement," Barnes pointed out. "They did come to discuss the funeral arrangements. Honestly, sir, I didn't think the Church of England allowed one to have fifteen hymns and seven readings done at one service, even if you're a baronet."

"That does sound a bit extravagant, doesn't it?" he agreed.

"Not as extravagant as having a ten-foot-tall marble headstone."

"And I expect having the Four Horsemen of the Apocalypse carved on the top of the thing will set a few tongues wagging as well," Witherspoon replied.

"He's being buried at the local church?" Barnes asked.

Witherspoon nodded. "Oh, yes, the family has a very prominent spot in the front of the churchyard. The funeral is tomorrow at ten. It's at St. Andrews, which is right off Richmond Green."

"That's the day before Christmas Eve." Barnes clucked

his tongue. "They'll be lucky if they can dig the hole to bury the man, the ground is still pretty hard."

"I expect they'll manage somehow," Witherspoon replied. "We'll have to be there, of course. Before I forget, make sure we've a few lads available in case we need them."

"You're expecting something to happen at the funeral tomorrow?" Barnes asked eagerly. "You're close to an arrest?"

"I wish that were the case," Witherspoon admitted. "Actually, I was thinking we'd need them to keep the traffic sorted out properly."

Everyone was on time for their meeting that afternoon.

"Shouldn't we wait for Lady Cannonberry?" Wiggins asked as they settled themselves around the table.

"She sent her butler over with her regrets," Mrs. Goodge said. "A friend of hers has come down with influenza, and Ruth has gone to sit with her."

"I hope the lady gets well soon," the footman said sympathetically. "Feelin' poorly at Christmas doesn't seem right."

"If no one 'as any objections, I'll go first," Smythe offered.

Betsy gave her beloved an irritated glance but didn't protest. She had talked to every shopkeeper in Richmond today and hadn't heard anything except old bits that they already knew. "Go ahead. I've nothing to report."

"Go on, Smythe," the cook urged. "We've got to start somewhere."

As no one else said anything, he plunged straight ahead. "One of my sources told me that on December fifteenth, three days before the murder, Charlotte Braxton bought a third-class ticket to New Zealand."

"That's a long ways away," Wiggins said.

"Did your source know why?" Mrs. Jeffries asked.

"Not for certain," he replied. "But he thinks it was because of her gambling. My source says the ones that run those games can get right nasty when you don't pay up."

"But Charlotte Braxton is the daughter of a baronet," Mrs. Goodge protested. "Surely even the worst ruffian wouldn't have dared harm her person?"

"No, but they could 'ave made 'er debts public and ruined her in lots of other ways." He helped himself to a slice of buttered bread.

Mrs. Jeffries frowned. "When is the ship due to sail?"

"Tomorrow morning. I think we ought to let the inspector know about it."

"If she bought the ticket three days before the murder, then she had made up her mind to leave," Mrs. Jeffries mused. "So if that was her intention, why would she then kill her father?"

"Perhaps she decided she didn't wish to go," Hatchet suggested. "Perhaps she might have thought that if she left, her debts would become public. If that happened, Sir George could have cut her completely out of his will."

"But we don't know that," Mrs. Jeffries replied. She honestly didn't know what to do. "I don't think she killed him. Not if she had decided to flee the country."

"Are you goin' to tell the inspector?" Wiggins asked.

"Perhaps I ought to," she said hesitantly. "But I'll need to think of a clever way to do it." She glanced at the coachman. "Do you have anything else?"

He shook his head. "Not really."

"Can I go next?" Mrs. Goodge asked.

"You might as well, Mrs. Goodge," Hatchet said. "I've nothing to report. Despite my rather extensive network of resources, I've heard nothing new about this case, just a mishmash of old gossip and speculation."

Mrs. Goodge took a deep breath. "I think I know what Sir George had on Randall Grantham." She told them the gossip she'd heard from the delivery lad. She took care to tell them everything, making sure she left nothing out of her tale.

When she'd finished, Betsy said, "So Grantham was a pickpocket."

"And not a very good one," Smythe added. He wondered why Blimpey Groggins hadn't got wind of this tidbit. It was the sort of knowledge that was his stock and trade.

"Yes, it most certainly sounds that way," Mrs. Jeffries replied slowly. "Oh, dear, then that more or less eliminates him as a suspect."

"Eliminates him?" Mrs. Goodge repeated. "Why? I should think it would put him more in the running. He obviously hated Sir George."

"Of course he did," the housekeeper replied. "And fifty years ago, the word of a baronet would have been enough to bring charges against someone like Grantham. But times have changed. Braxton didn't lodge a complaint with the police when this incident happened, so after a few weeks of time had passed, it would have been Braxton's word against Granthams."

"But the lad's uncle saw it all," Mrs. Goodge protested. "He could tell the police."

"Tell them what? That he saw a scuffle between two men. Grantham could claim the purse fell out of Braxton's pocket, or that Braxton planted the thing on him. Oh, dear," she sighed impatiently, "I'm not explaining this very well, but after weeks had passed, I don't think the police would have been too keen to arrest Grantham just because Braxton claimed the man had tried to pick his pocket."

"And Grantham would 'ave known that," Smythe agreed. "His sort knows 'ow the police work. You're explainin' it fine, Mrs. Jeffries. Grantham could 'ave left anytime he wanted."

"Then why did he stay?" the cook demanded.

"Food and shelter," Betsy said. "It's the dead of winter, and he'd probably no place to go. At least he had a roof over his head and hot meals." She had once been poor herself and had had to survive on the streets. She knew what hunger and cold could do to a person. From under the table, Smythe squeezed her hand, and she gave him a quick, confident smile.

Mrs. Goodge's shoulders slumped. "Well, that's a right old kettle of fish, I finally get some information, and it's not worth anything."

"Of course it's worthwhile," Mrs. Jeffries said quickly. "You've told us something very important."

"I have?" the cook stared at her hopefully.

"Absolutely," Mrs. Jeffries laughed. "We can now eliminate Randall Grantham as a suspect. Whoever killed Sir George went to a great deal of trouble to lure him outside, cosh him over the head, and then chip a hole in an icy pond and shove his head into it. If Grantham had committed the murder, my guess is he'd have simply coshed him over the head and not bothered with the rest."

"I agree," Betsy added. "People like him don't bother to come up with elaborate plans. They're more the grab-and-run type of criminal."

"I concur," Hatchet said. "And I believe this is very good news indeed. This case has far too many suspects, it's nice to be able to eliminate one of them."

"Well, good then, I feel better."

"Excellent," Mrs. Jeffries beamed approvingly. "You always do your fair share, Mrs. Goodge, make no mistake about that. Now, does anyone else have anything to report? Wiggins?"

Wiggins had been dreading this moment. He had a story ready, but he wasn't sure it was one they'd believe. "I've 'eard a bit, but I'm not sure if it's true or not. I got it from a lad that used to walk out with one of the maids at the Braxton house." He paused and took a deep breath. "Anyways, this lad told me that the maid had told him that she knew the contents of Sir George's will. She claimed she'd overheard Sir George talkin' to 'is solicitor." He stopped and quickly scanned their faces. But they were watching him as they always did, and he couldn't tell if they believed him or not.

"Well, get on with it, lad," Mrs. Goodge urged. "We've not got all night. What's in Sir George's will?"

"Not much, really," he said quickly. "Just that the daughters get it all in equal shares. It's not very interestin'."

"How long ago did this young woman hear this?" Mrs. Jeffries asked.

"I didn't think to ask," he admitted. "But I 'eard something else as well. The lad, I'd bought 'im a pint you see, also told me that Mr. Clark gets to stay at the Braxton house for all 'is life."

"That was in Sir George's will as well?" Betsy asked.

"No, it was in 'is father's will. Neither Sir George nor 'is daughters can turf 'im out, so I reckon 'e 'ad no reason to do the murder."

Mrs. Jeffries thought about that for a moment and then said. "You could be correct, Wiggins. In which case, we might be rapidly running out of suspects. Anything else?"

"No." He was glad this was over. Pretending that the bits and pieces that Luty gave him to report were actually his own, made the telling very hard. He felt like he was lying. "That's all I've got. Uh, if we're finished, I'd like to take Fred for a walk."

"Mind you don't let him run off from you again," Mrs. Jeffries said. She rose to her feet. "I'm going upstairs to wait for the inspector. Hopefully, he'll have some more information on the case. Let's meet again down here before bedtime."

Witherspoon was dead tired when he arrived home, but he did consent to have a glass of sherry before dinner.

"Tomorrow's the funeral," he told her as he took a quick sip, "and we're no closer to finding the killer than we ever were. I don't know what I'm going to do."

"You'll keep on looking until you do find the murderer, sir." She smiled calmly. "Now, why don't you tell me about your day, sir. That always helps."

As he talked, she occasionally asked a question or made a comment. She had several ideas that she wanted to put into his mind, none of them were particularly brilliant, but like the inspector, she, too, was at a loss to know what to do next. But luckily, by the time they'd finished their Harvey's, his recitation of the day's events had given her food for thought.

"How are the plans for Christmas coming along?" he asked. He followed her out into the hall.

"Very well, sir. See for yourself." They had reached the dining room.

Witherspoon gasped. "Gracious, this is lovely."

Holly boughs and ivy were draped on the mantle piece. The table was covered in a lace tablecloth, and there were fringed silk shawls on the top of the cabinets and the side-boards. Delicate angel figurines and candles were entwined in the greenery.

"I'm glad you're pleased, sir. Everyone enjoyed decorating the house. But most of the credit for making it so lovely should go to Betsy. She's very clever at putting things together nicely. She found those figurines in the attic and gave them a good clean."

"And the result is wonderful. I'm so lucky to have such a dedicated staff, and I'm so looking forward to Christmas dinner with Lady Cannonberry."

"We're looking forward to Christmas as well."

He sat down at the dining table, and Mrs. Jeffries went to get his dinner tray. When she had him safely tucking into his boiled mutton, she dashed back down to the kitchen.

Betsy was washing dishes, Wiggins was drying, Mrs. Goodge was sitting at the table, resting her feet, and Smythe was pouring a large sack of flour into Mrs. Goodge special bin.

"Let's have a brief meeting while he's having his supper," she said. "I found out a few things, and I want to share them as quickly as possible with all of you. This case isn't going well, and frankly, I can't make any sense of it. I need all of you to be thinking about it as well."

"We're running out of time, aren't we?" Smythe put the sack down and slipped into his seat.

"Yes, and if the inspector doesn't catch this killer, it could seriously damage his career. Nigel Nivens has been waiting for him to fail, and a failure of this magnitude would be just what he wants. We're not going to let that happen."

"We certainly will not," Mrs. Goodge said. "Now, tell us

what you've learned, and we'll all put our minds to solving this puzzle."

She told them everything. Then she dashed back upstairs to get the inspector's supper tray. Betsy came with her. They were almost at the dining room when Mrs. Jeffries heard what sounded like dozens of footsteps outside their front window. She peeked out the window and laughed in delight. "Call the others," she told Betsy. "We've got carolers." She dashed to the dining room. "Inspector, come quickly."

They opened the front door and saw a group of warmly dressed men and women standing in a semicircle in front of their steps. The others had come up from the kitchen and were now crowded around the open front door behind the inspector and Mrs. Jeffries. Smythe slipped his arm around Betsy's waist.

They began to sing, and the quiet night was suddenly filled with the lovely words and melody of "Silent Night."

" 'Silent night, holy night, all is calm, all is bright.' "

The carolers sang beautifully, and the household of Upper Edmonton Gardens was soon completely caught up in the joy of the season.

Mrs. Jeffries heard Mrs. Goodge sniff and saw her dab at her eyes with the hem of her apron, Smythe pulled Betsy closer to him, and Wiggins was grinning so widely she feared his cheeks would hurt. Even the inspector had lost that worried, strained expression he'd come home wearing.

The carolers finished the song and Mrs. Jeffries thought they would move on, but then they began to sing "Good King Wenceslas."

She closed her eyes briefly, letting the music wash over her and lift her spirits. " 'Good King Wensceslas looked out on the feast of Stephen.' " This was so very nice, she thought. " 'When the snow lay round about deep and crisp and even.' " An image popped into her mind and her eyes flew open. " 'Brightly shone the moon that night, though the frost was cruel when a poor man came in sight, gathering winter fuel.' " But the idea, nebulous as it was faded away as the notes of the Christmas melody drifted through the air. Up and down Upper Edmonton Gardens other doorways opened, and people came out to stand on their stairs and door stoops. The singers finished the song, and with cries of "Merry Christmas" from everyone, they moved on down the road.

"Ought we to have invited them in?" Witherspoon whispered to Mrs. Jeffries.

"No, sir, I think they're the choir singers from St. John's Church. Perhaps an extra bit of money to the poor box on Christmas day would be a nice way of expressing our gratitude."

"Yes, I'll be sure to do that." He yawned widely. "Good night, all, everyone sleep well."

But Mrs. Jeffries didn't sleep well, she tossed and turned, and finally got out of the bed altogether and took up her spot at the window. There was something about that song, something about the image that had popped into her mind when the carolers sang "Good King Wenceslas."

She'd sung the old carol for years, so she went over the words silently, trying to get the idea back. Images came and went, but none of them were the one that had shaken her so completely, the one that she knew was the key to finding Sir George Braxton's killer.

Suddenly, the scene flew back into her head. She could see it as clearly as she saw the almost-full moon peeking through the clouds. But what did it mean? That's what she had to determine tonight.

She unfocused her eyes and let her mind wander as it would. Bits and pieces of the case came and went willy-nilly; Betsy saying that the only thing the butcher could talk about was the missing chicken livers. The bloodstain and hair in the greenhouse, Samson showing up the night his master was killed. Charlotte Braxton coming home perhaps just minutes before the murder. Mrs. Merryhill having to give up her child, Randall Grantham finding the body and rousing the household.

Everything came and went quickly. The kernel of an idea began to form, but it stubbornly refused to take shape and help her come up with the answer.

She sat there for hours, letting the clues come and go. But finally, she had to admit defeat. Whatever concept the image from the carol had started was completely gone. Dejected, she got up, wincing as her stiff joints reminded her she shouldn't be sitting motionless for hours in a cold room. She slipped back into bed and closed her eyes. Now that she had admitted to herself that it was hopeless, sleep would come. Tomorrow she'd have a meeting with the others, and she'd tell them the truth, that she had no idea who had killed Sir George Braxton and they weren't likely to find the answer before Christmas. Perhaps it would be best to concentrate on ways to keep the inspector's spirits up. Perhaps it would also behoove them to come up with some thoughts on how they might keep Inspector Nigel Nivens from taking advantage of their inspector's failure.

She yawned, rolled onto her side, and told herself quite sternly to go to sleep. But thoughts of the cat came back, and the words popped into her mind unbidden. She sat bolt upright as she suddenly understood what it all meant. That was it. Of course, how could she have not seen it before? That was the key to solving the case; that was what the image had been trying to tell her. Gracious, it was so very obvious.

She threw back the covers just as another piece of the puzzle fell into place in her mind: "It looked like some giant hand had reached down and yanked it off just to make the scene even more frightening." When Witherspoon had repeated that conversation and those words to her, she'd barely given them a thought, but she'd been wrong. Oh, yes, now it all made sense.

She sat up and fumbled under the bed for her slippers. She put them on, slipped on her heavy dressing gown, and then got up and lighted the lamp on her desk. Grabbing the top blanket off her bed, she sat down at her desk, arranged the blanket over her knees, and set to work. The room was cold, and she had much to do before she could sleep. Taking a sheet of paper out of the drawer, she picked up her pen and began to write. This was the only way to be sure, the only way to be certain that her idea was right.

Mrs. Jeffries was the first one downstairs the next morning. She put the kettle on, measured out enough tea into the big brown pot to insure it was good and strong, then went back upstairs to wake the others.

When she came back the kettle was whistling, and by the time the others had trooped down, she had the tea poured and the cups spread out on the table.

"What's wrong?" Wiggins asked.

"Mrs. Jeffries has thought of something," the cook yawned. "Why else would she have got us up at this time of the morning. Ah, lovely, you've made tea."

"Have you figured out who the killer is?" Betsy asked as she slipped into her seat. "I knew you would. I knew it was just a matter of time."

"I have an idea, but I'm not sure I'm absolutely right." She touched the paper in her pocket, taking encouragement from the account she'd written up in the wee hours of the morning. She'd done it to clarify things in her own mind, and she had no intention of showing this missive to the others. Despite everything, she could be dead wrong.

"Don't start yet." Smythe hurried into the kitchen, he was carrying his heavy gloves and his old brown scarf. "I thought I'd best bring these down in case you need me to go out."

"That scarf has seen better days," Betsy commented. "And those gloves could do with a clean."

"I don't wear them that often." He sat down next to her and reached for her hand under the table.

"I know, that's why your hands get so chapped in the winter," she chided. "You don't wear your gloves. But not to worry, I'll take care of them."

Mrs. Jeffries gave him a grateful smile. "I do need you to go out, that's why I've called everyone here so early. But first of all, I want to say that I'm not altogether sure of my conclusions in this case."

"Stop frettin,' Mrs. Jeffries." The cook took another sip of tea. "We've done this many times. You're never sure, but you're generally always right. Now, who's the killer?"

"That's just it," she said. "It could be several people. I think I know who it is, but there's a second suspect who could equally have done it."

"Then what are we goin' to do? We can't get the inspector to arrest 'em both." Wiggins said. He looked worried.

"Of course we can't, but I have an idea about how he can arrest the right person. Unfortunately, it's quite complicated, so I'm going to need some help." She turned to Smythe. "I need you to bring Constable Barnes here to the kitchen, I've got to talk to him. He's got to convince the inspector to do something very unorthodox today."

He started to get up, but she waved him back to his seat. "Finish your tea. We've got time, and this might be the only opportunity you'll have to get something in your stomach."

Mrs. Goodge got up and started for the dry larder. "If that's the case, I'll go get those buns I made yesterday so he can have a bite to eat before he goes."

"Can we 'ave some of that red currant marmalade as well?" Wiggins asked. "It's right good."

"I'm saving that for our Christmas breakfast. But I've some nice gooseberry jam, will that do?"

"That'll be fine," Mrs. Jeffries said firmly. She smiled at the footman. "As soon as you've had your breakfast, I want you to go to Richmond."

"Cor blimey, really? What do ya want me to do?" His eyes sparkled with excitement and all thoughts of red currant marmalade vanished.

"Keep watch on the Braxton house," she instructed. "After the funeral everyone will go back to the house. If any of our suspects leave, follow that person."

Wiggins gaped at her. This was generally the sort of task Mrs. Jeffries would give the coachman. "What should I do? I mean, 'ow far do I follow 'em?"

"I don't think it'll come to that," she replied. "But just in case, stop by Luty's and get Hatchet. Take him with you. That way he can get a message to us if someone disappears unexpectedly."

"What about Charlotte Braxton?" Betsy asked. She got up and went to the pine sideboard for the breakfast plates. "Did you manage to let the inspector know about her plans to leave for New Zealand today?"

"No, and I'm taking a great risk. If I'm wrong about the

identity of the killer, and it turns out to have been her, then she will have already gone. The ship leaves from Liverpool so she would have had to have left last night."

"If she's not at the funeral, then we'll know." Mrs. Goodge put the tray of food on the table and yanked the tea towel off the plate of buns. "But somehow, I don't think she's our murderer."

"But what if she is," Betsy asked softly, "and she's already gone?" She reached for a bun, popped it on a plate, and and put it in front of Smythe.

"The ship stops in Cherbourg before it goes to New Zealand," Mrs. Jeffries said. "I checked the Shipping Intelligence in the *Times* yesterday, so if Charlotte Braxton is our killer, the inspector can send a telegram for the French police to detain her. Smythe, as soon as you bring Constable Barnes here, go to Howards' and get Bow and Arrow at the ready. Now everyone hurry and eat, we've much to do."

They finished their small breakfast in record time. Wiggins put on his heavy coat and gloves. As he started for the back door, Mrs. Goodge handed him two more buns that she'd wrapped in brown paper. "Here you go, lad. Put these in your pocket for later. I'll not have you goin' hungry."

"Thanks, Mrs. Goodge."

"And mind you and Hatchet be careful at the Braxton house," Smythe warned as he pulled on his coat. "Richmond's not London, and there's not many places to hide. But as it's a funeral reception, there might be enough comin' and goin' so as you're not noticed."

"Let the lad go," Betsy cuffed him on the arm. "He knows what he's about."

"Right, lass." He grinned at her, dropped a quick kiss on her lips, and followed the footman out. "I'll be back soon."

When the back door closed behind the men, Mrs. Jeffries

turned to Betsy. "I've a task for you as well, I want you to go to the foundling home in Twickenham. I want you to find out what happened to Mrs. Merryhill's baby boy."

"Is that where she sent him?" Betsy looked surprised by the request.

"I don't know, but it's the logical place. It's the only establishment of it's kind close to the Braxton home," Mrs. Jeffries replied. "I don't think she sent the boy off to live with relatives because in all the information we've heard, no one has ever mentioned the boy."

"And if he were living with her relations, someone would have said something about him." Mrs. Goodge added. "That makes sense."

"Do you think they'll tell me anything?"

"They will if you give them this," Mrs. Jeffries drew a five-pound note out of her pocket. "Tell them it's a donation. I'll leave it to your discretion to come up with a story that sounds reasonable as to why you're asking about the child."

"That's a lot of money, Mrs. Jeffries," Betsy exclaimed.

"It is, but I've not given very much to charity this year. Whether we find out anything useful or not from them, I'm sure they'll put the money to good use."

Betsy grabbed her coat and hat. "I'll be back as quick as I can."

Twenty minutes after she'd gone, Smythe returned with Constable Barnes. "Good morning, ladies," he said. "Smythe has told me you wanted to see me."

Mrs. Jeffries gestured for him to sit down. "Thank you for coming, Constable."

"If you don't need me anymore, I'll go get Bow and Arrow," Smythe said. "Do you want me to bring the rig back 'ere?"

"Just a minute, Smythe. That will all depend on whether or not Constable Barnes agrees to help us."

Barnes raised an eyebrow. "Mrs. Jeffries, how could you possibly doubt that I'd help? Of course I will. Now, tell me what it is you need for me to do."

"I need you to convince the inspector of two things. The first is that you sent Smythe for the rig, and that you think he would be wise to use it today instead of a hansom cab. If I'm right, you may need to move fast."

"I think I can do that," he replied. "And the second thing?"

"That's a bit more difficult, I'm afraid." She took a deep breath. "And what's more, you'll have to convince him that the whole thing is his idea."

"Whole what thing?" Barnes asked. He nodded his thanks as Mrs. Goodge put a cup of tea in front of him.

"Oh, dear, this is getting far more complicated than I thought," she replied. "You must convince him to have everybody from the Braxton household show him their arms and hands. You've got to make sure he's the one that comes up with the idea, otherwise, it'll not work very well at all. You see, Samson knows how to put up a good fight."

CHAPTER 11

"I hope you don't mind me takin' such a liberty, sir, but I knew we were going to be pressed for time." Barnes opened the door of the inspector's old-fashioned carriage and waited while his superior climbed inside before entering himself.

"Actually, it was very good thinking on your part, Constable," Witherspoon replied. "I ought to have thought of it myself." He settled back in the red, tufted seat, determined to remember that he owned this contraption. But as he'd not been raised to travel in such conveyances, he always felt a bit odd riding in the big old thing. He didn't use it much; hansoms and trains were really so much more convenient and comfortable.

"You've a lot on your mind, sir," Barnes replied. "I was thinking about what you said the other day, sir. You're playing this one very clever, sir. Very clever indeed."

Witherspoon stared at the constable. "I am? I don't quite

understand." He grabbed the handhold as the carriage bounced over a hole.

Barnes hoped he could do this properly. "Well, sir. Remember what you said about the cat?"

"The cat?"

"About how it was sad that the old thing had come home on the night his master had died. I should have realized what you had in mind then, sir, but it only occurred to me later. Of course you're right, sir. It wasn't a coincidence about the cat coming home that night. Samson didn't come home that night. The killer finally let him out."

Witherspoon gaped at him, and Barnes was sure this wasn't going to work. But then the inspector's expression changed, he shut his mouth and his eyes lighted up. "Of course, that's how the killer lured Sir George out of his bed and into the back garden."

Relieved, Barnes said, "Now, sir, I'm sorry if I've ruined your surprise, but I've worked with you a long time. I know your methods, and I know when you're listenin' to that famous 'inner voice' of yours."

"That's most kind of your Barnes, er, uh." He tried to think of what to do next. The constable was correct, of course, it all made sense now. Samson was the perfect explanation as to why Sir George went out that night. The killer was no doubt lying in wait for him. "Let's see . . . uh—"

"Now, now, sir, don't tell me, let me guess," Barnes interrupted. Mrs. Jeffries had told him this trick, and he hoped it would work. The inspector was an innocent, but he wasn't stupid.

"Guess? Uh, certainly, do go ahead." Actually, the inspector had come up with a very good idea of what it would be best to do, but he didn't want to spoil the constable's obvious pleasure in exercising his reasoning abilities.

"Well, knowing you as I do, sir, and knowing that both of us heard about how mean that cat is, I'd say there's a good chance that whoever took Samson and kept him away from the house for those days he was gone, ended up getting pretty badly scratched. As Randall Grantham said, that cat knows how to put up a fight."

"Yes, I was thinking along those lines myself," the inspector agreed.

"So I expect you'll wait until after the funeral reception, and then you'll insist on looking at the arms and hands of the principals in the case. Am I right, sir?"

Witherspoon nodded. "That's precisely what I was thinking. I'm not sure we can force anyone to disrobe, but I don't think asking people to roll up their sleeves is likely to get us into difficulties. Have you noticed any scratches on anyone?"

"No, sir, but that doesn't mean anything, as we've not been looking." Barnes replied. He couldn't believe how easy this had been, but then again, Mrs. Jeffries had laid a good foundation. She'd made a few remarks and asked a pertinent question or two while the inspector was eating his breakfast. "That's one of the reasons I was glad you let us bring the carriage, sir. If you're right, someone may try and run for it. We've had that happen a time or two."

"Unfortunately, that is all too true," he replied somberly. "But this time we're prepared. I don't know that my idea will work, but it's a sound enough theory to give it a try." He leaned back, and the two men rode in silence.

Ideas and theories were now flying into his mind with great speed, and he was sure they were on the right track. Mrs. Jeffries had been correct, all he had to do was to wait for his "inner mind" to ascertain as many facts as possible, and then the solution to the case would become apparent. A good night's sleep helped as well.

"We ought to be at Richmond soon," Barnes said as he looked out the window. "We're crossing the river."

Witherspoon took his watch out of his coat pocket and snapped open the case. "Let's go straight to the house. I want to have another word with the servants. I've an idea where the killer might have hid Samson for those days he was missing. Mrs. Jeffries asked me a question this morning, and it got me to thinking."

"You don't want to go to the church, sir?" Barnes looked away to hide a smile.

"Oh, no, Constable, it'll be far too long a service for my bones. We've got lads stationed at the church. I doubt that our killer has any idea we've figured out that Samson was the key to luring Sir George out that night. The killer will come back to the house, I'm sure of it."

"Let's hope our murderer isn't the sort of person that heals quickly," Barnes replied. "But then again, healin' fast is usually reserved for the very young, and all of our suspects are heading nicely into middle age."

Betsy dashed into the house, taking off her coat and hat as she walked. Mrs. Goodge looked up from the table where she sat peeling turnips. "Did you have any luck?"

"I'm not sure," she admitted. "Where's Mrs. Jeffries?"

"I'm right here," the housekeeper replied. She'd been upstairs polishing the brass fittings on the third-floor landing and had heard the back door slam. She had wanted to keep busy today in order to hold her nerves at bay.

In the clear light of day, her theory about the murder seemed more and more fanciful. She was afraid she'd sent her inspector and the good constable on a fool's errand that would ruin both their careers. "What did you find out?"

"The warden at the home was quite nice. Her name is Mrs. Shelby, and she seems a kindly soul." Betsy giggled. "When I came into reception, I think she thought I was bringing in a baby. She seemed quite surprised when I told her I wanted to make a donation. I told her I'd come to find out if my brother had been brought there thirty years ago."

"You had a good story ready, did you?" Mrs. Goodge asked.

"I told the truth," Betsy explained, "it seems to work so much better. Of course, I pretended that Mrs. Merryhill was my mother. I didn't use her name or anything like that. But I kept to the facts as much as I could. I said my mam had been seduced by her employer, got with child, and then forced to give it up. I said she'd left the child there about thirty years ago, but I didn't know the exact dates or anything like that. I tossed in a bit that my mam had met my father much later and they'd emigrated to America."

"Very good, Betsy," Mrs. Jeffries said, "and obviously, the warden believed you."

"Oh, yes. I said that my poor mother had always wanted to find out what happened to her son, but she had to wait until my father passed before she could make any inquiries."

"Didn't the warden notice you don't have an American accent?" Mrs. Goodge asked.

Betsy grinned. "I told her I was born in Baltimore, but that we'd come home to England fifteen years ago. My father did very well in America, you see, and we've a nice house in Coventry. But despite believing me, Mrs. Shelby wasn't as much help as I'd hoped. She'd only come to the foundling home a few years ago."

"But don't they keep records?" Mrs. Jeffries was sure they did.

"The old records were destroyed when the cellar flooded ten years ago."

"That's too bad," Mrs. Goodge remarked, "especially after you went to all that trouble to come up with such a good tale."

"But I did find out something," Betsy said. "One of cooks has been there for a long time, so Mrs. Shelby asked her if she remembered anything. The woman said about thirty years ago, a carriage drew up in the middle of the night, and a man got out, banged on the door, and demanded they open up. When they did, he shoved a wicker basket with a baby wrapped in some old bunting in it and handed them a pound note. Then he stomped off and got in his carriage without so much as a by-your-leave. He didn't speak to them, wouldn't even answer when the warden's husband called out to him. That's why the cook remembered it so easily. Usually people bring the children during the day, during proper hours."

"That sounds like something that old blighter would do," Mrs. Goodge muttered. "What happened to the baby."

"It died the next day," Betsy said sadly. "It was a little boy."

It was almost four o'clock in the afternoon by the time the last of the guests left the funeral reception. But Witherspoon and Barnes had been very busy. Barnes had gone to the local station and got some lads to do a bit more searching of the grounds.

"We've found this, sir." Barnes came into the butler's pantry, carrying a large piece of butcher's paper. "It was stuffed in behind the cooker."

The inspector took the paper, examined it thoroughly, and then took a whiff. "It still smells like chicken livers. Good work, Constable. We'll take this into evidence."

"I expect this was how the murderer kept the beast quiet." Barnes glanced around the decrepit pantry. "Has anyone seen the animal? Too bad he can't talk, sir. He could tell us everything."

"Indeed, he could," Witherspoon replied. "Samson is alive and well. One of the kitchen staff is secretly feeding him. Apparently, the daughters loathe the animal and have instructed the housekeeper not to waste any more food on it. But Mrs. Merryhill, to her credit, is ignoring that instruction."

"Good for her. Did you have a look at her arms and hands, sir?"

"Not a scratch on them," he smiled. "Nor on any of the other servants, except for one of the maids. But hers are recent, and she got them because she's the one feeding Samson. The rest of the staff vouches for her, and she'd no reason to murder Sir George." He surveyed the decrepit, ugly pantry where the staff took their meals. "He really was a dreadful man, wasn't he? The facilities for the servants are shameful, utterly shameful; the furniture is falling apart, the light is miserable, and I'd bet my pension there is barely any heat in here. Still, Sir George didn't deserve to be murdered. His lack of compassion and mercy is between him and the Almighty."

"And I'll warrant the Almighty had plenty to say on the subject," Barnes murmured.

"I've finished here." Witherspoon started for the door. "Mrs. Merryhill has told the family and the others we need to speak to them. She's waiting for us outside the drawing room."

Barnes followed the inspector, stopping only long

enough to step out the side door and give the butcher's paper to one of the constables. They had constables unobtrusively stationed at all the doorways.

The inspector and Mrs. Merryhill were in the hall outside the big double doors of the drawing room. The housekeeper acknowledged him with a faint smile.

"Let's keep our fingers crossed that this will work," Witherspoon said as he opened the doors.

As he followed them inside, Barnes was suddenly filled with grave doubts. What if this didn't work? What if Mrs. Jeffries was wrong? What if the theory was nothing more than fancy, and they'd find nary a claw mark on anyone? Then he caught himself, for goodness sakes, they weren't hanging an innocent at the yardarms, they were looking for a few scratch marks.

If this didn't go as planned, the Braxtons would complain, but by then it wouldn't matter. Inspector Witherspoon would be off the case and maybe even back on his way to the Records Room. No matter how many cases he'd solved in the past, the top brass at the Yard wouldn't forgive him for messing up this one.

"What's the meaning of this?" Clarence Clark demanded as he turned and saw the three of them. He was standing by the fireplace. He'd discarded his jacket and was in his shirtsleeves, as was the only other man in the room, Raleigh Brent. The women had all discarded their shawls and gloves as well.

"I'll handle this, Clarence." Raleigh Brent got up from the chair and stomped over to the inspector.

Clark glared at Brent. "I'll thank you to remember your manners, sir. You're not married to Lucinda yet and as such, you're only a guest in this house."

"Don't speak to Raleigh like that!" Lucinda leapt to her

feet and charged over to her fiancé. "How dare you, Cousin Clarence. Raleigh has every right to take charge."

"Oh, for God's sake." Charlotte Braxton rolled her eyes.

"Do be quiet," Nina said. "You're all making fools of yourselves."

"I'm engaged to Lucinda," Raleigh cried, his voice shrill.

"For a house in mourning, you do make a lot of racket," Fiona Burleigh commented to no one in particular.

"Excuse me," Witherspoon shouted to make himself heard over their quarreling. "But I've something to say that is most important."

Everyone looked at him in surprise.

"I'm sorry to have to bring you all here, especially on such a sad day, but I think I might know who murdered Sir George."

"What are you saying?" Brent demanded. "If you know who did it, just go ahead and arrest that person. There's no reason to inconvenience the rest of us."

"Really, Inspector, couldn't this wait until tomorrow?" Fiona Burleigh complained. "It's been a long day, and I'm tired."

"It could wait until tomorrow, but you're leaving tonight, isn't that correct, Miss Burleigh?" Witherspoon asked. "Mrs. Merryhill said you've hired a hansom to take you to the train station at six o'clock."

"That's none of your business, Inspector." Her eyes narrowed angrily, and she glared at the housekeeper, who gazed back at her without flinching. "My coming and going isn't anyone's concern but my own."

"No one's trying to stop you from leaving." Lucinda smiled cattily.

"Of course, no one's stopping you from going about your

business," the inspector said. "But before you go, could you please show us your hands and arms."

Fiona's jaw dropped in surprise. Barnes quickly scanned the faces of the others and realized that everyone was equally stunned by the inspector's demand.

"I beg your pardon," Fiona said. "What did you say?"

Witherspoon smiled kindly. "I know it's a very odd request, but if you'll do as we ask, we can eliminate you as a suspect, and you can be on your way. If you're uncomfortable rolling up your sleeves in our presence, Mrs. Merryhill has consented to help us."

Fiona stared at them for a long moment, then she moved over and stood directly in front of the inspector. She stuck her hands out. After a moment, she reached over and began unbuttoning the cuffs on the sleeves of the black dress she wore.

"If the rest of you ladies will unbutton your sleeves as well, this will go much faster," Barnes said to the others. He kept his position by the door.

"This is outrageous," Clark sputtered. "My cousins will do no such thing."

"I don't mind." Nina Braxton had already began to undo the small studs on her cuffs.

"Neither do I." Charlotte had got up and was doing the same as her sister.

"Well, I for one am not disrobing in front of the police," Lucinda announced.

"Have you got something to hide?" Fiona asked. She'd unbuttoned both cuffs. She shoved the sleeves up each arm and thrust them at the inspector.

"Don't be ridiculous," Lucinda snapped. "Raleigh, do something. This is an utter outrage."

"I think it would be best if we did what they asked,"
Brent said softly. "We don't want them thinking we've
something to hide."

The inspector nodded. "Thank you, Miss Burleigh. We
very much appreciate your cooperation."

"Can I go now?" she asked. "I think I'd like to leave immediately."

"Of course, we've your address if we need to ask you any
more questions."

Fiona gave Lucinda and Raleigh a withering look as she
stalked out of the room.

Charlotte Braxton stepped over to the inspector and
thrust her hands and arms out. "Is this what you needed to
see." She rolled her wrists back and forth, exposing her arms
completely. Her plump arms were clear of blemish.

"Thank you, Miss Braxton. That's fine."

"Good." Charlotte went back to her seat. "Now everyone
can stop suspecting me." She stared at her older sister. "I
know that's what everyone was thinking, just because I was
out late that night. Well, I wasn't fond of Father, but neither were any of you. Why don't you go next, Lucinda? Or is
Fiona right? Do you have something to hide?"

"Of course not," Lucinda yelped. She reached over and
yanked her left sleeve so hard that buttons flew every which
way. Then she did the same to the right.

She closed the short space between her and the policemen and thrust her hands virtually under the inspector's
nose. "Have a good look," she ordered. "There's not a mark
anywhere. Not that I've any idea what on earth it is you
think you're going to find."

"Thank you, Miss Braxton." Witherspoon ignored her
tirade.

Nina Braxton stepped forward next. The sleeves of her dress were already open and neatly folded back.

She, too, was clear of any claw marks.

Raleigh Brent came next, rolling up the cuffs of his and shaking his head. "If you'd just tell us what it is you're looking for," he complained. "We'd be able to help a great deal more with your inquiry. I don't want you to think Lucinda and I aren't anxious to catch her father's killer."

"Do be quiet, Raleigh, and show them your bloody arms," Lucinda snapped. "Oh, dear, please forgive me, darling, I'm so distraught I don't know what I'm saying."

"I know what came over her," Nina said to Charlotte. "Fiona's gone."

"I understand, dearest." Raleigh smiled weakly at his fiancée. He gamely stuck his arms out in front of the policeman. "I do hope you're happy, sir. This exercise has so upset my fiancée that she's not even aware of what she's saying."

"Thank you, Mr. Brent," Witherspoon said kindly. He felt badly for the poor fellow. Whether the man realized it or not, he'd just had a preview of what marriage to a rich woman with a nasty temper was going to be like.

Rolling down his sleeves as he walked, Raleigh went over to stand next to Lucinda. "It's your turn now," he said to Clark.

Clarence Clark snorted derisively. "You're not master here yet."

"And when I am, you'll not be here long," Brent shot back. He took Lucinda's arm and herded her toward a love seat as far away from the others as possible.

"I wouldn't count on that," Clark smiled slyly. "Or hasn't your precious fiancée told you?"

Brent stopped. "Told me what?"

"That I've a lifetime interest in this house. I can stay here until the day I die."

"Mr. Clark, will you please roll up your sleeves?" Witherspoon asked. He struggled to hold back his disappointment. He'd been so sure, the idea had been so logical. He'd not known the identity of the killer, but he'd been sure the killer would be marked.

"I most certainly will not." He whirled around and went back to stand by the fireplace.

"You will," Lucinda shouted. "Or I'll make damned certain you never step foot in that greenhouse of yours again. You have a right to live here, but you've no right to the conservatory. I know Nina and I promised we'd not sell it off, but if you don't do as I say, I'll burn it to the ground, and your precious orchids with it."

Clark's eyes widened, and his hands trembled in rage. "You're as bad as your father. He's not even cold in his grave, and you're stepping into his shoes."

"Mr. Clark," the inspector shouted. He just wanted to get this over with and get away from these odious, terrible people. "Please, just show us your arms so we can be done with it."

Clark unbuttoned his cuffs and shoved away from the fireplace. He stalked toward the inspector, his eyes were blazing with rage, and his expression was so fierce that Barnes, fearing for Witherspoon's person, hurried over to stand by his inspector.

Suddenly, Clark veered sharply to the left, leapt over an embroidered footstool, and was out the double doors.

"Come back!" Witherspoon shouted as he charged after him. Barnes blew into his police whistle and then ran after the two men.

"Mr. Clark, I demand that you stop!" the inspector yelled

as they rushed down the hall. Clark was heading for the side door. "Stop, stop I say!" From behind him, he could hear the pounding of feet as the others came running after them.

Clark was fast, but just as he got to the bottom of the back stairs, something shot out from the shadows and went directly under his feet. Clark stumbled and then slammed down against the slate floor with a loud crash.

Witherspoon almost fell onto the fallen man, but he managed to catch his balance at the last second. He grabbed Clark by the shirt collar and hauled him up to his knees.

Clark had slammed his head against the botton step, and it was bleeding profusely. Barnes pulled him to his feet, reached over, and shoved his shirtsleeves up to his elbow. His right arm was covered with scratch marks. They were healing, but they were plain for everyone to see.

"Mr. Clarence Clark, you're under arrest for the murder of Sir George Braxton."

"The bastard was going to sell it," Clark cried. "He didn't need the money, he was just doing it for meanness. Just to make a few more pounds to add to his coffers. He didn't care that he was taking the only thing that made my life worth living. He didn't care a whit what he did to his own flesh and blood."

Two constables from outside raced in through the side door and skidded to a halt. It was Constable Goring and Constable Becker.

"Mr. Clark, you'll soon have an opportunity to make a statement." Witherspoon motioned to the constables. "Take him to Richmond station and charge him with the murder of Sir George Braxton. Constable Barnes and I will be along shortly to take his statement."

"Yes, sir," Goring replied. He took one arm, and Constable Becker took the other. Goring nodded respectfully at the inspector as they led the man off.

"You were right, sir," Barnes said with a grin. "Samson does know how to put up a good fight, he even knows how to trip up his enemies." He pointed to the corner.

Samson was sitting on his fat haunches, staring at the two men.

"What's taking them so long?" Betsy complained. "It's been hours."

"It always takes a long time," Mrs. Goodge replied. "Catching murderers is hard."

"Oh, dear, I do hope I'm right." Mrs. Jeffries' stomach was in knots.

Betsy suddenly stood up from the table. "Someone's coming." She ran down the back hall and threw open the door. "It's about time. What happened?"

"Just a moment, lass," Smythe said as he, Wiggins, and Hatchet stepped into the warm house. "Let's get inside so we only have to tell this once. The inspector is right behind us, so Mrs. Jeffries better tell us her bit right quick."

They hurried into the kitchen, took off their heavy coats, and took their seats.

"I'll make tea," Mrs. Goodge said. "I've got the kettle ready to boil, and I can listen while I get things ready."

"We 'ad to wait about for hours," Wiggins said. "But once we saw them leadin' 'im off, we went along to the station and waited till Smythe got there with the inspector and Barnes. We're about froze to the bone."

"That is quite true," Hatchet agreed. "It got very cold, especially when one is hiding outside in a copse of trees."

"It was good of you to be so dedicated. Did he make an arrest?" Mrs. Jeffries asked bluntly.

Smythe nodded. " 'E did."

"Was I right?" she asked.

Wiggins laughed. " 'Course you were right. He went a bit bonkers and tried to make a run for it. But he didn't get very far."

"Clarence Clark confessed," Hatchet said. "Or so says our good man Smythe here, who got it out of the inspector when he was driving him to the police station in Richmond. Now, tell us how you came to the correct conclusion."

Mrs. Jeffries had already told the Betsy and Mrs. Goodge who she suspected was guilty, she thought it only fair as the men were on the scene to see it happen, so to speak. "I wasn't sure I had," she admitted. "It was really the carolers that put the idea in my mind."

"The singing from last night? The Christmas carols?" Betsy exclaimed.

"That's right," Mrs. Jeffries replied. "It was 'Good King Wenceslas' that actually did it. When they started singing the first verse, the bit about 'When the snow lay round about,' and the part where it goes, "When a poor man came in sight, 'it reminded me of Sir George going outside that night."

"Sir George wasn't poor," Hatchet interjected.

"Yes, I know," she explained. "But it wasn't about him exactly, it was the image that sprang into my mind. A man walking outside in the snow. It was hours before I could understand what the image was trying to tell me, but once I did, it all fell into place."

"I don't understand," Mrs. Goodge complained. "What's that got to do with anything?"

"The key to the murder was Sir George going out alone that night," she continued. "What would make him do such a thing? He was a mean, nasty, selfish man, and if he'd merely heard something that bothered him, he'd have called one of the servants. The only thing he cared about, the only thing he showed any concern for was his cat, Samson. Then I realized something we should have seen from the very beginning."

"The cat came back the night Sir George died," Hatchet nodded in understanding. "I see where this is leading."

"That's right. Samson coming home was no accident. The killer had, well, for want of a better word, catnapped Samson. His plan was really quite clever: he knew that the minute Sir George heard the cat crying, he'd come rushing outside. That's when he made his move."

"So Clark took Samson and kept him somewhere? But how could that be? Sir George had the servants out there searching the grounds all the time?" Betsy asked curiously.

"That was the clue that pointed me toward Clarence Clark," Mrs. Jeffries said. "He was the one who searched the carriage house, and that's where he kept the cat. It was your clue about the butcher complaining about the missing chicken livers that helped bring it together in my mind."

"Of course, he stole them to keep the cat fed," Betsy said. "It all makes sense now. But you haven't told us why Clark wanted Sir George dead."

"I know," Mrs. Goodge said. She poured boiling water into the teapot. "It was because Sir George was sellin' the conservatory."

"That's right," Mrs. Jeffries beamed approvingly. "And it was your clue that put it all together in my mind."

"Which one?" the cook set the teapot on the table.

"The delivery boy told you that his Uncle Ennis had once seen Sir George's cousin cuff a porter because he'd dropped his flowers. Coupling that bit with everything the inspector said about Clark's devotion to his plants, it all seemed to fit."

"But what about the daughters?" Hatchet took a cup of tea from the cook with a nod of thanks. "They all had motives. What made you realize they were innocent?"

"I didn't know for sure," Mrs. Jeffries confessed. "Actually, up until you men came in and said that Clark had confessed, I was of two minds about the resolution of the case. My other suspect was Lucinda Braxton. She was the one daughter that had the most to lose."

"And she could have catnapped the cat," Wiggins finished. "But she couldn't have kept him in the carriage house. Not if Clarence Clark searched the place."

"No, but she could have kept him elsewhere," the housekeeper replied. "Once we found out that Charlotte Braxton had plans to leave the country, I was fairly certain that she wasn't the killer. Nor did I think Nina Braxton guilty."

"But she'd lost a lot of her father's money," Mrs. Goodge pointed out, "and the brokers were coming that day to tell him so."

"Yes, but when you think about it, Sir George had lost money before. That's why he'd given Nina the task of managing the investments. He might have gotten angry at her, but he'd not have tossed her out into the cold or cut her out of his will. No, the only persons who were really at risk were Lucinda Braxton, who stood to lose the man she loved, or Clarence Clark, who stood to lose the thing he loved, the conservatory."

"So you knew that whoever catnapped Samson would have gotten badly scratched." Wiggins grinned. "That was right good thinkin' on yer part."

"Samson was famous for putting up a good fight," she

laughed. "For goodness sakes, he even scratched the hand that feeds him. Look what he did to that poor maid who got too close to his food dish. So I knew that even if the killer had worn gloves when he tried to handle him, that was one cat that would manage to get his licks in somehow."

"'E did it again today," Smythe said. "He tripped up Clark as he was makin' a run for it."

"Clever cat." She took a sip of tea.

"What about the murder weapon?" Mrs. Goodge asked. "They never found it."

"I don't think it can be proved, but I'll warrant that the murder weapon melted." Mrs. Jeffries said calmly.

"Melted?" Wiggins exclaimed.

"How could that be?" Betsy asked.

"Go on, tell us 'ow you sussed that out," Smythe urged.

"It was an icicle. Clark pulled it off the side of the garden shed where Randall Grantham was sleeping and bashed Sir George's head with the thing. I expect that was the noise that Grantham heard that originally woke him up that night."

"I know them big ones are 'eavy," Wiggins said doubtfully, "but 'ow could someone 'ang onto one of them slippery things with enough force to really 'urt someone?"

"He wore gloves," she replied. "Then he pulled Sir George to the pond, chipped a hole in the ice and stuck his head down in it. As soon as he was sure Sir George was dead, he went into the greenhouse and tossed the icicle under a table. By the time the police searched the area, the icicle had melted."

Wiggins looked at Mrs. Jeffries with unabashed admiration. "Cor blimey," he said, "that does make sense. How'd you figure it out?"

"The hair and the bloodstain that was found later in the greenhouse. The icicle melted, but it left the blood and the hair behind. The only explanation that I could think of was an icicle. Also, I remembered a case my late husband had once investigated. In that crime, a wife stabbed her husband with an icicle. Mind you, she didn't kill him, it was just a flesh wound, but it could have been deadly if she'd not been drunk and had hit an artery or a vital organ."

Smythe looked at Betsy. "I 'ope you never get that angry at me."

"Don't be daft," she laughed. "But if I do, you're in for it. I don't drink."

"I'm right glad this case got solved by Christmas," Wiggins said. "It makes it nice and tidy. One of these days, I shall write an account of our adventures, and this one'll be called 'The Last Breath of a Silent Knight'. That sounds good, doesn't it?"

"I hate to point this out to you, Wiggins," Hatchet said apologetically. "But Sir George was a baronet, not a knight."

"I know that," Wiggins replied. "But there's not much difference between 'em, exceptin' that one's hereditary, the other usually isn't. They're both 'sirs'. Besides, 'The Last Breath of A Silent Baron' just doesn't have the same ring to it, does it?"

They all agreed that it did not.

Later that evening, after everyone had gone to bed, Mrs. Jeffries came downstairs. Wiggins, who was slipping out of his hat and coat, whirled around as she came into the kitchen. "Cor blimey, you gave me a fright. Uh . . . I was . . . uh . . . just takin' a bit of air."

She stared at him.

"Oh, blast, I'm not good at this. I slipped over to see Luty and tell 'er 'ow things turned out. She made me promise, Mrs. Jeffries."

"I know," Mrs. Jeffries smiled. "How is she feeling?"

"She's right as rain," he said, relieved that the housekeeper wasn't angry. "I'm sorry. I didn't mean to deceive anyone, but it meant so much to 'er, and I didn't want you lot gettin' angry at me 'cause we agreed to keep 'er out of it. She's old, Mrs. Jeffries. She told me she might not 'ave many cases left, and she didn't want to miss even one. She did all her investigatin' right from 'er room."

"Wiggins, it's all right. I'm not angry, and I won't tell the others. Now get on up to bed and get some sleep. Tomorrow is Christmas Eve, and we've much to do."

"Ta, Mrs. Jeffries." He started for the back stairs. "Uh, Mrs. Jeffries there's just one more thing I've got to ask you."

"What is it?"

"Well, it's about that cat. Even with the servants feedin' 'im, I think 'is days at the Braxton house are numbered."

"You're not suggesting what I think you're suggesting?" She couldn't believe her ears.

"I think we ought to adopt 'im, Mrs. Jeffries. 'E can't be as bad as they say, and I'm sure 'im and Fred would get along real good."